THE INDUSTRY

Wooldridges $18.99

THE INDUSTRY

ROSE FOSTER

Angus&Robertson
An imprint of HarperCollins*Publishers*

Angus&Robertson
An imprint of HarperCollins*Publishers*, Australia
First published in Australia in 2012
by HarperCollins*Publishers* Australia Pty Limited
ABN 36 009 913 517
harpercollins.com.au

HarperCollins*Publishers*
Level 13, 201 Elizabeth Street, Sydney, NSW 2000, Australia
31 View Road, Glenfield, Auckland 0627, New Zealand
A 53, Sector 57, Noida, UP, India
77–85 Fulham Palace Road, London W6 8JB, United Kingdom
2 Bloor Street East, 20th floor, Toronto, Ontario M4W 1A8, Canada
10 East 53rd Street, New York NY 10022, USA

National Library of Australia Cataloguing-in-Publication entry:

Foster, Rose.
  The industry / Rose Foster.
  ISBN: 978 0 7322 9330 7 (pbk.)
  For young adults.
A823.4

Cover design by Matt Stanton, HarperCollins Design Studio
Front cover images: Face © 2011 Jaydee Artsen; hands by shutterstock.com
Back cover image by shutterstock.com
Typeset in 10/14.5pt Sabon by Kirby Jones
Printed and bound in Australia by Griffin Press
60gsm Hi Bulk used by HarperCollins*Publishers* is a natural, recyclable
product made from wood grown in sustainable plantation forests. The
manufacturing processes conform to the environmental regulations in
the country of origin, Finland.

5 4 3 2 1   12 13 14 15

For you, Ellie,
For every reason, least of all being that the
other 6.95 is here

CHAPTER ONE

MATCH

They had been waiting almost a week when the match came through. A computer, one among many cluttered on a long desk, gave a tiny, muted beep.

The three men in the room didn't hear it the first time. They were gathered around one of the other computers, scrolling through a news bulletin, collecting snippets of information and scrawling them down in a file. One man was small and thin; one was young and tall; and the third was in charge. The small man and his boss were deep in discussion. They were so accustomed to the idea of waiting that the beep reached their ears and passed through their minds unnoticed. It was the youngest of the three who thought he might have heard something. At first he ignored it and returned to the bulletin. A second beep regained his attention, but he pushed it away, thinking he was hearing things. It was too soon, after all. When a third beep sounded, he knew he couldn't be imagining it.

He straightened up and turned slowly. Outside, snowflakes fluttered past the window. He stood very still, glaring across the room. At the next beep he went to the offending computer — the one at the end of the row — and bent low to frown at the monitor. A small link appeared in the form of a text box that offered only one word: 'MATCH'. He stared at it for a very long time. Could it be true? Could they have found a match in only a week's time? It was borderline ridiculous. In fact, it felt impossible. What were the chances?

'Latham,' the young man said. His boss glanced at him. 'Latham, look at this.'

Latham left his chair and came to stand at the beeping computer. The small man, Ramien, followed suit. It took a moment for them both to fully understand what the word in the text box meant.

'Show me,' said Latham hungrily. 'Show me.'

Ramien pulled the mouse towards him and clicked on the link. It opened up a page and showed them a sequence of fourteen characters. They stared at it.

'Where's the prototype?' Latham asked.

Ramien yanked a folder off the desk and began rifling through it. After a moment he pushed a sheet of paper into Latham's hands. Latham looked between it and the screen several times.

'It's a true match,' he said.

The youngest man read the sequence over Latham's shoulder and found that it did indeed match the one on the monitor perfectly.

'Who is it?' Latham asked. 'Who did it?'

It took Ramien many tense moments of typing to

unearth the person who had, unknowingly, sent them the matching sequence. The other two stayed by his side, unable to tear themselves away. Finally, Ramien located the source of the match. A computer in a high school half the world away. The three men stared.

'She's young,' Ramien said finally, looking through the candidate's computerised high-school records. 'Too young, really.'

'That's not a problem,' Latham said.

Ramien turned to look at him, surprised. For a moment, he thought he must have misheard. Any person who was able to match the prototype would save all their jobs. He or she would become the most hunted person in their business and would soon be worth millions, perhaps even billions, of dollars … and Latham wanted to pin all their hopes on some teenager?

'It's not a problem?' Ramien asked uncertainly.

'No,' Latham said. 'In fact, it's better. The young are weak, Ramien, and far less resourceful. When we take her, she won't fight back.'

CHAPTER TWO

CRACK THE CODE

It was the first lunchtime of the school year when Kirra Hayward sat down at a computer in the air-conditioned Hewitt Hollandale Memorial Library. Her school, Freemont Grammar, had named the library in honour of the only famous person ever to fumble their way out of the suburb of Freemont: a local politician from half a century ago. It was rumoured that the man in question hadn't actually even attended Freemont Grammar but had instead received his education at Ingram High, the public school around the corner. This was something the Freemont school board chose to ignore. After adjusting her swivel chair, Kirra logged onto the computer with her student code and password, and rifled through the homework she'd been assigned in her morning classes.

At sixteen, Kirra was in Year Ten, but several years ago she had been given special permission by the principal of Freemont Grammar to study maths and science subjects two years above her grade. 'Exceptional' was the word the principal had used to describe Kirra when he'd discussed the advancement with her parents and, of course, they'd allowed the move to go right ahead. Kirra was the only student in the school permitted to make such a jump and she figured doing her homework on time was a way of ensuring they didn't remove her from the classes. She didn't think she could bear to go back to Year Ten maths. It would almost be like being shoved back to primary school.

With such a frightening thought in mind, she flipped through her notebook and settled on the first task she saw. 'Come up with your own equation!' Mr Gummer had exclaimed that morning, far more excited by this prospect than his new Year Twelve maths class appeared to be. 'Any sort of equation you choose! Extra marks for a puzzle, like the ones you find in the paper!'

Kirra gritted her teeth. The task had no academic purpose whatsoever and was exactly the sort of thing she'd had no time for in the past. Why Mr Gummer couldn't have done something worthwhile with his class on the first day, like revising the Euler method from last year or introducing them to trigonometric identities, was a mystery to Kirra.

She typed *puzzles* into a search engine, her fingers smacking against the keys as she felt her resentment towards Mr Gummer intensify. Only this morning he'd announced to the class that Kirra Hayward was the sole student to get perfect results in the previous year's final exams. Kirra had felt the contempt of her classmates — all of whom were two years older than herself — blasting at her from all sides. She had slipped a little lower in her seat, all the while staring very hard at her desk, and regretted her decision to get every answer right on that stupid exam. She usually remembered to answer a couple incorrectly so she could avoid uncomfortable moments such as these.

And now she was stuck doing Mr Gummer's useless homework task. Unlike many others in her classes, Kirra wasn't normally a student of plagiarism — the idea of stealing someone else's work made her very uncomfortable — but she simply couldn't stomach the idea of putting effort into something that was such a mammoth waste of time. Old Mr Gummer was renowned for being technologically inept and notoriously easy to hoodwink; he'd never know if she copied someone else's puzzle.

A page of results loaded before her eyes, some leading straight to Sudoku puzzles, others advertising children's learning games. Finally, she came across one interesting link. *CRACK THE CODE!* it blared at her. Did a code count as a puzzle? She scrolled over the link and clicked.

The page loaded with surprising speed to reveal a simple site with numbers and letters filling the page in tight columns. They were in no particular order and made no sense at all and Kirra frowned. At the bottom of the page was a blank field to submit the answer; however, there were no instructions given and no key to follow. She made to exit the site — there were bound to be plenty more puzzles to copy; no need to fixate on this one — when a number four caught her eye. It was in one of the middle columns, close to the bottom, and for a reason Kirra couldn't entirely explain it stood out as though it were in bold font. It wasn't, of course. It looked exactly like every other character in every other row. Still, there was something about it.

She scrolled to the bottom of the page and hesitated, unable to explain to herself why this particular number meant so much. Every answer in her maths class came from working it out in her head or on paper, from following tried and true methods. But this puzzle? The code seemed to be beyond understanding ... and yet ...

She typed the number four into the answer field and glanced back at the code. Nothing.

She rolled her eyes. This code wasn't a code at all. It was complete nonsense. She gave it one last indignant glance before going to exit the page ... and froze.

A letter V in one of the last columns was ablaze on the screen. The four seemed somehow linked to it, as though it was the most obvious character to follow. It was almost as though the four naturally equalled the V, as though this was a standard mathematic conclusion to come to. It wasn't, of course. Why should it be? How could it be? It was just the letter V.

Kirra did nothing for a moment, her fingers hovering above the keyboard as though attached to invisible puppetry strings. The library seemed weirdly still and silent as she blinked at the computer, and then, almost of its own accord, her index finger struck the V key. She stared at the screen, transfixed. The number and the letter coupled together perfectly, as though meant to be. Suddenly, the letter R, in the top row, nagged at her, as though she'd worked out by a process of elimination that it was the correct character to go after the first two.

The four and V were equivalent to it, all three characters somehow synonymous. She gnawed her top lip, her fingers trembling slightly. She couldn't help herself: she hit the key.

To her immense surprise, more numbers and letters offered themselves up to her at a much faster rate than before, each tied to the last in what seemed to be an inexplicable mathematic bond. She tried to keep up; each figure fading just as soon as she'd typed it in; a new one blaring at her in its place. And then, before she truly realised what had occurred, a fourteen-character code fitted neatly into the answer field: 4VR93F7E4NS6D6.

Kirra raked her gaze over the neighbouring computers and the few other students in the hushed library, all of whom were immersed in their own private lunchtime ventures. Two small boys were giggling between the shelves over a printout of something and a group of Year Eleven students were hovering quietly around the photocopier, making colour copies of the best art projects from the year before. A girl who smelled faintly of chlorine and a boy with an impressive amount of facial hair for someone his age stood whispering together by one of the grimy windows that looked out onto the oval, where hundreds of students milled around in the sweltering February heat. The pair's eyes roamed over the library as they gossiped, switching targets and topics, but it was quite clear that Kirra, safely hidden behind the computer monitor, escaped their interest.

She turned back to stare at the submit button. This sequence was correct. There was no doubt in her mind. She would have bet her life on it.

She drummed her fingers against the desk for a moment, and then, without another thought, clicked the submit button. She knew it was right — of course it was — she just needed to see it for herself. She waited, anticipating the arrival of some sort of congratulatory notice, but nothing happened. The page failed to refresh itself. It stayed white and blank, her answer apparently lost to cyberspace, sucked away for good.

Scowling, Kirra exited the site. She rose from her chair, logged out of her student account and left the library, feeling dazed and annoyed. She went and stood outside the science lab, waiting impatiently for the bell to ring for chemistry. She felt quite sure the subject would take her mind off what had just happened, but as she spent the afternoon quietly immersed in the principles and applications of spectroscopic techniques, she found that she couldn't quite forget about the code and its confounding answer.

CHAPTER THREE

BARRIE AVENUE

David Hayward eyed his dinner plate longingly. He refused to start his meal until Kirra's mother, Sandra, was at the table, though at the moment it looked as though it was costing him dearly.

Kirra sat opposite him, still in her school uniform, swinging her legs under the table as she waited. Sandra was upstairs, trying to wrestle Mitchell, Kirra's younger brother, away from his video game and gently attempting to convince Kirra's sister, Olivia, that her fresh nail polish wouldn't be tarnished during the process of eating dinner.

David glanced at Kirra, seeming almost startled to find her sitting before him. 'So, how was your first day back?' he asked.

'It was alright,' Kirra replied, nudging the end of her fork with her thumb.

'Good. Excellent,' he said, pursing his lips for a moment, trying to cover up the enormous effort it took for him to carry on a conversation whilst ravenous. 'And ... ah ... and your special Year Twelve classes?'

'Pretty good.'

'Easy stuff for you, right?' He smiled, tapping his foot in an intense percussion solo beneath the table. 'Easy-peasy.'

For a moment Kirra thought of telling him about the code on that site; about how she'd somehow known the answer, and how it had swallowed up her submission without any sort of explanation; but instead she let the conversation dwindle and die. Her father was busy counting down to the arrival of dinner and the appearance of Mitchell, whom he so loved to talk AFL with. No, Kirra thought firmly, she wouldn't tell him about the code. There was nothing really to tell anyway.

David shot an aggrieved look at his plate, pushed away from the table and strode upstairs to investigate the hold-up. Within moments, Mitchell had been forced into a chair and Olivia sat herself gracefully down beside him.

Amid the commotion, the phone rang from its place by the fridge and Mitchell shot off his seat to answer it.

'Oi, Olivia!' he barked as he came back to the table, holding the telephone at arm's length. 'I think it's for you.'

Olivia gave a sharp squeal, clapped her hand over her mouth and flew off her chair. She seized the phone from Mitchell and hurtled around the corner and out of sight, emitting a name under her breath that sounded a lot like *Steven*, only to emerge a moment later looking enormously deflated. She plopped back down in her seat.

'Who was that, Livy?' Sandra asked.

'Don't know,' she said, her nose wrinkling. 'Someone asking if I've entered any competitions lately. I told them about the Hargraves contest, but they hung up. I just ... I don't know ... I really thought they might be ringing to tell me that my charm design won.'

'Oh. Well, no matter, darling,' cooed Sandra. 'They'll ring back, I'm sure. I saw your design, I know how perfect it was. The glitter was a fantastic touch.'

'It was in the end, wasn't it?' Olivia agreed happily.

Mitchell sniggered into his casserole, but covered it up by pretending to choke on a particularly big bit of potato. Kirra patted him weakly on the back, trying to keep a straight face. In the last few months Olivia's sickly girlishness had well and truly reached galactic proportions, but if they laughed out loud at her their mother would reprimand them for the rest of the evening, especially as it seemed she was nothing short of thrilled with Olivia's irritating developments. Instead, Mitchell settled for a quick knowing look and turned away. Olivia, however, looked up just in time to see Kirra quell her smile.

'What? What is it?' she asked, her eyes narrowing immediately.

'Nothing,' Kirra said.

'You were laughing.'

'No, I wasn't.'

Olivia turned to their mother. 'Kirra was laughing at me!'

'No, she wasn't!' Mitchell piped up.

He stuck a pea on the end of his fork, pulled it back and let go. The pea flew at Olivia and bounced lightly off the end of her nose. By the time Sandra looked up and caught Olivia on the verge of bursting into tears, Mitchell had managed to look perfectly innocent again. Kirra took a sip of water, just to look occupied, and their father was too busy with his food to be aware of the exchange at all.

'Mitchell, eat your dinner,' Sandra ordered, peering suspiciously between him and Kirra. 'Kirra, don't be jealous of your sister.'

Kirra nearly spat her water all over the table. *Jealous? I'm not — that's not —*'

'Oh, yes,' Olivia said, looking delighted to be getting to the bottom of things. 'You are. I don't hear Steven ringing here for *you*.'

'I wouldn't want —' Kirra spluttered. 'Even if I could, who'd want —'

'And the Hargraves competition is about fashion, so you'd hardly understand that.'

'Fashion?' Mitchell interrupted. 'Hate to tell you, Olivia, but just because something's pink doesn't mean it's fashionable.'

He nodded at the fuchsia coloured jumper she'd changed into before dinner, a sequined pattern on the front.

'Mum!' Olivia cried, looking distraught.

'Mitchell,' Sandra said, setting down her fork, 'be quiet! Kirra, apologise to Olivia this instant!'

But Olivia wasn't finished. 'You shouldn't laugh at me,' she said, gazing fiercely at Kirra. 'All *you've* got is maths. All *you've* got is algebra and typography and —'

'Topology,' Kirra heard herself saying. 'It's topology, not typography.'

'Exactly!' Olivia said, looking smug. 'Exactly. That's all you have and it's nothing really. So you shouldn't be laughing at me. If anything, *I* should be laughing at *you*, but I feel too sorry for you to do that.'

'Kirra knows that, Livy,' Sandra said, her voice growing stern. Kirra knew their mother detested dinner-table confrontations. 'I'm sure she's sorry for laughing. Now, tell me about what happened this morning on the bus with Steven.'

Olivia's face brightened, and she acted as though Kirra had spontaneously ceased to exist. 'Oh, yes,' she said, and launched into a detailed description of her twenty-minute journey to school: 'I sat down at the back, but made sure the seat next to me was free, and then he got on and sat down and —'

While Sandra listened with rapt attention, Kirra turned back to Mitchell, who gave her an almost imperceptible shrug, a look of saddened camaraderie on his face. Kirra responded with a reassuring smile, the sort that plainly said she didn't care about Olivia or any of the things she had said.

Unsurprisingly, it was David who finished the meal first. He cast his eyes back to Kirra, who was picking absently at her plate. Everyone else was still busy eating.

'So, do you want to have some friends around on the weekend?' he suggested benignly. 'You could have a sleepover.'

Kirra grimaced to herself. A sleepover? For a moment she imagined asking Phillipa Corbel and her docile, well-mannered friends, Joanne Gaskell and Sarah Novak, to stay at her house. They were nice enough to let Kirra sit with them at lunch when she wasn't ploughing through homework, but they generally wriggled out of any further association as politely as they possibly could. Kirra, with all her aggravating cleverness, was considered unfashionable company.

'Sounds good,' she said in a cheery voice, prodding at a chunk of onion. 'I'll check if they aren't already doing something.'

She tried to say this as quietly as humanly possible. Olivia had been absolutely right when she'd said that all Kirra had was maths. Kirra just didn't want her to know that.

Monday lunchtime, a week after she'd come across the strange code, Kirra settled on a lone, splintery bench in the shade. She spotted Olivia sitting by the basketball court with some other Year Nine girls. She tucked a sandy curl behind her ear and grinned at one of her friends, a stringy girl with teeth so prominent she looked capable of eating her lunch through a tennis racket. The grin changed to a stunning smile as a couple of gangly boys roamed by.

'What are you staring at?'

Kirra shielded her eyes to find Mitchell standing by her side, frowning deeply and attempting to follow her line of vision. His socks were crumpled around his ankles and his shirt was a good four sizes too big for him.

'Nothing,' Kirra lied. She looked around as he crouched beside her. 'Where are your friends?'

'At the canteen. I've met some guys who've just started at Freemont, which is cool because I don't have to hang around with Rowan Maretti anymore. He's become an arsehole over the holidays. How 'bout you?' he asked shrewdly. 'You made friends yet?'

Kirra focused on her sandwich for a moment. 'Nope. Not yet.'

'Oh. Well, you haven't been here very long,' he joked. 'Just got to give it time.'

'Yeah,' Kirra agreed. 'It's only been ten years. Can't rush these things.'

Mitchell fiddled with the laces of his polished, oversized shoes. 'Want me to stay with you?'

'Stay?'

'Well, yeah,' he said, determinedly casual. 'We can hang out together at lunch now because … you know … I'm finally here.'

Kirra smiled grimly. She had indeed been waiting for Mitchell to start at the Freemont high-school campus for some time. Three years, in fact. Now primary school was well behind him and he was a week into Year Seven. The idea that he would stick with her at lunchtimes was touching, but not one she'd ever consider seriously. He had friends to make and things to do without Kirra tagging along.

'Won't your new friends wonder where you are?' she asked.

'Probably, but it doesn't matter,' he said, and shoved his hands deep in his pockets. 'They're new friends. I've had you a fair bit longer.'

Neither of them said anything for a few moments.

'You'd better go,' Kirra said finally, pushing him away. 'I've heaps of work to do.'

He nodded, trying not to look too relieved, and knocked shoulders with her before jumping up and racing off, his enormous shirt flapping as he went.

Kirra went back to picking over her sandwich. As she used a bit of lettuce to wipe off the tomato relish her mother persisted in including day after day, she found herself wondering if there was any way she could speed up the three years she had left at Freemont Grammar, or if she could somehow hibernate until it was all over. Time, it seemed, was moving deliberately slowly. She gave a small, humourless smile and tossed the soiled lettuce in a nearby garden bed — and froze. The most alarming sensation pooled at the bottom of her spine and travelled slowly upward, tingling as though the many legs of an insect were scuttling along her vertebrae.

If it weren't for the disturbing incidents of the past week, Kirra might have ignored the feeling, might have passed it off as something else. But this wasn't the first time she'd felt it.

The first time had been the Wednesday evening just gone, when she'd accompanied Sandra to the supermarket to help her with the groceries. As she heaved a bottle of detergent from the trolley into the car boot she'd felt something distract her. It had been an unnerving sensation: almost as though she was being watched. But as Kirra peered around the half-full car park, she realised she was being an idiot. There was no one watching her at all.

'What are you doing?' Sandra asked impatiently, glancing at her gilded wristwatch and reaching for a bag of cheesy crackers and a large tub of yoghurt.

Kirra did another quick scan of the area. 'Nothing. Sorry.'

Sandra squinted at her through the dusk. 'Right. Well ... get a move on, Kirra. Olivia needs her shampoo.'

It was ludicrous to think someone was watching her. What possible explanation could there be for such a thing? Who could be that interested in her? No one, that's who.

But as she watched Mitchell play in his under-thirteens AFL game at Maitland Park on Saturday afternoon, it happened again. Standing there between her parents in the sun, Kirra had to acknowledge for the first time that she might actually be going mad. There wasn't a breeze to speak of, no drop in temperature, and yet she felt that odd alteration in her surroundings again, a shiver that she could only equate with the sensation brought on by being under close surveillance.

'Kirra! Mitchell's about to kick a goal,' David said, shaking her elbow.

She looked back at the field just in time to see Mitchell miss by several metres. He laughed it off and ran back to his position.

'Sorry,' Kirra said.

'Better luck next time, champ!' David hollered across the field. He peered curiously at Kirra. 'You nearly missed it! Everything okay?'

'Yeah. Yeah, fine.'

He looked concerned for a moment, then smiled. 'Thinking about all your tricky sums at school, I suppose.'

'Yeah.'

passengers with her heavy bag on the way and wincing when she heard a soft, sneering giggle from the back.

Once she had alighted and crossed the busy Waverly Road she looked around for Cassie, who normally strode ahead or lagged behind, outright refusing to even seem to be an acquaintance of Kirra Hayward's.

It appeared, however, that Cassie wasn't going home tonight as the bus chugged off in a cloud of exhaust with her firmly still on board.

Kirra kicked a flat stone ahead of her for a few paces, before it skittered off course and into the gutter. She dawdled along the street, paying much more attention to her music than to where she was going, having taken this route home more times than she ever cared to remember. It was only when she turned the corner into the quieter Barrie Avenue that she slowed and came to a halt. Standing by the blossoming yellow rose bushes that filled the garden of the house on the corner, she felt goose bumps sprout along her forearms despite the afternoon warmth, and the all-too-familiar shudder trickled down her spine. This time the feeling was much stronger and far more threatening than before, and her brow crinkled in a frown. She *was* being watched. She was certain of it.

But there was no one around. The street was empty except for a stationary bright gold Honda, a blue Jeep with a dent in the driver's door, and a dark green van. The faint clanging of a piano resonated from one of the houses, the roar of traffic from Waverly Road continued, and a dog yapped in the next street.

It's nothing, Kirra told herself firmly, replacing her headphones and almost digging them into the canals of her ears in the hope that music at a high enough volume might force the menacing feeling away. She turned towards the safety of her house on Lowe Road, her stride far more purposeful than before. She couldn't help feeling that the faster she got away from Barrie Avenue, the better.

But something made her stop again. She yanked the headphones from her ears and looked back, the hairs on the back of her neck tingling. The green van, so unremarkable before, had now become the centre of her attention. The windows were tinted and it was motionless, but Kirra was sure — no, she was *positive* — the engine had started in the time she'd replaced the headphones and taken those few steps. Now it sat very still, simply watching her.

Not watching *you*, she chided herself silently. Don't … don't be paranoid.

She'd taken a few more steps, still teasing herself for being foolish, when, out of the corner of her eye, she noticed the green van pull out onto the street. It crawled along behind her and Kirra increased her pace. It was entirely plausible that the van had nothing to do with her at all. Perhaps it was purely chance that it had pulled out behind her. But her heart sank as it accelerated with her stride. Another few steps proved the van was indeed tailing her. It wasn't merely her imagination on overdrive. Her mouth went bone-dry.

She stopped and stared at it openly for a moment. A nervous little laugh bubbled up in her throat.

Blood roared in her ears and her heart thumped in her chest as she looked between the buzzing main road she'd come from, where cars and buses still zipped past, and her house just around the corner. Which was closer? Which could she sprint to faster? The road was a slightly shorter distance, but the path towards her house was downhill. Her mind raced to calculate her chances as the van hovered before her, like a chess piece waiting comfortably for her next move.

Kirra gulped and, making a split-second decision, hurled her weighty school bag to the ground and ran for her house.

The van roared into the chase.

As it sped closer Kirra screamed, at first without realising it, then again on purpose, willing someone — *anyone* — to help her. It felt as though she was running through a ghost town. No one emerged to stop her pursuers. No one peeked out of a front window to see what was wrong.

The van sped ahead of her and slammed to a halt. Kirra tried to stop and instead skidded into a lavender bush. She untangled herself furiously from the plant and stumbled to her feet, her heart hammering, lavender buds tangled in her hair. Whipping around, she started off in the opposite direction, back towards the main street.

It was then that the van's side door burst open and a masked man shot out to chase her on foot. She looked back. He was twenty metres behind her. Ten. Five.

Kirra only made it back to the house on the corner and its glorious rose garden before she was snatched around the waist and hoisted high into the air. The music player was knocked from her hand and smashed on the footpath; the headphones shattered beneath the thick rubber sole of the man's boot.

'HELP!' she bellowed, clawing at the arm around her waist, wriggling desperately. 'HELP ME!'

She kicked out, thinking the man might slacken his grip if she caused him enough pain, even just for a moment, just for a second, so she might be able to run into someone's front garden, hammer on the door and yell — beg, even — for help. She felt her heels connect briefly with his kneecaps before she was passed into another set of arms where she watched the first man fish her old black wallet out of the front pouch of her schoolbag and flick through its contents. He discarded her bus change, her birthday money and her house key, then found what he was looking for: her student identification card. He ripped it from its slot and reviewed it carefully.

'It's her,' he said.

At this affirmation, the other man dragged Kirra, her arms flailing furiously, towards the van, muffling her screams with a huge, sweaty hand. Her panic reached its peak as she realised her struggles were useless. No matter how ferociously she twisted, lashed out and thrashed around, her abductor would not release his grip on her. In a last desperate attempt, she latched onto the side of the van's door. She was pulled away quite easily a moment later, her fingernails leaving ten little chips in the dark green paint — a surprising sign of the strength she didn't know she had.

Inside the vehicle, she looked up to find one man in the driver's seat and another in the back with something that looked suspiciously like a syringe. All of them wore ski masks. Her eyes widened at the sight of the needle. She barely noticed that her schoolbag and her destroyed music player were tossed in beside her, the street wiped clean of her presence. Horrified, she racked her brain to come up with an explanation for all this. Why would anyone kidnap her? What possible reason could there be?

Two other men jumped into the van and slid the door shut with a heavy clunk. Barrie Avenue vanished from view as the van started to pull away.

The men gripped her limbs and held her down, one of them pinching her skin tightly between his fingers. The man with the syringe turned to her and leaned his hand on her knee, trying to steady her for the injection. Kirra cried out as she felt a sharp stab in her thigh; fluid warmth dispersing beneath her flesh. Her scream died, unheeded, as she fell limp and silent.

On the corner of Waverly Road and Barrie Avenue a man with a steel cane stopped by the yellow rose bushes. He was out of breath, his broad chest heaving in the summer heat. He had only just managed to catch the tail end of Kirra Hayward's kidnapping, and now, as he panted, he extracted his phone from his breast pocket, dialled a number he knew by heart and brought the device to his ear.

'We were too late,' he rasped. 'They've already got her. We need to call Des.'

He snapped the phone shut and limped away just in time to escape the attention of a woman from the house across the road, a couple from down the street, and a pair of teenage boys, all of whom emerged into their front yards, curious as to what all that yelling had been about.

CHAPTER FOUR

LATHAM

A low roar filled Kirra's ears, accompanied by a strange, dull pressure she found vaguely familiar. She stretched out a little bit at a time, feeling sluggish and exhausted. Her eyes were far too heavy to open just yet, and a stiff ache was registering horribly from somewhere in her body, although she wasn't sure exactly where.

The incident on Barrie Avenue had been a nightmare, of course. A twisted, terrible nightmare. Kirra stretched out, feeling stupid. Why on earth would anyone ever kidnap her? Finally, she mustered the strength to open her eyes, stifle a yawn and squint around. Immediately, she felt the blood drain from her cheeks. The room was unfocused and unfamiliar.

She blinked and sat upright. Fear rose in her throat like bile. Barrie Avenue had been real? That meant she was … where? And who were those men? What did they want with her? Perhaps there would be a ransom for her. Yes. Yes, that was probably it. What else could they want? What kind of money would they demand? Could her parents afford to pay it? *Would* they?

Did they even know she'd been kidnapped yet? Maybe they wouldn't realise for some time. No, they would have realised something was wrong at dinnertime. Kirra was always home by dinnertime; she never had anything to keep her away. Would they be looking for her right now? Had anyone told the police yet? How long would she have to wait before being rescued? Hours? Days, even?

Willing herself to move, to do something, anything, she crawled across the carpeted floor and flopped against the wall. Barely audible over the unidentified roar was the low drone of voices. Male voices. The men who had taken her! She wanted to yank the door open and demand an explanation, wanted to ask them what right they thought they had in kidnapping her, but instead she stayed where she was. She wasn't sure she was brave enough for something like that.

The room was small and stark and full of suitcases and packing boxes. Unexpectedly, she was moved off balance. At first she assumed it was her fuzzy head trying to recover from the drug the men had injected her with, but, as another hard jolt hit, she froze. She was moving. Actually moving. Her ears popped uncomfortably. She got to her feet, a task exceedingly harder than usual, and stepped over to a small oval window. She opened the shade.

A shriek of surprise and terror escaped her before she could stifle it. Below, as far as she could see, were clouds; an infinite white blanket of clouds stretching off into the horizon. Above them, the sun was bright and strong and the sky a perfect clear blue. Her stomach plunged horribly. She was in a plane, in some sort of storage compartment. The shock of it hit her like a punch to the face.

Kirra backed away from the window and inhaled unsteadily, telling herself to be brave. Much to her disappointment, however, she found all she could do was to bury her face in her hands and bawl.

Keller, one of Latham's associates, was flicking through a file. 'Since Spencer's death, as far as I can tell, we are the only Contractors to have discovered the prototype,' he said. 'Thank god for that tip-off.'

'And no one else knows about the Translator girl?' Latham asked, dabbing with a perfectly folded napkin at the ring of moisture his glass had left on the tray table before him.

'No, but word will spread quickly, and when it does we can expect to be hunted. You will have to increase security as much as possible.'

'I've taken on more staff to handle it.'

Latham sat back in his plush chair and watched the clouds flutter past the window, feeling delighted with himself. How satisfying it was to know things were going just as planned. Amid the low hum of the engine a new noise punctured the air. Crying? Wailing, almost. He rolled his eyes. The Translator girl was awake.

'I thought she'd be out for the whole flight,' Keller commented, glancing over his shoulder.

'So did I.' Latham sighed and rose from his chair.

'What are you doing?'

'Going to see if she'll make things easy for us.'

At first Kirra, with her head tucked firmly in her arms, didn't hear the door open. She only realised the man was there once he'd addressed her.

'Kirra Hayward?'

She gasped. Her head jerked up. 'Who are you?' she demanded, though it came out as a squeak. 'What's going on?'

The man observed her closely and Kirra stared back. He was dressed neatly in black pants and a charcoal grey shirt and looked to be in his mid-forties. He was tall, slightly overweight and had dark eyes which bore into hers beneath a thick honey-coloured fringe. He also had an accent of some sort, though Kirra couldn't tell what it was yet. 'Are you Kirra Hayward?' he asked.

Kirra wasn't about to tell the man who had kidnapped her anything. Instead, she concentrated on keeping her tears at bay.

He sighed when she didn't answer. 'We know you are Kirra Hayward. We know you recently turned sixteen on the first of January. You live at Nine Lowe Road in the suburb of Freemont and you have attended Freemont Grammar School for the past ten years. Your father, David, works in community development, and your mother, Sandra, works in advertising. You have a younger sister, Olivia, in Year Nine at your school, a younger brother, Mitchell, in Year Seven, and a golden retriever named Oscar. You are the only student at your school taking advanced subjects and we've found that most afternoons you supervise Mitchell as he attempts tricks on a black and blue skateboard outside your house.'

Kirra stared at him, horrified. 'How do you know all that?' she finally breathed.

'My name is Latham. I own an agency and I require your assistance.'

But Kirra wasn't listening. 'But ... but when are you taking me home?' she spluttered.

'If you are good and you help us, there is the possibility of some day being reunited with your family.'

Kirra's throat seemed to close up. Her chest felt as though it was collapsing, as though she were being crushed beneath several tonnes of concrete.

'Some day?' she choked quietly, a single, traitorous tear threatening to spill. '*If* I'm good?'

Latham acted as though he hadn't heard her. 'Last week you completed a puzzle code you found via an internet search engine,' he said calmly. 'Do you remember that, Kirra?'

She stared blankly at him. What did that code have to do with this? With anything?

'Do you remember?' he urged.

She nodded. If she was good, they would take her home. She just had to keep telling herself that.

'Yes, I remember.'

'The answer you submitted was correct,' Latham told her, his tone implying she should be pleased. 'There are very few people who have that skill.'

'But I ... I d-don't know how I did it. It just h-happened. It just —'

'Made sense?' Latham suggested. He smiled. 'Yes,

the Spencer code is quite fascinating. It doesn't require an algorithm, despite its complexity. You can either translate it into a workable sequence, or you can't.'

Kirra suddenly felt a glimmer of hope. They obviously had the wrong person. She knew she had few hidden talents and nearly no noteworthy skills. Being simply clever at maths didn't mean she was a genius code cracker.

'It's not me,' she said, almost feeling sorry for all the trouble she seemed to have caused the man. 'I can't do anything like that. You've got the wrong person.'

Latham smiled again. 'No, Kirra,' he said. 'Yours was the correct answer.'

'It couldn't have been,' she said. 'I've never done anything like that before. It must have been someone else!'

'Someone else who logged into a computer at your school library using your student number and password?'

Kirra gaped at him. 'You can find all that?' she whispered.

Latham seemed to be tiring of the conversation. 'We can find anything. Indeed, any*one*.' This was said with a substantial amount of smugness.

'Can you do it?' Kirra asked. 'Can you break the code?'

'If I could, I wouldn't need you,' he told her.

Kirra frowned. Some of her dread gave way to confusion. 'What do you need the sequence for?' she asked slowly.

'A question I've often asked myself,' said Latham, a strained smile on his lips. 'My reasons for needing the sequence need not worry you too much. What should worry you, however, is your safety, which all depends on whether or not you'll cooperate with me.'

'Cooperate with you? You kidnapped me! My family will call the police! They'll come looking for me!'

'I'm positive they will,' Latham agreed. 'Absolutely positive. They'll never find you though. I can promise they won't.'

Kirra goggled at him for a moment.

'What are you?' she breathed.

'A Contractor,' was the answer.

Kirra blinked. She wasn't sure she knew what that meant. Her bewilderment must have been apparent because Latham sighed and elaborated.

'A Contractor is someone who does things for normal people — for a price, of course.'

'What sort of things?'

'Whatever. People often want things done but don't want to get their hands dirty. For the right price, they can hire my agency, which has a reputation for incomparable efficiency. You, Kirra, are going to help me maintain that reputation.'

He studied her for several moments. The air between them buzzed, the plane's engine a blaring roar.

'Do you kill people?' Kirra asked eventually.

'I do whatever I'm hired to do.'

She felt her eyes widen. He was a murderer!

'I'm not going to help you,' she said, feigning bravery.

'I think you will.'

'No. I won't. Not ever.'

'Then you will never be reunited with your family,' Latham said, an edge to his voice. 'Not that it matters.

32

My employees aren't afraid to use force in order to gain your cooperation.'

Force? Kirra tried not to think about what that meant.

'You kill people,' she said. 'That's all I need to know. I won't help you. You can do whatever you want to me, but I won't help.'

Latham's smile was patronising. 'Kirra, far braver and stronger people than you have succumbed under force. Be assured, I will make you help me.'

He seemed so certain that Kirra couldn't help but feel terrified. She was neither brave nor strong, so perhaps he was right. Perhaps he would be able to force her to help him.

'Now,' he said charmingly, 'I have work to attend to. We'll be landing soon, so make yourself comfortable until then. Goodbye, Kirra.'

He disappeared through the door, locking it with a smart click behind him.

The nausea that had plagued Kirra since she'd woken flared, and she just made it to an open packing box in time to vomit into it.

She mopped her mouth with the back of her hand and crumpled to the floor, where she replayed the conversation in her head, again and again. Not one bit of it made sense. She'd been kidnapped because she'd submitted a correct answer to the code. But what *was* the code? And what did the answer do? It was crazy. It couldn't be real. This couldn't be happening, not to her. It was a dream. It had to be a dream. She would wake up in bed in her tidy room with its blue carpet and curtains, and she would get up and get ready for school. It would happen any second now. She knew it would.

Latham stood by his seat, his fingers caressing its leather upholstery. For all the many who succumbed to physical force, there was always one person who stayed strong and died because of it. Latham was fairly certain the pitiful creature in the storage compartment wouldn't be one of those strong people, particularly not under duress ... and yet he couldn't afford to take the chance. The only thing he knew for absolute certain was that Kirra Hayward could not die.

'Everything alright?' Keller asked, glancing up from his papers.

Latham nodded, moving slowly to resume his seat. He looked from Keller and the many files in his hand, to the small band of men sitting together at the back of the plane, where his gaze hovered for a moment, and, finally, to the clouds that whispered past the window. A brilliant idea suddenly struck him, an infallible idea, and he turned to Keller with a growing smile.

'It will be.'

CHAPTER FIVE

THE HANGAR

When the plane finally touched down, Kirra scrambled to the window and pressed her nose flat against the freezing pane. Her vantage point only told her what was already obvious: they had landed on an airstrip in a field somewhere. She did a double take when she saw a thin layer of ice blanketing the grass. Ice? She stared. In the distance were fields of white. Snow? Kirra had never seen snow before, but much more unsettling was the fact that it was currently the height of summer at home in Freemont. Beyond the fields, she could make out the faint outline of a cluster of industrial buildings, a long and empty highway, and nothing at all to help her identify her location.

Behind her, the door burst open with a bang. She whipped around as two men came towards her, snatched her under the arms and heaved her into the air. She tried to get a good look at them, as much as she could whilst being swung above the ground. Were these the same men from Barrie Avenue?

The trouble was, she had no idea what those men had looked like. They'd all worn ski masks the entire time. What Kirra seemed to remember most of the event was the sound of that piano and how the person playing it had failed so spectacularly to come to her aid. Now she was beginning to realise that her abduction had been over and done with in less than a minute. She wasn't even sure how much of that time she'd screamed for, meaning that anyone who might have helped her hadn't had long to do so before the van had swallowed her up and taken her away.

The moment she was thrust into the outside air a small, helpless yelp burst from her lips. The icy wind sliced through her school jumper and cotton dress, the summery garments a ridiculous opponent for this kind of weather. As she twisted and gasped within the men's grip, the air stung at her bare legs like tiny frosted pinpricks. If the two men flanking her were bothered by the dramatic drop in temperature, they certainly didn't show it. There was ice on the tarmac, small piles of snow in the places where bitumen met grass and the sky was a steely expanse of grey cloud.

Distracted by the cold, Kirra barely realised she was being carried towards the looming mouth of an aircraft hangar. The two men forced her through a side doorway into an extended concrete corridor, and marched her along it for some time before pausing at an open door.

Inside the room, a woman sat on a couch, talking happily with someone out of Kirra's view. The woman wore jeans, a dark crimson jacket and gloves, and had long dark hair draped over her shoulders. She looked up at Kirra and the two men, her expression curious.

One of Kirra's brutish escorts spoke in a language Kirra couldn't identify, and was answered in the same language by the other person in the room, a man Kirra couldn't see. Obviously the men had been given instructions of some kind, because they led her off in the opposite direction with a distinct sense of purpose, heading down another corridor before stopping at a wide metal door, once painted a silvery grey and now peeling and rusty.

One of the men punched a security code into the keypad on the wall and lifted the bolt, and Kirra found herself face to face with a concrete room full of nothing. She was pushed over the threshold, stumbled, and spun around just in time to watch them slam the door and hear them bolt it from the outside.

She sucked in a breath and tried to wrench the door open, not entirely sure why she was bothering. Whirling around, she noted a metal tap and basin and a frosted steel toilet in the corner behind the door. The water in the toilet was almost frozen over. She flushed it once and watched the liquid seep away and then reappear. Several flushes proved successful in thawing most of the ice.

Opposite the toilet and basin was a tiny window, high up in the wall: metal bars crisscrossed over a broken pane of glass. She tensed when an icy breeze whistled into the cell.

After concluding that escape was impossible via the little window, Kirra did a few quick laps of the cell. In four steps she could walk from one side to the other.

She was trembling with cold. She slipped her hands up into the sleeves of her jumper, crouched in the corner facing the door and wrapped her arms around herself.

Her breath curled away from her mouth in steamy spirals, and each inhalation felt like someone had her chest in a vice and was winding it tighter every few seconds. She glanced at her wrist, but remembered that back home in Freemont she'd stupidly forgotten to put on her little watch with its cobalt coloured wristband.

As night fell, Kirra started to panic in earnest when she thought she saw several dainty snowflakes float in through the window. The room grew colder and colder by the moment and the air pressed in on her. It felt like being shut up inside a freezer. She wondered for a frightening moment if she'd survive the temperature of the night. She wasn't positive she would and so she told herself that a rescue team had to be on its way. Any time now, they'd come for her. They'd wrap her up and give her a warm drink and take her back to Freemont. There was no need to panic about the cold. None at all. They were coming.

Kirra woke to the sound of voices. They sounded far off and for some reason Kirra processed their words at a much slower rate than she normally would have.

'You have made an unacceptable error,' a man was saying threateningly. It sounded like Latham.

'Me?' The second voice sounded ashamed. Kirra didn't recognise this man.

'Yes! You! I gave you a simple task: to keep her alive. Not challenging, is it?'

'No, but —'

'Not hard at all, really, and still this morning I very nearly find a frozen corpse in the room instead of a viable Translator.'

38

'That's not my fault. You can hardly blame me for hypothermia.'

Kirra wanted to open her eyes and see them, but when she did she was blinded by a bright light hanging directly above the bed she seemed to be lying upon. She shut them quickly. The men kept talking.

'I told you to check the room to ensure it was safe and escape was impossible —'

'I did! I just ... I just didn't think about temperature.'

'You don't seem to understand the severity of the situation. She must *not* be allowed to die. Her safety is *everything*. You must be prepared for *everything*. Do you understand?'

'Yeah, of course.'

'This is about to become an ongoing responsibility for you. The most vital responsibility imaginable.'

'I know. I know how important she is.'

'Good. Ensure you are more cautious from now on.'

'I will be.'

'Now go, before she wakes up and sees you.'

What they were talking about interested her, but not enough to open her eyes properly or attempt actual movement. She didn't know where she was or what was going on. Her body felt frozen stiff and her lungs were like iceblocks in her chest. Eventually she drifted back to sleep.

Kirra awoke the next time because she felt a mattress creak beneath her. Two things were very clear right away: she was trapped beneath a weighty pile of blankets, almost to the point of being smothered, and she was far from recovery. Her chest throbbed, her muscles felt like flimsy plywood and her limbs no longer seemed to be part of her body, as if they were weird foreign attachments her nerves couldn't recognise. Kirra didn't know much about hypothermia, but she did know she was lucky to be alive.

She jumped when something touched her hand. Looking up, she was met by a concerned face with huge dark eyes and recognised the woman she had spotted on her arrival at the hangar.

The woman sat on the edge of the bed, still dressed in her red jacket, her long dark hair over one shoulder. She said something in a language Kirra didn't understand and gave a tiny, timid smile. She was pale, and her hands were dry and chafed, her neck splotchy and rough with what looked like wind rash.

She seemed to realise Kirra was incapable of movement and propped her up into a half-sitting position with an extra pillow. She picked up a stained ceramic mug, raised it to Kirra's lips and murmured another foreign word.

Kirra inspected the woman closely. She didn't seem threatening. Not at all. She was young and sweet and seemed hell-bent on helping Kirra drink. And really, what did Kirra have to lose? Parting her parched lips, she took a shallow sip. The tea scorched as it swept down her throat, but the woman seemed so delighted that Kirra was drinking, she didn't have the heart to complain.

The woman then draped another blanket over the bed and tucked Kirra in so that she was only visible from the chin up. Voices could be heard occasionally beyond the door. With each murmur, the woman glanced up, her hair floating around her worried face. It was plain that she was there in secret, and the sooner Kirra drank the tea, the sooner the woman could go.

Kirra obliged, and couldn't help but feel a tiny bond with the woman. Perhaps she was a prisoner too. After the last sip the woman set the mug down, removed the extra pillow and straightened the blankets. She took Kirra's hand between her own for a moment, then got up and left, closing the door quietly behind her. Kirra wanted to shout after her, wanted to ask her to stay. She wanted to know what was going on and what was going to happen to her, but stopped herself just in time. She didn't want to get the woman in trouble, especially as she seemed just as afraid as Kirra was.

Kirra was kept in the low cot bed in the infirmary for nearly a week. She was, for the most part, left alone to recover from her near-fatal bout of hypothermia — the result of a single night spent in the cell. Every so often a man came into the room to fetch something from one of the cabinets. He was young, with wavy blond hair and dark circles beneath his weird, staring eyes. He checked Kirra over twice a day, monitored her breathing, her heart rate, her temperature, and then left her alone. He never looked her directly in the face and never said anything to her, his eyes strangely empty and his face disturbingly soulless.

Kirra knew he was a doctor, or had at least some training, because one day two injured and bleeding men had stumbled into the room, and he had treated them both without a moment's hesitation and prescribed medicine from a cabinet high up on the wall.

Every day Kirra told herself to expect Latham, an event she regarded with an acute sense of terror. She wondered anxiously how he might force her to cooperate with deciphering the code, and what he wanted it for. But he never showed up.

The person Kirra saw most often was the woman. Always in her jacket, the precise colour of blood, she came with plates of food and mugs of tea and assisted Kirra in whatever way she could. She always seemed nervous and never stayed very long, but Kirra looked forward to her visits as much as she did her cooking. She guessed the woman made the meals herself, because whenever Kirra managed to get through one she seemed almost flattered. For breakfast, she brought bowls of cereal and toast, sometimes even eggs, and, once, pancakes. For lunch, she made thick sandwiches packed with chicken and cheese. Dinners were by far the best. She made soup and spaghetti dishes, roasts and vegetables, rice and chunky stews, all of it warm, comforting and delicious.

After almost a week of immobility in the infirmary, Kirra began to feel restless. She had recovered to an extent and regained the full use of her limbs, but tried to hide it from the woman and the doctor for fear they might return her to the cell if they knew she was well enough. The idea of going back there frightened her immeasurably, and she wasn't sure she would survive the cold for another night.

Her efforts were all in vain, however, because one day, after the doctor had completed his second examination, another man barged through the door, grabbed Kirra out of bed and set her on her feet. He steered her out of the room, stopping only to grab a large paper bag from the top shelf of a cabinet, and forced her down the corridor.

Kirra did her best to catch quick glimpses into the other rooms in the hangar. Many were computer labs, some were storage rooms, and others were filled with equipment in black and silver cases. Occasionally she passed a room with a couch, a rug or a mirror; simple items that tried and failed to lend the hangar a sense of domesticity. One room, its door only slightly ajar, was painted a sickly shade of violet. Frowning, Kirra twisted back to get a better look, but was wrenched onward.

Finally, they came to a door she recognised. The man typed the code into the keypad on the wall, lifted the bolt and pushed Kirra back into her cell. He tossed the paper bag in after her and slammed the door shut.

Kirra was pleased to note that the broken pane in the window had been removed, a new one in its place. In the corner now lay several blankets, for which Kirra was grateful, though she couldn't help thinking a mattress wouldn't have gone astray. She cautiously opened the bag the man had thrown onto the cement, and expelled a sigh of relief as she pulled out two scuffed boots, a pair of faded jeans and a dark fleecy jumper. All the clothes looked and felt as though they'd been worn before. Kirra wondered if they belonged to the woman in the red jacket. The jeans were a bit too long, and the jumper very tatty, but they were warm and soft and Kirra was grateful. She slipped off her blue school dress and put the new clothes on. She bundled up the uniform and shoved it into the corner, thinking it would make a better pillow than none at all.

CHAPTER SIX

BALCESCU'S DRUG

A week had passed since Kirra had been returned to her cell. She made sure to count the days, and tried to count the hours too. The boredom she felt was so intense that she wouldn't have been surprised to find herself going mildly insane. Latham had yet to make an appearance and she didn't want to worry about what might happen when he did. Instead, she spent the time wondering about her family. She tried to imagine what they were doing, and how an evening in the house might unfold now that her disappearance was approximately two weeks old. Did they still sit down at the dining table for dinner? Did Olivia have to be wrangled into her chair? Did she talk non-stop about Steven? Did Mitchell have to be extracted from his video game? Or did they all sit at the table quietly, ears on alert for a knock on the door or a phone call that might tell them where Kirra was?

If only she'd told her father about the code at dinner that Monday night, as she'd thought to. Maybe it would have made all the difference, might have pointed them in the right direction, perhaps even got them to her almost as soon as she'd been abducted. They had to be close now. They just had to be. Any day now, she'd see them again.

The woman in the red jacket, Lena, had continued to visit Kirra after she'd been returned to her cell. The first time Kirra had seen her post-recovery, she had pointed to herself and said her own name, then pointed to Lena and looked questioningly at her. Lena had understood immediately and rewarded Kirra with the word in a strong accent. Their time together was usually brought to a close by one of the men, who would come to the door, throw it open and issue a harsh command. Lena seemed to dislike the men intensely, her dark eyes resentful as they led her out of the cell like a child who'd done wrong and slammed the door after her.

Sometimes Lena remained in the cell even after Kirra had finished eating. Occasionally she brought her extra bits of clothing, sneaking in a glove or a beanie or an undershirt, one at a time. She started bringing a newspaper with her, always the same scrunched edition, as though she had been toting it around for years. Though Kirra couldn't identify the language, let alone read it, the pictures were enough: of stern men in suits, of crime scenes, of protests and ceremonies. Lena read the paper out loud, providing Kirra with long and animated explanations in her own language. Sometimes she giggled softly at what Kirra guessed were jokes of her own creation, and Kirra often found herself giggling along too. Frequently Lena flipped to one of the last pages to point at a picture of a city skyline at night, lit up and glittering prettily. She'd take Kirra's hand in her own and talk about the picture far more than any other photo or article, gazing at it and thumbing the tattered corner of the page. Though Kirra had no idea why Lena was so obsessed with the tiny photo, she did have a feeling she was trying to tell her something important about it.

One morning, the bolt lifted and two men entered the cell. Kirra had worked out their names — Marcam and Bjerre — from listening hard to their interactions with Lena. They pulled her to her feet and escorted her down the corridor and into a long, mouldy bathroom.

It was there they extracted her from her clothes and tossed them, one by one, into a rattling washing machine, before pushing her under the icy jet of water slamming out of a rusting showerhead. At first, Kirra had tried to fight the men off, horrified at the idea of being naked in their presence. Of course, between the two of them her struggling was a slight inconvenience, and they'd easily succeeded in removing her clothes by force in under a minute. After several moments in the freezing shower a flimsy towel was tossed her way, her clothes were dried in a wheezing tumble dryer and she was finally allowed to step into them once more. The men unashamedly observed the entire process from their places by the door.

Hours later, Kirra was still choking back hot tears of humiliation. When the cell door opened and Lena appeared, she hurried to hide the moisture around her eyes, and was grateful when Lena pretended she didn't notice. Instead, she grinned and pressed a finger to her

46

lips. Kirra felt annoyed by her jubilant mood. What the hell was there to be cheerful about?

Lena crouched down, her hands held behind her back, and tilted her head from side to side. Kirra stared at her. Lena rolled her eyes and continued to nod towards each shoulder with increased enthusiasm. Suddenly, Kirra understood.

'That one,' she said, indicating to Lena's right hand.

Lena revealed an empty palm.

'Okay then, that one.'

Lena smiled widely and produced a hairbrush, probably her own. Kirra reached for it, but Lena gently pushed her hand away. Without a word she took Kirra's stringy hair between her fingers and began working out the knots.

Kirra stayed very still, struggling to contain the painful sobs sitting hot and heavy in her chest, until she could hide them no longer. She wasn't sure why this simple kindness produced such emotion in her; she was crying harder now than she had just after her shower. It wasn't merely the incident in the bathroom though; it was everything. Weeks were passing and still no rescue. No sign of help at all. The longer she spent here, the further away help seemed and she was fast losing hope.

Lena let her cry as much as she wanted. She wrapped her arms around Kirra's neck — a surprisingly sturdy grasp for someone so wispy — and hugged her for a long moment before going back to her hair.

The next afternoon, Marcam and another man Kirra had never seen before collected her from her cell and took her into a long, dark room. There was only just enough light for her to distinguish a single chair surrounded by trolleys and tables. The men dumped her into the chair and proceeded to strap her arms and ankles down with black belts built into the upholstery. Kirra started to panic. What exactly were they going to do to her?

Less than an hour before, Lena had come into the cell — not to present Kirra with a meal or to sneak her a woollen scarf, but to administer a frantic, desperate hug. She had looked stricken, as though she'd been crying, and had held Kirra for a very long time. Kirra had clung to her, feeling terrified, sure that the hug heralded something truly awful and there was nothing she could do but wait for it to happen. Lena had seemed not to want to let go, but the men had called her to leave, so she'd stood up and given Kirra a fierce, bolstering look, her distress too great for anything more. Now, strapped into the chair, Kirra realised Lena had been trying to tell her to be brave.

'Good afternoon, Kirra.'

The light above her chair was switched on. She strained her neck around to watch as Latham entered the room, closely followed by the blond doctor from the infirmary.

Latham placed a piece of paper and a pen on one of the tables by the chair and she glanced at it. It was another code.

'If you wouldn't mind, I need your help with this.' Latham's voice was light and even, almost pleasant.

'What do you need it for?' Kirra said, her voice wobbling.

Latham's eyes narrowed. 'It makes no difference to you, Kirra,' he said smoothly.

'Tell me.'

He lifted an eyebrow. 'Each sequence acts as a security PIN. Each PIN unlocks a door behind which something of value is hidden.'

'Something of value? What?'

'Would it be better if I told you we were bank robbers?' Latham asked, looking amused.

'I just want to know,' Kirra said, sounding pathetic even to herself.

'Yes: you *want* to; you don't *need* to. Now, look at the code. Does anything jump out at you?'

She shook her head, her eyes glued to the paper. 'No.'

'Lying won't help,' Latham said.

'I'm not lying!'

He gave her a sceptical smile and turned to the blond doctor, who, up until then, had been standing silently to one side. Latham said something in another language and the doctor came forward to hook Kirra up to a heart monitor. He attached a little clamp to her left index finger and fastened a belt around her arm. He fixed a catheter into a vein in the crook of her elbow, then took a syringe from one of the trolleys and filled it carefully with some kind of clear medication from a vial. He double-checked the dosage and turned to Kirra.

'This is an interesting drug,' Latham commented. 'The opposite of a painkiller. I've not tried it myself, but the sensation is apparently so acute that after only a minute death would come as a welcome release. Decipher the code, Kirra, and Balcescu will discard the dosage. Now, take another look for me.'

Kirra swallowed, eyeing the doctor nervously.

'Please don't,' Kirra pleaded quietly. It seemed, however, that he couldn't hear her; his eyes stared vacantly as he came ever closer.

'He won't,' Latham assured her, 'as long as you decipher the code.'

'You need it to kill people. You said that on the plane.'

Latham tapped a plump finger against his chin, looking frustrated. 'You have a moment to make your choice,' he said, his voice far less patient than before.

Kirra stared at the paper, unwilling to look at Latham, unwilling to look at Balcescu. The sequence was already forming. She could see it. First the letter H, and then a six, and then —

She looked away. She had to be brave, just like Lena wanted. After all, Latham was a murderer. She mustn't give him the sequence, not under any circumstances. And anyway, how painful could this drug thing be? She'd broken a finger once. It had been jammed in the bathroom door one morning as Olivia had fought with Kirra over whose turn it was to go first. How much more painful could it be than that?

'I won't help you,' she said, feeling oddly brave. 'I won't.'

Latham merely nodded. He murmured something to Balcescu, who took a firm hold of Kirra's arm. Her throat dried up and she tried to wriggle away, but the bonds held her tightly, inescapably, to the chair. To budge even a centimetre in any direction was impossible.

Balcescu injected the syringe into the catheter, and Kirra felt the drug empty into her body and wash right into her blood. She bit her top lip and shut her eyes tightly, bracing herself.

After several seconds, she opened her eyes. She waited, blinking under the light. Nothing was happening. Nothing at all. She almost wanted to laugh, all the tension draining from her body to leave her feeling victorious. It wasn't working! She felt nothing! Perhaps, in the inexplicable way she could decipher the code, she was also immune to the drug. Maybe the drug had a horrific effect on others, but none whatsoever on her. Perhaps she was mysteriously special in all sorts of ways.

But then she saw Latham look at Balcescu and Balcescu look back, fanatical anticipation gleaming in his eyes. And, finally, she felt it.

A terrible shriek ripped from her throat as an invisible knife stabbed at her heart, twisting and seemingly digging it out from her chest. The agony continued downward, circulating through the veins in her legs, flooding into the soles of her feet. It spread out to her arms, her hands, her fingers, and up into her neck, shooting spikes into her head. Her blood boiled and her skin felt as though it was blistering. It felt as if she'd been injected with poison, and now it raged within her, scalding and furious, as though searching for a place to escape.

Kirra heard herself screaming, a high-pitched, frenzied sound she'd had no idea she could produce, as she writhed in the chair. It had to stop. *It had to stop!* She was going to die! She was certain of it. She couldn't take much more. Any second now her body was going to give in. But it couldn't. She didn't want to die. She wanted to live! She wanted to survive long enough to get back to her family, long enough to make it back to Freemont Grammar, and then even longer so she could leave it. She wrenched her head up and gazed imploringly at Balcescu.

'Please,' she rasped, surprised she could speak at all. 'Please … just *stop it*!'

Balcescu said nothing, but it hardly mattered. Latham had his own reply ready.

'It can stop at any moment, Kirra. We have the antidote ready. Agree to decipher the code and it will stop and you can go back to your room. Refuse, and Balcescu will increase the dosage.'

Kirra's skull was being sliced in two. She crumpled forward, with only the restraints to keep her from falling. Her mouth hung wide open; she had no control over the muscles in her face. She gasped for air and struggled furiously to keep her brain functioning.

'Alright,' she panted. 'Alright! Please … *please* just make it stop …'

She was barely aware of Balcescu holding her arm and injecting something else into the catheter. Within an instant, the fire inside her was extinguished. Her whole body was drenched in a cool wave of relief and her lungs found air, her eyes regained their sight. All she felt now was violently ill, but that was a glorious improvement.

Her relief was short-lived, however, as Latham pushed the piece of paper in front of her, followed by a pen, which he pressed into her hand.

'Balcescu is preparing another dose, Kirra, just in case you change your mind.'

Kirra couldn't even raise her head to answer him. Exhaustion such as she had never known overwhelmed her.

'No,' she breathed. 'No, I'll do it.'

She scrawled the code as best she could. With her wrist still bound tightly to the armrest and her fingers quaking, her handwriting was atrociously messy, but each digit, each letter, was just legible along the bottom of the document.

H6JF9A37UV5N2B

She dropped the pen, her hand collapsing with it, and slumped back, feeling wretched and sickly. To have aided Latham was more agonising than any physical pain, but of course it was too late now.

'In time, Kirra, I believe this will get easier,' Latham said, slipping the piece of paper into the breast pocket of his suit. He said something Kirra didn't understand and she felt the restraints loosen. She was lifted from the chair by two men and carried out of the room and back into the corridor.

Out of the corner of her eye she caught a swift glimpse of red, and, looking back, saw Lena pressed against the wall outside the room, her cheeks wet with tears. Kirra wondered if Lena had expected her to refuse Latham, to be far more courageous than she'd been. But then she caught Lena's eye and they shared a silent moment of understanding. They were on the same team, the same side, not to be disappointed by each other, but to be beaten as one.

CHAPTER SEVEN

LENA'S DEPARTURE

Hours later, in the dead of the night, Kirra was still awake. Her body seemed unwilling to give in to sleep, though it felt as though she'd just run a marathon. Her hands were trembling, her throat was still hoarse from screaming, and for the first hour back in her cell she had crouched by the steel toilet, vomiting without respite. Finally, she'd been able to wash the taste of sick from her mouth and retreat to the blankets in her corner, her tongue burning and her forehead bathed in sweat.

Was it Monday today? She was losing track. It was as likely to be any other day as it was to be Monday, but today had a Monday sort of feel to it. At least she was missing out on PE at school then; that was something to be thankful for. On the other hand, she was also missing out on maths, something that would have felt wonderfully comforting. She wondered if her class had realised she wasn't there yet. The students in the Year Twelve maths class paid about as much attention to her as they did to the stain on the carpet in the corner of the room, left over from when a Year Seven had lobbed a balloon filled with an undetermined substance through an open window just before the summer holidays one year.

Kirra registered the sound of hushed footsteps travelling down the corridor. She frowned. Nobody ever came to her cell in the middle of the night. A night-time visit struck her as very worrying. The five-digit code was entered into the keypad and the bolt lifted, all with as little noise as possible, and Kirra braced herself for the worst.

Lena appeared in the doorway, swooping down to hold Kirra in a tight embrace for several long moments. Kirra exhaled happily and returned the hug. Then Lena was fumbling for her hand and pulling her to her feet, a definite air of haste about her. Kirra held back. She had expected Lena to be bringing her a hot drink, as she often did in the evening, or to suggest a game of cards with the deck she carried with her. She hadn't expected to be taken somewhere.

She frowned at her through the darkness. 'Lena, what are you doing?'

She ignored Kirra.

'Lena!'

'Shhh!' Lena pressed a finger to her lips and motioned for Kirra to follow her out the door.

Kirra froze. What was happening? Lena turned back, her eyes huge and imploring. She clasped Kirra's hands and gazed at her fiercely. Kirra knew if Lena had the words she would be pleading with her to cooperate.

Kirra nodded and followed. It was against her better judgement to venture out into the freezing corridors of the hangar at any time, but she trusted Lena implicitly. She was the greatest friend — the only friend — she'd ever had.

The hangar seemed deserted. There were no lights on, nor any other signs of life, as Lena dashed silently through the corridors, peering around corners and tiptoeing past doorways, looking over her shoulder to ensure Kirra was following. Kirra wondered what on earth they were doing. The corridor ended, and Lena inserted a slim silver key into a side door. It clicked softly, the noise magnified in the tense silence, and Lena pushed the door open.

The cold blasted over Kirra's face with the force of a hurricane, almost throwing her back into the passageway. Since the window pane in her cell had been replaced, she'd forgotten just how cold it was outside. It didn't take long for her to start shaking, goose bumps parading up and down her forearms, the tips of her fingers searing in the wind.

Lena shrugged off her red jacket and draped it around Kirra's shoulders. Kirra immediately went to shove the coat back, but Lena ignored her with a strained smile and helped — almost forced — Kirra's arms into the sleeves before moving on.

She kept close to the side of the building, her long hair billowing around her as she turned a corner and entered the great, gaping mouth of the hangar. Several cars were parked just inside, and Lena turned to Kirra to fish in the pocket of her forfeited jacket. Suddenly, Lena's intention dawned on Kirra and she halted, her heart almost stopping along with her.

'We're leaving?' she gasped loudly.

Lena jumped a few centimetres into the air and dropped the car key, her hand, coarse and red with an irritation of some sort, clutching her chest in fright. She looked around, her eyes wide, mistaking Kirra's sudden realisation for an alarm.

'Lena? You're helping me escape?' Kirra asked again.

Lena frowned, but grasped Kirra's arm and motioned for her to stand by a shiny teal-coloured sedan. She scooped up the key from the ground and placed Kirra's hand on the passenger door, silently urging her to be ready for a quick getaway.

Lena winced as she pressed the button on the remote key and the beep that indicated the unlocking of the car resonated loudly inside the hangar. Kirra flinched. Surely someone would have heard that. Lena didn't hesitate to find out. She flung the driver's door wide open and scrambled inside. Kirra followed suit, shutting the door behind her.

A light flicked on further back in the hangar. Kirra could hear shouting, people rushing about, orders being made with desperate urgency.

Lena's hands trembled as she tried to jam the key into the ignition, missing several times. Finally, the car roared to life. Kirra looked back over her shoulder. She could see several silhouettes pouring into the hangar, sprinting towards them.

'Lena!' she yelled. 'Go!'

Lena didn't need telling twice. She released the handbrake, hit the accelerator and the car sped off into the night. In the distance, Kirra spotted a dimly illuminated highway: their path to freedom. Once they reached it, she assumed Lena would drive to the nearest police station, explain the situation and then the appropriate calls would be made. Within days, Kirra was going to be home.

She stole a glance at Lena. Her eyes were on the road ahead, her knuckles stark white as she gripped the steering wheel. Kirra felt a pang of misery at the prospect of leaving her. She was certain Lena would want to go back to her own family once she was free, and so she knew their freedom meant their goodbye.

Just as Kirra was lamenting the impending loss of her friend Lena looked in the rear-vision mirror and gasped. Kirra whipped around. They were being chased. Two sets of headlights were tailing them, growing steadily closer with each tense second. Kirra looked back at the highway. Once they reached it, she was sure nothing could hurt them. So long as they got there, they would be safe.

A sharp crack pierced the air and Kirra couldn't help but yell out in surprise. Were they being shot at? She didn't want to believe it — *couldn't* believe it. She turned back to look, but couldn't see anything except the ominous pairs of headlights. Another crack sounded out.

Lena was crying now. Silent, terrified tears streamed from her eyes as they sped onward, though the highway didn't seem to be getting closer at all. More gunshots rang through the night and the back windscreen exploded, shards of glass soaring into Kirra's hair. She ducked and slipped further down into her seat, her body seeming to operate on adrenaline alone. A louder, closer bang, different to the gunshots, sounded and the car lurched wildly. Lena fumbled for the steering wheel, but the swerving was beyond her control. Kirra felt herself bump around in her seat. Another ear-splitting bang, another tyre blown, another dangerous zigzag.

A silver car effortlessly overtook theirs, slowing in front of them and forcing Lena to slam on the brakes to avoid a collision. She tried to veer around it and keep going, but the second car, a black one, blocked them in.

Lena yelled something to Kirra, then sprang from the car like a cat as two men clambered out of the silver one. Kirra froze. She couldn't move. Those men had guns.

Lena glanced back to see Kirra still in her seat. She came to a slow standstill in the middle of the road, studying her resignedly. The chase was over. The two men ran to her and she didn't struggle as they took her arms and twisted them behind her back.

'No!' Kirra yelled, finally moving from her seat. It was far too late, of course. One of the other men was already by her side and removing her from her seat. He dragged her towards the black car as Lena was deposited into the silver one.

'Lena!' Kirra shouted.

But she had been swallowed up by the vehicle, lost behind its tinted windows, and was already on her way back to the hangar.

The ride back was short and silent for Kirra, who was drowning in disappointment. They had been so close. She gazed gloomily at the car ahead. Lena had done so much to get them away and Kirra desperately wanted to tell her how much it meant, how thankful she was, how brave she thought Lena had been. Maybe they would try it again someday. They could plan it carefully together, work out every detail to ensure they weren't ever caught again.

All too soon the cars were parked and Kirra and Lena found themselves back in the hangar. A single light high up in the ceiling gave the area a deceptively welcoming glow — until Kirra saw Latham waiting for them.

He looked tired and supremely inconvenienced by their near escape. Kirra couldn't help staring at the small handgun resting in his grip. Was he going to kill her? The terrifying thought collided with what he had said about how important she was. Latham needed her. He wouldn't kill her.

'Kirra,' he began wearily, 'you must know that this will be your last attempt at leaving us. Security will be improved greatly from this moment on. Be assured, you won't get so far next time.'

Kirra felt Lena reach for her hand and hold it tightly; her fingers were cold but remarkably reassuring nonetheless. Looking up, Kirra saw a strange emotion in her friend's eyes. Acceptance perhaps, or something akin to it. Standing there with her, shoulder to shoulder, Kirra wanted to tell her it didn't matter. They could try again. They *would* try again.

She heard Lena take a long, slow breath as Latham started speaking very softly to her in what sounded like her own language. When he'd finished, he motioned for her to go to him. Lena looked at Kirra once more and, with an encouraging smile that seemed to communicate there would indeed be another escape attempt some day soon, she stepped forward.

She had barely left Kirra's side when Latham raised the gun. Kirra must have screamed. She must have. Who else could have made the terrible sound that accompanied the gunshot?

Not Lena. Of course not. How could she? She was sprawled on the floor and she wasn't moving. Blood was running thick and fast into her hair, as though it had a life of its own. Kirra wanted to believe she wasn't dead. She wanted it so much more than she'd ever wanted anything in her life. But Lena was motionless, her blood was everywhere and her big dark eyes were glassy and still.

Kirra was in her cell. She didn't recall leaving the mouth of the hangar and had no idea how she'd got back here. She supposed someone had carried her, or possibly dragged her, but it didn't really matter. The only thing that mattered was that Lena was gone.

Kirra's chest tightened as the thought repeated itself over and over in her head, each time more excruciating than the last. She had never in her life known such kindness from a stranger, and because of that kindness Lena was dead. No, that was wrong, Kirra thought. Lena hadn't died. She'd been murdered — by Latham.

Latham, Kirra thought. He needed to die. He needed to be killed as soon as possible, and Kirra was the one to do it. It didn't matter that she came from Freemont or that she was still in high school. It didn't matter that murder had never once crossed her mind before. Latham had killed Lena, and Kirra was the one who was going to avenge her. She was certain of it.

It wasn't until dawn that she realised she was still wrapped in Lena's dark red jacket. She remembered how Lena had given it to her the instant she'd realised Kirra was trembling from the cold. Even now, it was still keeping her warm.

CHAPTER EIGHT

MILO FRANKLYN

A bleak sort of haze descended upon the cell, hanging like a thick, weighty fog. Kirra barely moved in the day following the escape attempt, and couldn't keep her thoughts from turning to the matter of Lena's body.

She knew, of course, that Lena would not be given a funeral, and her family, wherever they were, would never know what had happened to her. In all likelihood, her body had been dumped someplace where it would be impossible to find, with the only person in the world who cared about her death unable to scrape together anything at all to honour her.

The injustice of Lena's death, combined with her own guilt, festered within Kirra like a disease. It never relented and it never eased. It was the kind of thing someone might be admitted to hospital for, where they'd be administered a constant supply of pain relief, because no one could be expected to function in this kind of agony. It felt like Balcescu's drug raging inside her, but this time there was no antidote. The only thing that could possibly help was if Lena appeared at the door, alive and safe. Kirra just wanted her back. That was all. She just wanted that to be somehow possible. She wanted to rewind time so she could stop Lena, or convince her to run away by herself. She wouldn't have done that, of course. Kirra knew that. Lena had died because of her selflessness. If only she hadn't been so generous, hadn't been so loyal, so kind.

Kirra noticed she was no longer being provided with meals. Clearly, Lena had been solely in charge of Kirra's well-being, because, as soon as she was killed, Kirra seemed all but forgotten about. In her grief, though, she didn't really care.

Late in the afternoon, two men came and pulled her from her cell. She'd never seen either of them before. The constant turnover of guards used to interest her: where did the old ones go? How did they hire the new ones? She'd wondered in particular about those she saw regularly. Did they have parents, wives and children? Were any of their families aware of the nature of their jobs? Now, her lack of familiarity with them helped; it made it easier to keep hating them.

The men steered her towards the shower room, and Kirra readied herself for the humiliating process to come. As they went they passed two other people in the corridor. One was a guard, wearing the dark clothes they all seemed to favour — a sort of uniform Latham had probably prescribed for them. The other figure caught her attention: a male prisoner stumbling along in a pitifully disoriented fashion, wrists cuffed tightly together at the front, a black bag tied securely over his head.

Before Lena's death, Kirra might have twisted back to get a better look. She might have been curious, might have wanted to know more. But the new prisoner wouldn't change anything. He wouldn't bring Lena back. He wouldn't help Kirra get home.

When Kirra was returned to her cell, she slid onto her blankets in her usual corner. Her hair was still damp and frosty and she began the tedious task of combing it out, remembering how Lena's hands had once carefully untangled the strands as though they had been spun gold. Lost in the memory, it took a while before her gaze fell on the adjacent corner. She froze.

The new prisoner was there — there in her cell — pressing against the wall as though the room was six sizes smaller than its actual size. The cuffs hadn't been removed and the black bag was still tied firmly over his head. He was tall — taller than her by a foot at least — and broad. His fingertips were bright white in the freezing cold and each fingernail was encrusted with a lining of dirt. His clothes were bulky and weatherworn, indicating that he was quite used to cold weather. His padded jacket had holes in one pocket and lint balls infesting the collar, and his jeans were marred with grass stains. He brought a strange, alien smell into the cell: a mixture of sweat, dirt and fresh air.

Kirra stayed perfectly still, examining him very closely for many minutes, before she considered him safe and got to her feet. Instantly, he recoiled.

'Who's there?' he demanded, his head jerking around.

Kirra stopped. He spoke English. She supposed that made things easier.

'Who's there?' he repeated, struggling to stand up.

Kirra frowned down at him. 'Stop moving,' she said quietly.

He did, and froze against the wall.

'Good,' she said, and crouched down.

'Who are you?' he asked.

For a moment, Kirra said nothing, her face very close to his hooded one. She frowned at him, though he couldn't see, and dropped her gaze.

'Just stay still,' she ordered finally, and began to work at the knot keeping the bag secure. He allowed her to take it off and discard it on the cement by his side. The moment it was gone, he squinted in the light, scarce as it was, and looked around.

His skin was black, his eyes tired and bloodshot and he had a short mop of tightly curled brown hair. His cheeks were dotted with a few of what she supposed were old acne scars. He was older than her, though not by too much.

'Who are you?' he repeated, as though Kirra mightn't have heard him the first time.

She said nothing.

'Well?' he asked. 'What's your name?'

She sighed. He wasn't going to back off. 'Kirra,' she answered.

'Kirra …' he repeated, as though trying the word out for size. 'Where are you from? Why are you here?'

'I'm from Australia,' she mumbled. 'I'm here because I can crack a code.'

'The Spencer code?' he asked immediately.

Kirra looked up. 'Yes …'

'That's why I'm here!' he said. 'That man said it's really rare, being able to do that code. I've never heard of anything like it before. Were you kidnapped?'

'Yes … Were you?'

'A week ago, I think.'

Kirra nodded. 'I've been here longer,' she told him, leaning her head back against the wall.

He studied her for a long moment.

'My name's Milo Franklyn,' he offered, a crooked smile on his face. 'I'm from Southampton. That's in England. I'm eighteen,' he continued when she said nothing. He seemed to have calmed down considerably, slumping against the wall and looking too long for the small space they were now required to share. 'How old are you? You look really young …' He glanced at the bundled-up school uniform serving as a pillow in the corner.

'Sixteen,' Kirra said, pinching the bridge of her nose. His chatter was starting to annoy her.

'Oh. Well … don't worry. My government is coming for me. When they come, you'll be rescued too.'

'I've been here for weeks,' Kirra said. 'If anyone's police are coming, it's mine.'

'All the way from where? Australia, wasn't it?'

Kirra could detect the hint of a sneer in his voice. 'Yes,' she challenged.

'Don't get your hopes up,' he countered. 'Australia isn't exactly close by. It could be quite a wait.'

She glared at him.

'Your people aren't coming,' she said flatly, picking at her nails.

Milo blinked. 'I'm sure they are,' he said in a forced tone. 'I'm surprised it's taken this long, but they'll arrive soon.'

Kirra frowned. 'They aren't coming for you. No one's coming for you. They don't even know where you are.'

The truth of it almost floored her, because they weren't coming for her either and she'd only just realised it.

Milo was glaring at her.

'You know what? You're very annoying,' he said suddenly.

Kirra didn't reply. She resented having to share her cell, resented having her private grief for Lena disrupted by this boy. She'd never have imagined feeling this way before; permanent company was something she'd craved. But now that it had arrived in the form of Milo, she really wished the hangar came with two secure cells instead of just the one.

Milo shrank away into his own corner and ignored her for the rest of the night, which suited Kirra perfectly. She wrapped herself tightly in Lena's coat, which, despite being washed in the bathroom earlier that day, hadn't lost all of her smell. Breathing in deeply, Kirra curled herself into her corner and closed her eyes.

The next morning Kirra awoke to find Milo sprawled across the floor. In her sleep she had forgotten all about him. He was lying on his back, his mouth wide open and his jaw dark with stubble. He seemed even longer all stretched out like that. His hands were still cuffed together tightly and every few moments he let out a snore.

Kirra didn't move. She wanted to savour her time alone before he woke up, precious as it now seemed. It was barely dawn. She never slept full nights anymore — the long days of inactivity saw to that — but she supposed it had its upsides. Sunrise was something she'd never experienced before, due to the fact that she'd never had any kind of sports training to get her up early enough to glimpse it. She moved her feet distractedly, watching the weak shadow they formed, and wondered if daybreak had always been so glorious and why on earth she'd slept through it all these years.

In the silence, she considered what she would be doing today if she were at school. Sitting alone, probably, worrying about how friendless she looked and whether Cassie Cheng was going to stare her into a state of profound insecurity on the bus ride home. She almost managed a smile when she realised something: none of it mattered. Not now, anyway. She vowed silently to never worry about such stupid things again if only she could go back.

'How often do they bring food here?'

Milo was awake. He was struggling with the cuffs again.

Kirra ignored him and busied herself by wondering which of the guards had been assigned to deal with Lena's body. Had they been careful with her? Respectful? She glanced at Milo. He was staring at her pointedly.

'It used to be all the time,' she told him, avoiding mention of her lost friend. 'But it's been a while now.'

Milo nodded, and ruffled his hair with his cuffed hands as though frustrated with its length. 'It was fairly regular at the factory,' he explained, as though Kirra had wanted to know. 'Not too bad, either.'

'The factory?'

'Yeah. This sort of hollowed-out warehouse they use. It's where they kept me before.'

Kirra wasn't really listening. She wondered if they'd covered Lena's face when they dumped her body.

'He's an assassin, you know,' Milo continued, scrutinising her from the corner of his eye as though interested to see if she was impressed with his deduction. 'I could hear his recruits talking sometimes, from my cell in the factory. They need the code to get past security systems. To … you know … kill people.'

Kirra closed her eyes, still thinking about Lena. She hoped that they had at least taken the time to bury her properly, but maybe that was too much to hope for.

'Yes,' she said. 'They kill people.'

She was beginning to feel very ill, and her neck no longer felt up to the task of holding her head in place. When had she last eaten?

Milo examined her for a moment. 'You alright?'

'Fine,' she murmured, the room spinning. 'Just leave me alone.'

By the afternoon Milo was still struggling with his cuffs, more determined than ever to get them off. He was growing agitated, his teeth grinding as he thrashed around. The cuffs weren't made of steel but a tough nylon cable.

'Got to be kidding me! What?' he bellowed, catching Kirra studying him.

'Nothing,' she said with a shrug.

'Good!' he spat and resumed his task.

Kirra fought off the desire to laugh at him.

'It's just plastic. Bite through it,' she suggested snidely.

He glared at her. 'It takes more than that. These are police-issue cuffs! They're not designed to give in to teeth!'

Kirra shrugged once more, wondering how he could possibly know whether they were police-issue or not. He probably just wanted to sound impressive. It seemed like the sort of thing he might do. She closed her eyes, willing the hours to pass, wondering hopefully if Milo's imprisonment in her cell might be only temporary whilst they set up another.

The next time she looked over, he was chewing into the cable. She smirked and resisted the urge to say something childish.

A week passed, during which Milo seemed to become more annoying than before, something Kirra hadn't thought possible. He remained adamant that it was only a matter of days before some rescue team burst through the door, arrested Latham and his men and escorted Kirra and Milo to safety. In fact, he rarely stopped going on about it. For Kirra, the hope of rescue had died alongside Lena.

'Have you ever tried escaping?'

She looked over at him. He had long since worked off his cuffs, but always stayed in his corner. Kirra had not offered him one of her blankets, reasoning that he'd ask if he really wanted one. His hair now hung limply around his ears, as though curling was too much effort for it.

She turned away. The last thing she wanted to discuss with Milo was Lena.

'Well? Have you?' he prodded.

Kirra ignored him. She got up and stretched her legs. She was so hungry. Too hungry, really. The recruits were now taking it upon themselves to bring in food, but it was mostly raw or unassembled and they often forgot. It had been a day, perhaps more, since they'd last remembered.

'Why don't you speak to me?' he asked after a moment, his voice low and his eyebrows knitted together. He too clambered to his feet. 'When I was alone I would have given anything for someone to talk to. Figures that I'd get some brat who doesn't want to speak.'

'Stop,' Kirra said quietly. Her head was spinning and her stomach was twisting. 'Please stop talking.'

'You are so frustrating!' he snarled.

Somewhere in the aircraft hangar someone started hammering something and the sound of metal scraping against metal ground into Kirra's head.

'They're probably fitting a new door or something,' Milo speculated, scratching a caked piece of earth from the knee of his pants.

Kirra dropped her chin to her chest. The room seemed to be shifting gently, tilting as though they were on board a ship. She blinked once, twice, and felt a bead of sweat trail down her spine. The swaying sensation was growing stronger, the metal clanging continued with increased enthusiasm, and all the while the pain in her stomach grew. She reached out to the wall to steady herself.

'You could at least acknowledge me,' mumbled Milo. 'You could at least do that. Wouldn't be too hard.'

Kirra wanted to say something to him, but found that the words got lost on the way to her mouth. Suddenly, the room tilted further and faster than it had before and, without warning, plunged into darkness.

Her eyelids felt like stones against her eyes. Her head was heavy and her muscles sore, but then she felt something soft and wet against her forehead. The sensation was odd ... and wonderful.

She opened her eyes a fraction and came face to face with Milo, who had torn off his coat pocket, doused it in the freezing water from the tap and was now dabbing her forehead with it. She was lying on her side, sprawled on the concrete, and he was close, much closer than he'd ever been. It was then Kirra realised he was holding her head in his other hand. On the floor beside him were two plates, one full and the other empty.

'Are you alright?' he asked.

Kirra's reply emerged in the form of a strangled groan. Milo yanked off his coat and bundled it up. He stuffed it beneath her head and sat back to review his effort. Kirra had to concede that it was a much more comfortable pillow than her scrunched-up school dress. He slid the plate of food across the concrete. The tips of his fingers were still white from the cold.

'How'd you get this?' Kirra asked softly.

He shrugged. 'Dialled three for room service.'

He waited for her to laugh. When she didn't, he said, 'They brought it in while you were out.'

'Oh,' was all she could manage.

Without meeting Kirra's eye, he folded his pocket into a perfect rectangle and laid it across her forehead. She examined him closely. He looked strangely distressed. Why should he care about her at all, especially when they annoyed each other so much?

When Kirra's head stopped spinning, she heaved herself up and found the wall to lean against.

'How long was I out?' she asked, her voice croaky.

'Not long. A few minutes maybe.' His hands were balled into clenched fists.

'You should eat,' he told her after a while, breaking the weird moment in which there seemed to be almost no mutual dislike.

Kirra scrutinised her plate. It was unusually full.

'I ate already,' Milo said.

Kirra frowned at him. In a flash, she pushed half the meal — tinned tuna and plain slices of wholemeal bread — back onto his plate.

'No! It's not … I had mine!'

'Don't lie,' she muttered, drawing her plate into her lap.

'You should have it,' he said weakly, though he looked longingly at the meal. 'Gotta keep you alive.'

'It could be days before they remember again. Just eat it.'

He sighed and took his plate. They ate together in silence and, to Kirra's surprise, she found she didn't mind that he hadn't returned to his corner straightaway.

CHAPTER NINE

THE OTHER INCENTIVE

Kirra awoke with a start as two hands grabbed her and lifted her swingingly towards the door. She saw Milo wake just as the door to the cell was slammed shut between them.

The recruit hauled her to the long, darkened room she despised so much. She expected her heart to explode into a flurry of panic as he strapped her into the chair, then left her to contemplate the approaching agony of Balcescu's drug, but, strangely, she was completely composed. Losing Lena had changed things, she guessed.

Balcescu was already placing vials on the tables around her, hooking her up to the heart monitor and finding a vein for the catheter. As always, he seemed detached from his environment and his work, only glancing at Kirra once before Latham strode into the room.

'Good morning, Kirra.'

She said nothing.

Latham laid a piece of paper on a table and cleared his throat. 'Now, you know the drill, Kirra. Balcescu has your dose ready.' He handed her a pen. 'Be a good girl.'

She studied him closely for many seconds before she spoke.

'Why did you kill her?' she asked, her voice barely more than a whisper.

Latham frowned. 'Why did I ...? Oh, I see. Lena meant something to you. Well, Lena broke the rules trying to escape with you, Kirra. She had to be punished. It was unfortunate, but necessary.'

Lena had to be punished? Punishment was something that involved after-school detention. What Latham had done to Lena wasn't punishment.

'Let me tell you something,' he continued, crouching to her level as though she required eye contact to retain critical information. 'Connections are dangerous in this world you now live in, Kirra. They will only serve to limit you and hurt you. You see, you too had to be punished for trying to flee, and so Lena's death also satisfied that requirement. And now you understand why friends are such an impractical idea, don't you? Particularly for someone as extraordinary as you.'

Kirra stiffened slightly in her seat. 'I'm not helping you today,' she said, steadying her voice as much as possible.

Latham did not seem particularly bothered by this. 'Have you forgotten what Balcescu's drug feels like?'

'No. I haven't.'

He watched her carefully for a moment.

'Balcescu, if you wouldn't mind,' he said, clasping his hands behind his back.

Balcescu injected the drug into the catheter and stepped back. Kirra braced herself, knowing that while it would be agonising, what was coming could not possibly hurt more than losing Lena.

As the drug took effect her body lurched forward. Her fingers spasmed uncontrollably and her body parts felt weirdly sectioned off from each other, each straining in a different, but no less torturous, way than the last time.

She looked up at Latham and found him watching her curiously because she wasn't yielding. What he didn't know was that Kirra had decided the night Lena was killed that she wouldn't give in. She knew, somewhere deep inside her, that they would kill her when they were finished with her. Perhaps … perhaps better sooner than later?

White-hot flames blazed within her. They licked at her veins and slid across her eyes like shutters over a window pane, but she wouldn't give up. Her lungs screamed, her heart thudded, and suddenly, without warning, the very thing she had been waiting for — *praying* for — happened. She was free and falling into a pitch-black abyss, her eyes rolling back in her head, her body sagging into unconsciousness.

'Kirra?' Latham's voice was soft and very close to her ear. She strained to regain awareness, her mind sifting through the lasting effects of the drug. She prised her eyes open.

'That was very foolish, Kirra. You shouldn't push yourself like that,' Latham said admonishingly, as though she had injected the drug herself. 'It can be quite dangerous.'

Kirra watched Balcescu from the corner of her bleary eye. He was drawing more of the drug into a syringe.

'Do we have to give you another dose?' Latham continued, sliding the paper towards her once more.

'I won't do it,' she mumbled groggily, fighting to keep herself upright. 'You'll just have to keep going 'til it kills me.'

'We can't have that,' said Latham mockingly. 'We need you. You are vital to us.'

It was then Kirra noticed a second chair adjacent to her own that hadn't been there before. In it sat Milo, strapped in place, twisting his neck to look over at her.

'Translate the code, Kirra,' Latham said, looking over at Milo.

'Or what?'

Latham didn't answer her, but indicated something to Balcescu, who advanced on Milo, held down his arm and injected him. For the first moment, nothing happened, but Kirra knew the drug needed time before it could hit with full force, time to slither its way into the bloodstream and find the most vulnerable spots, which was exactly what it did. Milo gasped and bolted forward in his chair, the muscles in his forearms contorting and his veins suddenly prominent beneath his skin. Kirra was horrified. Every ache, every pang, every stab of pain was reflected in his expression and his disjointed body movements. His eyes rolled back in his head and his mouth sagged. For an instant, she wondered if she looked that manic when she was injected.

'Give me the sequence and we'll provide him with the antidote,' Latham said. Kirra had almost forgotten he was there. 'Refuse and the dosage will be increased. It's all up to you.'

Milo was bellowing now. He seemed to be having a seizure, and his yells evolved into outright screams. Kirra looked away, traumatised. She didn't want to give in. That was the last thing she wanted ... But she couldn't ignore the fact that Milo was just like her. He was a normal boy, from a normal life, and it wasn't his fault he could do the code, just as it wasn't hers. Besides, the memory of his hand cradling her head last night had not dimmed completely, and it was with that memory in mind that she spoke to Latham.

'Alright,' she mumbled, fumbling for the pen. 'Alright, just make it stop.'

She scrawled the sequence beneath the code, and allowed herself to be unstrapped and forced down the corridor. Milo was given the antidote, his screams stopped, and he was released from his own chair and brought with her. Instead of returning to the cell, as she expected, they were taken into the mouth of the hangar. A jet was waiting, its engine rumbling. They were pushed up the stairs and into the cabin, and Kirra found herself back in the storage compartment she'd woken up in on the very first day of her abduction. The door was closed and locked, escape, as per usual, impossible.

She didn't care where they were heading or why. The thought of helping Latham still stung sharply, and the after-effects of the drug hadn't worn off — after-effects that seemed to be plaguing Milo too, although differently. He looked unsteady on his legs and was sweating profusely, whilst Kirra had to work hard to ignore the growing nausea in the pit of her stomach. That turned out to be more difficult than she'd anticipated, and she lunged for another small packing box, wondering vaguely who had cleaned up the last one, and emptied the contents of her stomach into it.

She jumped a little when she felt Milo place his trembling hand on her shoulder. He kneeled by her side and gathered her hair in his hands to bunch it at the nape of her neck.

When the nausea ceased, Kirra wiped her mouth and backed away from him, her hair unravelling and spilling across her shoulders. She missed Lena, suddenly more than ever before.

'Kirra ... I —'

'No,' she whispered, wiping a stray tear away and shutting her eyes tightly. 'Just leave me alone.'

The plane taxied out and took off, and Kirra turned away without another thought for Milo or their mysterious destination.

CHAPTER TEN

THE BACHMEIER BUILDING

Milo spent the flight standing against the wall, his arms crossed tightly over his chest, occasionally rubbing at his eyes. Kirra didn't pay him any attention. The last thing she wanted was a conversation that might result in him trying to thank her or attempting to discuss what had happened at the hangar.

She slid open the closest window shade and looked down to see an infinite blue gulf beneath them. They seemed to soar above the ocean for hours. Kirra knew she ought to be trying to establish her location; but really, she thought, what difference would it make?

She kept her place by the window, and saw when the sea finally gave way to land. They were still in the northern hemisphere: the fields below were coated in layers of fresh snow. This didn't really tell her anything useful, however, as the northern hemisphere happened to be quite extensive. All she knew was that she was as far from Freemont as it was possible to be; as far from her family as she'd ever been before.

Perhaps by now they'd assumed she'd been seized by a crazy man. Murdered and thrown in the Yarra River. There was nothing to link her to an assassin and the ever-mystifying Spencer code, so what chance could they ever have of understanding it all when she still didn't herself?

It was still light when the plane landed. The door snapped open and a familiar recruit, Marcam, stood at the threshold, a gun dangling in his oversized hand. He wasn't a good-looking man; in fact, his face looked as though it had been struck with a ping-pong paddle, and his teeth reminded Kirra of the mottled knuckles of a skeleton hand she'd once seen on a biology excursion.

'Up. Now.'

She got to her feet and crossed to the door with Milo behind her. Marcam followed them down the stairs and out into the wind. Kirra sighed when all she found waiting for her was another hangar. However, instead of being dragged inside, as she expected, she was forced into the back of a grey car, Milo beside her. An agitated-looking Latham sat in the front seat, next to a driver Kirra didn't recognise. Another car followed them. Kirra frowned as the hangar disappeared behind them. Where were they going?

Milo stayed silent, content to stare at the passing trees and grassland. Kirra did the same, until Latham's phone rang. She looked up.

'Yes,' he answered curtly. 'What? The meeting's been moved?'

Kirra snuck a quick glance at Milo. He was listening intently.

Latham raised his voice. 'Ensure you have the correct floor! We need to do this now. It has to be today or we won't be compensated. It'll have to be deciphered on-site.'

Latham ended the call and massaged his forehead aggressively.

Milo looked sideways at Kirra. She had a sinking feeling they were about to witness something catastrophic.

Fifteen minutes later, the passing fields had become city streets, trees giving way to skyscrapers and office buildings. The car turned into an underground car park. The recruits pulled Kirra and Milo out of their seats and set them on their feet. Latham turned to them, looking stressed.

'Occasionally, plans change,' he told them. 'We always endeavour to be prepared for that. Today, however, caught us off guard. I am going to make something very clear to you — both of you. You are about to enter a building where you are going to translate codes, separately, and then we are leaving. You will not fight us and you will not draw attention to yourselves. Are we clear?'

Milo stood with his brown eyes trained on the opposite wall. Kirra stared at her boots, almost overcome with dread. What was in this building? What or who was Latham after? Was she going to see another person die today?

'Good,' Latham said, even though neither of them had answered him.

The two recruits prodded them towards the car park's exit. After spending so much time in the darkened cell, the city street and its glaring sunlight came as a nasty shock to Kirra.

As her eyes adjusted, she spotted a man standing on the kerb on the other side of the road. She only noticed him because he stood stock-still amid the bustling crowd. He looked like the type of man who wasn't easily pushed around, a fact reflected in the behaviour of the passers-by, who gave him a wide berth, some even sidestepping to stay out of his way. He was scrutinising Kirra and her companions very closely. Short-bearded and stout, he wore a grey suit and was leaning on a steel walking cane, his fingers gripping it tightly. He didn't seem nearly old enough to need a cane. Something vague and distant tugged at Kirra's memory. She narrowed her eyes. Who was he? Why was he so interested in them?

She snuck another glance at Milo. He seemed oblivious to the odd spectator; and Latham was clearly too preoccupied with the task at hand to take any real notice of what was going on around them. Kirra looked back. The man didn't move at all as they crossed the street and entered the revolving door of a vast building with the word Bachmeier printed on the side in giant white lettering. Kirra craned back and was sure she saw the man take off in the opposite direction down the street as soon as they were safely inside.

Latham preceded them into a stark white reception area, empty save for two security guards sitting at a desk. He pushed the elevator button and waited. Kirra looked expectantly at the security guards, waiting for them to look up so she could get their attention. She was horrified to find neither guard took any notice at all.

The elevator doors opened and then closed with Latham's group tucked safely inside, Kirra wedged between two recruits. They exited on the third floor, where Latham punched a number into his phone.

'Where are you?' he asked impatiently. He listened for a moment. 'Alright, Cochran will go with the girl. Keller? Do not let anything go wrong.'

He hung up and turned to his two recruits. 'Keller has the equipment and the codes,' he told them. 'He'll meet you in the stairwell.' Then he strode back into the elevator and disappeared.

Marcam and Cochran led Milo and Kirra through a grey door into the stairwell. A man Kirra guessed to be Keller was standing against the wall, a large black sports bag at his feet. He took a sheet of paper from his pocket and handed it to Cochran.

'Take the girl and disable the system at the end of this floor. Get back here as soon as it's done.'

Cochran took the code and grasped Kirra's arm, forcing her back into the corridor and away from the others. She turned back to see Keller remove a gun from inside his jacket. Her heart jumped into her throat. What were they going to do to Milo?

The corridor was white and mostly empty, with many small side passages running off it that seemed to go on forever. Glass-panelled doors revealed glimpses of huge open-plan offices, meeting rooms and the occasional cafeteria. Finally, Cochran stopped at a cabinet set into the wall by a doorway. He forced it open without difficulty; inside was a small touch screen showing a keypad.

He turned to Kirra. 'Give me the sequence,' he said, brandishing the paper at her.

Kirra ignored him.

He raised his gun and pressed it against her neck. 'Do it.'

Kirra felt him force a pencil into her hand.

'Do you want to die over this?' he said.

Kirra blinked at him. She'd had an abundance of time in the past few weeks to consider death, and, really, she had to admit to herself that her answer was 'no'. Did she want to give her life for something she didn't even understand? Did she want to die for someone she'd never met before? Could she really just allow herself to be killed? In the safety of the cell, it was easy to believe she might have that sort of strength (or perhaps it was foolishness?), but when faced with the choice between her death and someone else's, she knew she'd choose someone else's. She wasn't proud of it, but it was the truth. Then, as the recruit pressed the gun further into her throat, a thought came to her.

'You can't kill me,' she said. 'You need me.'

It seemed he'd been expecting her answer. 'All I have to do is make a phone call and they'll kill the other one.'

Kirra glared at him. She'd been expecting his answer too.

'Fine,' she muttered, taking the paper from him. Within moments she'd scrawled the code across the bottom of the page.

Cochran tore it away from her and punched it into the touch screen. A moment later the screen read 'SYSTEM DISABLED'.

Cochran pulled out his phone. 'It's off. You can go in,' he said quickly.

He snapped the phone shut and grabbed Kirra's arm. 'Move,' he said, pushing her down the corridor.

He marched them straight ahead, ignoring every passing door, every corridor, every elevator, his focus on getting back to the stairwell as quickly as possible, but as they went Kirra caught glimpses of people at work, people making coffee, people in meetings. She chewed her top lip. Someone in this building had only moments to live. She suddenly felt ill. Some person was about to die because of her.

'NO!'

Kirra lunged towards the wall and yanked open a small glass case by a door. Inside was a red switch — a fire alarm — and she pulled it down as hard as she could. At once, a siren blasted through the building, great sweeping wails that filled the corridor and alerted people to the imminent danger. Cochran froze. Kirra ignored him and watched impatiently as it dawned on the office workers that the alarm was cause for real panic, not a mere drill. All along the corridor, doors flew open and people tumbled out, looking around wildly.

There seemed to be hundreds of them, and Kirra was unexpectedly surrounded, the crowd jostling her forward. She was separated from Cochran, who had let go of her to fumble for his phone, and as the fire alarm screamed on and people fought for passage to the stairwell, Kirra seized her chance. She tore down the corridor, shoving through the mass of bodies with ease, adrenaline boosting her strength.

'No!' Cochran screamed after her.

She glanced back to see him struggling through the swelling barricade of workers, but it was too late. She was already whipping around a corner and dodging through the throng. She couldn't believe it. She was free!

'Kirra?'

Her head shot up. Milo was standing still amid the swarm, staring at her.

'What are you doing?' she panted.

'Looking for you!' he said. 'What happened?'

'I rang the alarm!' she yelled over the din.

He stared blankly at her as a gangly man bounded out of a door beside them and raced off in search of an exit. 'You did that?'

Kirra nodded. A girl shoved past them in a pinstripe suit, one of her high heels stabbing Kirra's big toe. She almost didn't notice.

'There's an explosive,' Milo said, his jaw set. Beads of sweat lined his forehead.

Kirra felt her heart seize. *An explosive?*

'What?' she spluttered. 'D-don't they just want to shoot someone?'

'No! They came to blast the whole building apart! They needed the sequence so they could plant the bomb in some central room or something.' Milo seemed oblivious to the effect this information had on her. 'We need to get out of here right now!'

'How did you —'

'I got away from them,' he cut in.

It was then Kirra noticed Keller's gun gripped tightly in his hand.

'What are you doing?' she yelled. 'Did you kill them?'

Milo frowned at her. 'Would you care if I had?'

She stared at him, unsure of her answer.

'I just got away,' he told her before she could say anything, shoving the gun in the waistband of his pants. He jammed his hands in his hair and stared at a spot over Kirra's shoulder. Then he seemed to come to some sort of decision. 'They're looking for us,' he said. 'Come on.'

He started down the main stairwell, taking the steps three at a time. Kirra struggled to keep up, her boots slipping on every other step, her hand sweaty on the railing.

Milo came to a halt on the stairs and she stopped just short of running into him.

'Shhh!' he whispered.

Peering over the railing, Kirra spotted one of the recruits racing up towards them. Milo cursed under his breath and grabbed her hand, then pushed his way back into another corridor. They were met with the same havoc, people shoving and yelling and almost climbing over each other as they flooded to safety. Kirra's heart was pounding and her breathing shallow and sharp. The need to exit the building was overwhelming, but avoiding the recruits was paramount. She didn't know how much more she could take of captivity. She didn't know how much more she could take of being away from home.

In the corridor, she turned just in time to see two recruits step out of the nearest elevator. 'Milo!' she yelled. He looked around and swore loudly ...

They shoved through the crowd and turned down a narrow passageway. A door to their left read 'SERVICE STAIRWELL'. Milo pushed through it and skidded down the stairs, Kirra following closely.

Another door burst open and a couple entered the stairwell from a lower floor. Kirra and Milo came to a stop, fearful they might be more recruits, but Kirra saw the fear etched across their faces, and knew they were office workers who had nothing to do with anything.

The couple flew down the remaining stairs, reaching the ground level before Kirra and Milo. They forced open a service exit, which led into a dusty alleyway cluttered with rubbish bins and discarded office furniture and when Kirra saw it she felt victorious. They could escape this way. If they were quick, they could make it to safety before Latham found them.

Above the noise of the alarm, a more terrible sound suddenly met Kirra's ears. She stopped, frowning. A thunderous rumble resonated down the stairwell and the building began to shake; only slightly at first, and then violently, as though it had sprouted legs and was taking great, lurching steps across the city. She looked down at Milo, who had raced ahead into the alleyway and was holding the door open for her.

'Come on!' he bellowed, staring at her like she'd gone mad.

She finally got a hold of herself and took the next step. At almost that exact moment, she was jolted off her feet by a force so powerful it knocked her down the last few stairs. The ceiling began to crumble, tiles and chunks of debris raining down on her.

'Milo!'

She fumbled around, trying desperately to orientate herself. She couldn't see him. She couldn't see anything. She sucked in a breath and spluttered it back out; the air was clogged with dust and smoke. She glanced up again, in time to see the ceiling collapse. She did the only thing she could: she shut her eyes and braced herself.

CHAPTER ELEVEN

A VISIT FROM VACLAV

At first, there was only silence. Maybe she was dead?

Then there was a terrific ringing in her ears, but that didn't mean anything. Maybe that was just what death sounded like? But then, permeating her dulled senses, came the ambulance sirens. They were muffled and distant, but Kirra was certain she could hear them.

She opened her eyes and took a shallow breath, coughing out amongst the smoke. She was in almost total darkness, lying flat on her back amongst the rubble. Out of the corner of her eye, she could see a tiny break in the concrete and plaster that provided a small shard of light. She tried to move her arms. One was trapped; it was tender and sore, perhaps broken. The other seemed alright. She reached out with it and a cold, smooth surface met her fingers. Slowly, her eyes began adjusting to the dark and she discovered the flat surface was a vast concrete slab. She was trapped beneath it, buried by the blast, protected in a small dark crevice.

Somewhere above her right shoulder a pipe had burst and icy water was trickling into her hair and down her neck. Her face was covered in thick, heavy dust and her cheek was stinging. She could feel a gash of some sort beneath her left eye and the airborne grime from the explosion was mingling painfully with her torn flesh.

The distant sirens continued, the sound confirming again that she was still among the living. Without them, she might have thought this was hell. The screaming of the frightened office workers had ceased. There was no sound, and she couldn't sense any nearby movement.

She gently twisted her head to the side. What had happened to —

'Milo?' she croaked. Her voice was tiny, muted from the smoke and dust. 'Milo?'

There was no answer. No sound at all.

She fumbled around in the darkness with her uninjured arm, hoping that she wouldn't reach out and find a lifeless body lying compressed amongst the rubble. When she found nothing, she told herself not to panic. Milo was still alive. She felt sure of it.

Somewhere in the distance, a drill started. Kirra's head was aching and there was something jagged sticking into her hip. She wondered how long it would take Latham and his recruits to dig her out. She was certain they'd get to her first. Her hope of being saved by a rescue team was minimal at best.

How many unsuspecting office workers had lost their lives in the explosion? She wondered how many had survived, and if any of them would ever know that a man named Latham was to blame, and that she, Kirra Hayward, had aided him.

She had no idea how long she lay there, trapped and chilly, until the tiny shard of light faded to black. Night had fallen and she still hadn't been saved. Dreadful thoughts scuttled around inside her head. What if they didn't dig fast enough? What if she remained down here, squashed in the darkness, until she died of thirst and starvation? What if word of her death never reached Freemont? What if her parents were left to wonder for years and years to come what had happened to their eldest daughter?

Kirra willed herself to be patient. She wasn't going to die here, trapped beneath the rubble of the stairwell in the ruins of this office building. Her life wasn't meant to end like this. How deeply could she be buried anyway? Surely Latham's recruits were close by now, and if not them, then the rescuers. She just had to stay calm. They'd rescue her. If not tonight, then tomorrow.

A voice screamed something in German. Kirra recognised the language from her first year of high school when she'd been made to sample the subject like the rest of the year level. Her eyes cracked open. There was a commotion somewhere above her. The drill started up again. Sirens blared. Dust sprinkled onto her face from the shifting layers above. She had no idea how long she'd slept for, but it sounded as though the rescue teams were close.

'Help!' she spluttered, finally finding her voice. 'Please help me!'

More yelling in German, and then she was blinded as someone shone a torch into the crevice. The sudden burst of light after so many sightless hours reignited Kirra's headache. But it hardly mattered. She was about to be rescued!

It took the rescue workers hours to sift through the rubble, but she waited, perfectly still, her heart beating wildly, patient to the very end. Finally the concrete was lifted off her and more dust poured onto her face. She gasped in the morning air, squinting in the sun. Hands gently examined her, people yelled orders, others murmured words of encouragement into her ears. The rescue workers lifted her onto a stretcher and she was carried away.

Kirra squinted from the stretcher at the wreckage. Some of the Bachmeier building was still standing, but the damage was extreme, and what was left of it was blackened and crumbling. She could hear a mass of people yelling, what sounded like desperate relatives being contained on the street. A few feet from Kirra a man covered in blood was holding a towel to his eye, watching as workers lifted a chunk of steel off the legs of a woman who lay motionless, coated in white dust. Kirra looked away. Any moment Latham would pounce and take her away from this terrible place, and not a moment too soon, she thought desperately.

Paramedics fussed over her, offered her oxygen, bandaged her sore wrist, and then she was on her way to the hospital, tucked safely inside one of the numerous ambulances waiting to transport survivors away. She almost couldn't believe it. Where was Latham? And where was Milo?

The emergency area at the hospital was like something from a horror film. One man was bleeding profusely from his chest, nurses and doctors attempting to staunch the flow. A middle-aged woman was holding a patch to her forehead, moaning quietly in a chair in the corner. An older man was rushed into an operating room, shards of glass protruding from his back, and a girl in a pinstripe suit and dusty high heels was lying on a stretcher to one side, uncovered though clearly dead. Kirra recognised her as the woman who'd rushed past her in the corridor before the bomb.

Kirra was immensely grateful when the nurses relocated her to a bed in a ward, patched the wound on her cheek and drew a curtain around her. She noticed many scrapes, bruises and bleeding wounds she hadn't seen whilst buried, though she didn't make any effort to cover them or have them seen to.

She fidgeted with the bandage on her wrist and thought about how no one, not the victims, the relatives or the frenzied hospital staff, knew that she had played a part in this carnage. She didn't know how many had been found dead, or how many were still buried; she only knew she ought to be one of them.

She was safe now, but for how long? She knew she was in Germany; probably Dusseldorf from the few signs she'd glimpsed as the ambulance had sped through the streets. This presented another problem: apart from extremely basic politenesses retained from a single semester at school years ago, she could speak no German. How could she ask about Milo? What was his last name? Had he told her? She struggled to recall, combing back through her memory as she waited for the nurses to return. What she really needed to do was ask for the police. Once she spoke to them, everything would be alright.

Suddenly sensing a presence at her bedside, Kirra looked up. She had been expecting to find a nurse wanting to patch up some other injured part of her, but instead a short, brawny man stood frowning down at her. Kirra expelled a fearful breath. It couldn't have been clearer that the man was not hospital staff.

His brown eyes were sharp, his face harsh and serious, his jaw lined with a very short and unkempt auburn beard. He was dressed in a suit and rested heavily on a steel cane and Kirra frowned, her fear replaced by the shock of recognition. He was the man she'd seen in the street before Latham had taken her and Milo into the Bachmeier building.

'Kirra Hayward?' he asked urgently.

Kirra swallowed her dread. He didn't seem like one of Latham's recruits.

'Who are you?' she asked softly.

'Vaclav,' he said. His voice was rough and very impatient. 'My name is Vaclav. Look … don't cause a scene, I'm on your side. Latham has sent a recruit for you and he's almost here, but before they take you away, I want you to know that I'm going to help you.'

'Help me?' was all Kirra could say.

'Yes. You've probably worked out by now that you're important — not just to Latham, but to many of us. All of us, really. Because of your interference yesterday you have become far more prized than you can know to people like me.' He gave her a strange look, as though he was most pleased with her. 'Help is on its way. It shouldn't be much longer now.' And he turned on his heel and stomped from the ward without another word.

Kirra gawked after him for several seconds. He was on her side? What did that mean? What was her side anyway? Maybe it just meant he was a police officer? No, that wasn't right. He sounded as though he was like Latham somehow, though it certainly didn't seem they were friends.

Then she remembered what he'd said about Latham sending someone for her. She scrambled to sit up, tossed the blanket off her legs and fumbled around for her boots. She needed to get out of there, right now, before whichever recruit Latham had sent arrived.

It was only once her feet touched the ground that she stopped. Milo. If she ran, what would happen to him? If he was dead, there was a possibility she might never know. If he was alive, then sure, she could point the authorities in the right direction, but it was unlikely they'd ever find him. No one would ever see him again. *She* would never see him again. It would be as if she'd never met him at all. The only way she could know for certain was if she returned to the cell. No, she couldn't do that. Of course she couldn't do that. It was absurd even to contemplate it — crazy even. By some glorious twist of fate she was alive. She had been handed this one chance to run, to be free. But ... what about Milo?

She flexed her hand gently, feeling incredibly alone all of a sudden, listening to the sirens of the ambulances arriving outside. She almost didn't notice the recruit enter her ward. When she did see him, all thoughts of escape faded instantly. She'd lost her chance.

CHAPTER TWELVE

THE FACTORY

The recruit took Kirra in the back of a car to a brick building that looked like a warehouse from the outside. Inside, it was grey and draughty. Kirra followed the recruit through a labyrinth of darkened passageways before he unlocked a door and pressed her inside. She had time only to register that it was another cell before she saw Milo spring to his feet and cross the room in two sweeping strides. Kirra let out a breath she hadn't realised she had been holding in. The thought of arriving back to an empty cell had sat with her all morning.

'You're alive!' he said, taking her hands in his own.

She gasped as he gripped her bandage.

He let her hands go as if he'd been electrocuted. 'I'm sorry. I didn't mean to —'

'It's okay. It's just a fracture,' she told him, touching the bandage lightly. 'At least I think it is.'

'I thought you'd been killed,' he said.

'I thought you had been too,' she admitted.

'Your cheek …'

He thumbed the flesh beneath the wound for a moment, assessing the damage. Then he seemed to realise what he was doing and withdrew his hand from her face.

'Yeah,' she said. 'Is it bad? I haven't seen it yet.'

'It might leave a scar,' he told her.

'Could be worse,' she said, tucking her hair behind her ear.

'Definitely,' he agreed, clearly relieved she hadn't become upset over it.

'How did they find you?'

'I wasn't really buried. Some recruits dragged me out of the alley a few minutes after the bomb. Then they started searching for you, but they took off when the rescue teams turned up.'

Kirra nodded and settled against the wall, dabbing at her throbbing cheek with her fingertips. The lock creaked and she looked up to see a recruit she'd never seen before swing the door open. He was tall and had dark, stringy hair, pale skin and tired eyes. A jagged scar tore from his bottom lip, down through his black stubble, and trailed below his collar. He studied Kirra closely but she ignored him.

Latham appeared in the doorway and looked between Kirra and Milo. He seemed calm enough on the surface, but Kirra wasn't convinced.

'I'm not certain of what happened yesterday,' he began, 'but I have a feeling that it somehow involved the two of you. My associate Keller is dead, as are the two men who escorted you, so I'll never have the full details. I am, however, going to take this opportunity to make something very clear. This is a business and nothing more. The fact that these three men are dead is unacceptable.' Latham paused to run his plump fingers through his hair. 'I heard you rang the alarm, Kirra. Very brave, of course, but ridiculously stupid. What were you expecting the outcome of such a stunt to be? Did you hope to run away?'

'If I'd rung the alarm earlier, more people could have escaped,' she said. 'I didn't do it just to save myself. Getting home would have been a bonus.'

Latham watched her for a long moment.

'I feel it's best to tell you this now, so we can circumvent any more of these attempts of yours. You must have realised by now that we know everything about your families. We know your street numbers, your siblings' hobbies, the cars your parents drive. Even now your families are under surveillance — constantly. My point is this: if you attempt to call them, to see them, to get in contact in any way, they'll no longer be safe.'

'Safe from what?'

Latham tilted his head to the side. 'Safe from me, of course,' he said.

He disappeared back into the corridor and called for Wyles — Kirra supposed this was the dark-haired recruit — to shut the door and follow him.

She slid to the ground once both men had left. 'Do you think he'd really hurt our families?'

'Yes,' Milo answered. 'If for no other reason than to show he means what he says.'

Kirra let out a shaky sigh and glanced around the cell. It was cool and bare except for another couple of blankets tossed in the corner and a toilet and basin by the door. It was just like the hangar, except this place carried no memories of Lena. Kirra realised with a jolt that she hadn't thought about Lena at all yet today. Not once. Feeling guilty, she turned to Milo.

'So … this is the factory, then?'

He glanced up. 'Yeah, this is it.'

'Home, sweet home,' Kirra mumbled, playing with her bandage.

'How's your arm?'

'Fine. Sore.'

He stared at the opposite wall, his face set. 'I really thought you didn't make it,' he said, his voice a little too casual. 'It was a long night.'

'It was a long night for me too.'

If Kirra ever had to make a choice between the hangar cell and the cell in the factory, the factory would definitely win. It was after they'd arrived there that things started to take an almighty turn for the better. The bitterest part of winter had passed, and the days began to produce a measure of sunshine that made it in through a little barred window.

'Hey,' Milo said one day.

'What?'

'Reckon I can do more push-ups than you?'

'Yes,' Kirra said truthfully.

'Oh.' He said nothing for a moment. Then: 'Do you think you can do a handstand?'

'With my wrist? No.'

'Oh. Yeah. No, don't do that.' He took a long, slow breath. 'I'm bored,' he said finally.

'Really?'

He glared at her. She gave a small smile.

'Okay, well, tell me ...' She fished around for something to ask. 'Tell me about the day you were kidnapped.'

Milo stared at his feet for a very long time before he spoke. 'I was waiting for a train to uni,' he finally said. 'Latham showed up with a couple of recruits.'

'Latham got you himself?'

'Yeah. No one saw it though. It was quick, and I wasn't really having a good day anyway ...' He gave a dull chuckle.

'You're lucky. Mine was horrible,' Kirra said. 'Don't think I've ever been so scared.'

Milo nodded. 'Sorry,' he said.

Kirra shrugged. 'What for? I've kinda realised there was nothing anyone could have done.'

Milo nodded in agreement. 'What time do you think it is?' he asked after a moment.

'Ten thirty,' Kirra guessed.

'Are you kidding? No way in hell. Look at the sun!'

'What would you say then?'

'Noon. Easily.'

'You don't know what you're talking about. It feels like we just got up.'

'Yeah, well, time flies when you're having fun.'

'You never learned to ride a bike?'

'No. So what? It's not so strange.'

'Yeah, it is actually.'

'I had a go on my sister's bike once and fell off and shattered my kneecap. I dunno, I guess I wasn't very good at outdoor things.'

'So what did you do instead?'

'I don't know. Nothing really.'

'What's your sister's name?'

'Olivia. She's fourteen, and my little brother, Mitchell, is twelve. This is his first year of high school.'

'Who were you closest to?'

'Mitchell. What about your family?'

'Uh … well … my father … he's lived in Southampton his entire life, and my mother's the same. I have two brothers. Josh is twenty-two. Eli is seventeen.'

'Do you miss them?'

'Not much … My parents weren't around a lot, and I've never been close with my brothers. They were both into sport. They used to win everything.'

'You didn't play?'

'When I was younger, but I was bad. Really bad. I was only good at science. Nothing else.'

'There are worse things to be good at.'

'I got into a chemistry degree — the only thing I could hold over my brothers. Josh's job isn't great, and Eli doesn't even want to go to uni, he just wants to play football.'

'So really you're doing the best of all of them?'

'Yeah … maybe. I still can't believe you never learned to ride a bike. Is there anything else you can't do?'

'I never learned to swim.'

'You were talking in your sleep before.'

'Was I?'

'Yeah. Mumbling something about "Lena". Who's Lena?'

'Oh … she's … I don't know.'

'Yes, you do. You were speaking about her.'

'I said I don't know.'

'Tell me about her.'

'No.'

'Go on.'

'No.'

'Why not?'

'Because there's nothing to tell! It was in my sleep. How am I meant to know what I was talking about?'

'You just don't want to tell me.'

'Maybe I don't!'

'Fine.'

'*Fine*.'

'I'll go first. Ready?'

'Yep.'

'Okay. I spy with my little eye … something grey.'

'I'm not playing this.'

'Morning.'

'Hi. Why are you all the way over there?'

'See this patch of sun? I'm just working on my tan.'

'Right.'

'It's getting so warm now. I don't even really need this jacket.'

'So take it off then.'

'No. I … No.'

'A watch.'

'A TV.'

'A mattress.'

'A book.'

'A brush.'

'Backgammon.'

'Don't know how to play.'

'I'd teach you. Coffee.'

'A radio.'

'The internet.'

'Really? The internet?'

'Oh yeah. I take that back. No internet.'

Kirra awoke to find Milo's fingers tangled with hers, his hand startlingly dark against the almost translucent pallor of her skin. The tips of his fingers were still stark white though, something left over from the cold. She frowned. Their hands hadn't been like that when she'd fallen asleep. Slowly she drew away and stretched, stifling a yawn so she wouldn't disturb her snoring companion.

The cell seemed almost homey now. Their shoes were lying in various corners, Milo's jacket hung from a tiny nail sticking out from the door, and over the weeks he had managed to smuggle towels from the shower room when the recruits weren't looking to use as pillows and extra blankets.

The room was warming quickly. Kirra got up to stretch her legs. She looked down at Milo, long as ever, sprawled ungracefully on his side, his mouth wide open. She smiled when he rubbed his nose in his sleep, and stopped herself just in time from reaching out to touch his face. He might wake up and catch her in the act and that would be bad. Kirra had to maintain her distance;

she had to remember Lena and how dangerous it was to get close to people. So she stayed away, difficult as that was with him lying there, his hair sticking up in places and his eyes scrunched up to avoid the sun in his sleep.

The day before, when Milo had been returned to the cell after his shower, he'd looked almost like a different person.

'What happened to you?' she'd asked him, her mouth agape.

'Got rid of some of my hair,' he told her with a shrug. 'Trimmed it in the bathroom.'

'What'd you use, a chainsaw?'

'A pair of scissors I found. Had to do it quickly before they noticed.'

'Yeah, I can see that.'

He scowled at her and resumed his usual spot in the adjacent corner. 'Needed to be done. It was getting longer than yours.'

'Prettier too,' Kirra teased.

He looked at the sock he was turning inside out to dry. 'I disagree,' he said very quietly.

Kirra had stared at him. She'd felt her cheeks burn, as though she'd just stuck two hot coals in either side of her mouth. She parted her lips to say something back, but nothing came out.

That night Kirra jerked awake from a strange dream in which Milo and Olivia were speeding away from the factory in the same getaway car Lena had once used, leaving Kirra for dead. Disoriented, she fumbled around for a moment, and jumped when she realised Milo was right by her side, pressing against her.

'What are you —'

'Shh!' His hand clamped down over her mouth.

She pushed him away and sat up, frowning through the darkness. He was sitting perfectly still, his eyes trained on the door, and he looked as though he hadn't moved in some time. Kirra saw moving shadows visible in the light coming through the crack beneath the door. A soft muttering of male voices was just audible.

'Don't make a sound,' Milo breathed. 'Stay very still.'

The murmuring grew louder, as though the recruits outside were having an argument, and Milo coiled his hand around Kirra's wrist. He seemed petrified, and was obviously interpreting the situation in a way she wasn't. She was merely confused. What were the recruits doing up at this hour?

The whispering ceased and the shadows moved away. Milo released Kirra's wrist and relaxed against the wall.

'What was that?'

'I dunno. Probably nothing.'

'Then why were you —'

'I said I don't know. Just go back to sleep.'

CHAPTER THIRTEEN

THREE WEEKS

Kirra, distractedly twirling a lock of hair between her thumb and forefinger, watched the same square of sunlight that appeared every day shift across the cell. Milo had been gone for almost three weeks now. The day they'd dragged him from the cell and slammed the door between them was etched firmly into Kirra's memory. She may have lost track of the weeks and months since she'd been captured, but the days without Milo were conspicuous and Kirra carefully counted each one. The cell had once felt crowded because of him, almost suffocating really. Now it was barren and bleak and the time stretched on and on. She knew three weeks was far too long for him to be gone. A few hours wouldn't have worried her. Not even a whole day. Not at first, at least. But three weeks? That was different. A small part of her knew she ought to accept that he might never return.

The long days and nights of solitude left her with nothing to do. In an attempt to distract herself from

Milo's glaring absence, she started to sift through all the things that had brought her to this dismal point. What if she'd just ignored Mr Gummer's assignment? Or tried to do it properly instead of looking for something to plagiarise? What if she'd gone home a different way that day, avoiding Barrie Avenue? What if she'd escaped successfully with Lena? Lena might still be alive.

Her mental tally of events always stopped at the visit from the strange man in the hospital after the Bachmeier bomb. What had he said his name was? Vaclav something? Kirra was sure that was it. Vaclav. Vaclav, with his walking cane and his words of encouragement. Hadn't he said he was trying to help her? Kirra was sure that months had passed since then, and still no sign of help, no hint of rescue. Occasionally she wondered if she'd just imagined Vaclav and convinced herself he was real. Maybe she actually *was* going mad.

When the cell door opened, her heart leaped into her throat, then took a wild nosedive. It was just the recruit Wyles, who never seemed to shave and looked as though he hadn't had a good night's sleep in a decade. Still, he was always weirdly sympathetic towards her when he brought her meals or escorted her to the shower; where another recruit would have shoved, Wyles simply guided.

'What do you call a kangaroo at the North Pole?' he said. He gave her a tentative smile.

Kirra blinked.

'A lost kangaroo,' he answered himself.

Kirra stared at him. Unless she was very much mistaken, a recruit had just told her a joke. She debated the merit of shaking herself, just to check she hadn't imagined it.

Wyles cleared his throat, an awkward, unsure look coming over his face, and gave a one-shouldered shrug. 'Come on,' he said, and took her hand and lifted her lightly to her feet.

Kirra yanked her hand away. No matter how different Wyles was from the other recruits, no matter how amiable he seemed, Kirra refused to become friendly with him. Yes, he treated her with a measure of kindness, but he was still a recruit.

He escorted her down the hallway, his hold on her arm feather light, and guided her into the dilapidated bathroom. He nodded in the direction of the shower and backed out of the doorway. Kirra watched him go. He never stayed to supervise her showers, not like the others did. Sometimes they congregated at the door to leer at her, saying things to each other in another language. Sometimes they laughed; other times they were silent and still, which frightened Kirra much more.

She had learnt to ignore them, but when Milo was still sharing her cell he'd always nagged her to tell him what had happened each time.

'Nothing,' Kirra would say. 'They just stand there and watch.'

'They never do anything?' he'd asked, over and over. 'They never say anything?'

'They say lots of things.'

'Like what?'

'How should I know? It's all in another bloody language.'

'Shower quickly from now on, okay? Get it over and done with before they have time to see anything.'

Kirra, unsure whether to be annoyed by his concern or touched by it, had shrugged. 'They never *do* anything.'

'Doesn't mean they won't.'

But Wyles was different. He never watched her himself, and he never let any of the others gather in the bathroom when Kirra was his responsibility. Kirra knew she ought to feel grateful for this, but instead it just made her slightly suspicious. A recruit showing kindness? It didn't feel right.

She removed her clothes quickly and showered under the weak spray. She dried off and threw the clothes back on. Her jeans no longer fitted — she had to hold them up when she walked — and Lena's jacket felt baggier than ever. She'd never once gone hungry in Freemont, and months of imprisonment and neglect were beginning to take a very physical toll. She was thankful there were no mirrors in the factory, for she was certain she'd be appalled by the person she saw looking back at her.

She hitched up her jeans once more and shoved her wet hair back. She was just slipping into her boots, which she'd always suspected had once been Lena's, when a voice rang through the room.

'Are you the code cracker?'

She looked up. Standing just inside the door was a girl of around fourteen years of age, wearing a black cotton dress and a cherry-red ribbon in her brunette hair. She was quite short, and her dress was ironed and her hair neat. She was considering Kirra expectantly, her plump lips pursed. 'Well? Are you?' she prompted.

She spoke with an accent Kirra was unable to distinguish, but it was very clear that she'd been educated in an English school. Kirra was openly puzzled. Who was she?

'Yes,' she murmured, thinking that wasn't the title she would have chosen for herself.

'I didn't know you were so young,' the girl mused.

Kirra thought this was an interesting comment coming from someone at least two years younger than herself.

'My father takes great care to keep us apart,' the girl said, checking the corridor for recruits. 'He says I shouldn't want to see things like you. He's not here right now, so I thought I'd take my chance.'

Kirra ran her fingers through her wet hair, thinking. 'Latham is your father,' she said quietly.

'Mm-hm,' the girl confirmed, tightening the ribbon in her long locks. 'I come to work with him during my school holidays.'

Kirra suddenly remembered the purple room she had glimpsed at the hangar all those months ago.

'Do you know who ... what ... your father is?' Kirra ventured carefully.

Surely the poor girl couldn't know the truth. The idea that she might accompany her father on his killing sprees was horrendous but, to Kirra's immense surprise, the girl merely raised an eyebrow.

'Of course,' she said with the air of someone who enjoyed shocking people. 'Of course I know. I'm not an imbecile.'

Kirra frowned, doubtful they were talking about the same thing.

'Your father ...' she began slowly, wondering how she could put it without alerting the girl to the truth.

The girl's plump mouth curled into a patronising smile. 'Kills people? No. My father doesn't kill people.

Rich people kill other people. My father's just hired in the middle.'

Wyles' sudden reappearance severed the tension in the bathroom.

'Simone! What are you doing here?' he barked.

'Meeting the code cracker. I haven't had the pleasure yet,' the girl said.

'You shouldn't be in here,' he said.

'If you tell me to leave, I'll tell my father you were trying to break her out,' Simone said, all the while staring at Kirra.

The recruit narrowed his eyes. 'What did you say?' he asked quietly.

'Don't tempt me!' she fumed. 'Now go away!'

Wyles seemed to be pondering the authority of her order. In the end, he stepped back into the corridor and left them alone.

Kirra's eyes skimmed over the girl thoughtfully as she in turn fixed Kirra with another expectant stare. As Kirra looked at the long dark hair cascading over the girl's shoulders, she felt her breath catch. Simone suddenly reminded her so much of … No, it couldn't be!

'Was … was Lena your mother?' Kirra asked, her heart almost bursting at the prospect.

Simone didn't seem to share in Kirra's excitement. Her eyes flashed dangerously. 'Lena was left here by an old recruit,' she said. 'My father kept her around to take care of the men. She was just a servant. Nothing, really, and certainly *not* my mother.'

She folded her arms. 'Wyles, you can take her back

now. I'm done with her.' Her long hair flicked over her shoulder as she left the room.

Kirra stood stock-still for a moment, feeling furious. When Wyles reached for her arm, she shrugged away and walked ahead of him. She didn't need to be guided back to her cell. She knew the way.

It was clear, thinking about it later, that Lena wasn't Simone's mother. Kirra had noted the hair and jumped to conclusions. Indeed, there were more differences than similarities between the two. Lena had had a round, happy face and thin lips, whilst Simone's face was thin and long, her lips fat and pouting. Plus, Simone had none of Lena's vivacity and certainly none of her beauty. Kirra felt relieved. Lena could never have deserved a child like that.

She glanced up distractedly when Wyles entered the cell a while later and placed a toasted sandwich and a small bottle of orange juice on the floor. Both were unusually good in comparison to most of the meals she got. Without a word he removed a shiny little package from his pocket and deposited it beside the plate before disappearing once more. Kirra found it was a chocolate bar filled with chewy toffee and softened biscuit. She stared at it for many minutes. Just when she thought Wyles' confusing behaviour had reached its peak, he went and did something like this.

Looking at the meal, she decided not to question it too much, and devoured the sandwich and nibbled at the chocolate, wanting to make her first real treat since Lena's death last.

CHAPTER FOURTEEN

GIFTS FROM OUTSIDE

The next day Milo returned. The door swung open and he was pushed inside. Kirra had been dozing, and struggled to get her bearings, in which time Milo knelt beside her, lifted her into his arms and held her tightly. It took her a moment of bewilderment to realise what was happening, but when she did she buried her face deep into his chest.

Neither said anything for the longest time. Milo touched her straggly hair, his chin pressed firmly against her temple, and Kirra clung to him. Something within the moment felt charged, and she shuddered against him. The sensation, whatever it was, was so alien to her that she seized up, unable to breathe for several moments, goose bumps trailing her arms. The surface of her skin seemed more sensitive than usual as Milo gripped her, and she wondered why they'd not hugged until now. It felt like the most natural thing in the world, a thing they should have done as much as possible. She finally disentangled herself from his grip to look at him properly, and was delighted and surprised when his fingertips dragged across either side of her face as she drew back, as though he hadn't wanted to let go so soon. She gazed at him. He was alive. She kept saying it to herself, over and over.

They sat together on the cold cement, Milo's face close to hers as he inspected her with an intense expression she couldn't label. He seemed different; harder somehow.

'I've brought you something,' he said, reaching into his pocket, his voice hoarse. 'They took me all over, but when I was in your country I found this.' He held out a flimsy piece of newspaper.

Kirra unfolded it carefully, holding her breath. It was a clipping from a newspaper, and in the bottom left-hand corner of the page was a small article.

NATIONWIDE SEARCH FOR
FREEMONT TEENAGER

Today the search for sixteen-year-old Kirra Harriet Hayward, who disappeared from the suburb of Freemont on 8 February this year, has been expanded to a nationwide investigation. Victoria Police believes she may have been taken interstate after a caller reported seeing a young girl believed to be Kirra Hayward in Sydney. This sighting is the first new lead in the case since Kirra's disappearance. In a statement from the Hayward family Mr David Hayward said, 'This new lead will be followed to its conclusion, and if the girl sighted was not our daughter then we will continue with the search. Until any more evidence surfaces, we remain hopeful.'

The Hayward family will fly to Sydney this week to aid police in their inquiries. Kirra, a Year Ten student at the private high school Freemont Grammar, was last seen by a classmate alighting from the 305 bus on Waverly Road in Freemont at approximately 5.20 pm on the day of her abduction. She was wearing her blue school dress, has blue eyes, brown hair and is 163 centimetres tall.

Anyone with any information regarding the disappearance of Kirra Hayward is urged to contact police.

Kirra skimmed her hand over the tattered clipping.

'They didn't actually take you to Sydney, did they?' Milo asked.

'No.'

It didn't matter that someone had made an incorrect identification of a girl who possibly matched Kirra's description in Sydney. It didn't matter that her parents were looking in all the wrong places. All that mattered was that they were still searching. They hadn't given up.

She glanced at Milo. He'd obviously gone to great lengths to secure this tiny bit of information, this precious comfort, and deliver it back to her. He couldn't possibly know how much this meant, and she couldn't find the words to properly tell him.

'Oh, and I have this,' he added, as though the article hadn't been enough. He pressed something flat and cold into her hand.

She found a tiny, chipped brass watch lying in her palm, the size of a ten-cent coin. It was dirty and scuffed and the wristband was missing. All three hands were loose and swivelled around the numbers instead of staying in place.

'You know, if things were different ... if we were different ... and I went away somewhere, I'd bring something for you when I came back. You said you wanted a watch.' He shrugged, his voice suddenly gruff. 'I found it ... I thought ... I don't know. It doesn't work ... but what's the point of time for us anyway?'

Kirra curled her fingers around the tiny timepiece, wanting to say so many things. Instead, she swallowed down the sore lump in her throat and took a steadying breath. 'Thank you,' was all she could manage.

He seemed to understand.

'What happened?' Kirra asked him, storing the watch in the pocket of Lena's jacket. 'What have you been doing all this time? I thought they'd killed you or something.'

'Really?' he asked.

'Well ... yeah. What was I meant to think?'

'Sorry,' he said, looking guilty. 'They didn't tell you anything?'

'Nothing.'

'Oh. Well, Latham had jobs, right, all over the place and he took me with him.'

'Why'd he do that? He hasn't done it before.'

'Not sure,' Milo confessed. 'Guess it was just easier that way, to take a Translator with him, especially as he was on the move. Anyway, a fair few people were killed — nothing like Bachmeier though. Just people here and there. One in Australia. A woman, in this huge office all to herself. She was shot at her desk. That's — that's where I grabbed the newspaper. It was on a table near the door, and I took it before anyone noticed.'

He was gazing at the floor, looking tired and disturbed.

'There were others,' he went on. 'These two men in Durban. They were shot in this secure car park — that's where I found that watch. Then this old man in his apartment in Boston.' He went silent for a moment before — 'It's July.'

'What?'

'Yeah. July. Can you believe that? Can you believe we've been stuck like this all that time?'

Kirra watched him sadly.

'Why didn't you refuse to give the sequences? We were separated, Latham couldn't use us against each other.'

'He did,' Milo said immediately. 'Said you'd be killed if I didn't do it.'

'Oh.'

He shrugged. 'Didn't know what else to do.'

Kirra nodded, suddenly feeling hopeless.

'Yeah. I'd have done the same thing.'

The very next day Latham had both Kirra and Milo steered out of their cell and into a wide room plastered with graffiti. Kirra was no stranger to this room. She'd visited it many times since her arrival at the factory after the Bachmeier bomb all those months ago. Every few days, it seemed, they were strapped into adjacent chairs and given alternating roles. One was handed the code, the other given Balcescu's drug, and Latham would wait patiently as his method yielded excellent results. Kirra couldn't bear to watch Milo face the torment of the drug for long, and would write the sequence as fast as she could so he would be released. He did the same thing when it was Kirra's turn to be injected, watching her struggle for only a moment before giving in.

Today, of course, started out the same way as all the others. Latham laid a page before Kirra, and indicated for Balcescu to torture Milo.

'Don't,' Kirra said. Balcescu halted. 'Don't bother. I'll just do it.'

Milo looked over at her.

'Really?' Latham asked. 'How considerate of you, Kirra. You've saved us a dosage.'

Kirra ignored him, wrote out the sequence and pushed the page away. Latham looked over it, a very satisfied expression on his face.

'Take them back,' he ordered the two recruits at the door.

That night, they fell asleep in their usual corners, but some time later Kirra awoke to feel Milo's hands in her hair. It felt as if he was attempting to plait it, though he didn't seem to know how, and Kirra decided to pretend to still be asleep, not wanting to interrupt or embarrass him. His movements were tentative, as though he was afraid of disturbing her, but with each of Kirra's deep breaths, he grew more confident.

Kirra felt her skin tingle as his thumbs trailed her hairline and grazed with agonising tenderness over her skin. Desire like she'd never known it unfurled somewhere in the pit of her stomach, and though she chose not to act on it, the awareness of it alone thrilled her. She kept her eyes tightly closed, enjoying each gentle tug of her hair, every brush of his fingers against her temple.

Something in Milo's ministrations also felt slightly wrong; as though Kirra was partaking in something her parents never would have allowed or approved of, as though she was taking something that belonged to someone else.

For a moment she wondered what her parents would think if they could see her now. She wasn't even sure they'd believe it was her, lying there, held firm in Milo's embrace. It was the sort of situation reserved for Olivia, who was always encouraged to relay the details of her growing relationship with Steven to their mother.

In an instant, Kirra felt an eternity's worth of affection for Milo rising up inside her. He didn't care about who she used to be. He had no idea about any of it, and for once Kirra was entirely glad to be stuck in the cell. She shifted very slightly and felt his hands freeze amongst her tangles. He seemed terrified that she may be waking up, but she continued with her deep breaths and lay perfectly still, and he started up again, oblivious to the smile she was struggling to keep from her lips.

One particularly warm evening, just as it was getting dark, Kirra spotted two moving shadows beneath the door. Milo saw them at the same time. His jaw clenched and he reached out to wrap his hand around her wrist. They stayed perfectly still and silent, Kirra's heart in her throat. Milo's reaction to the men outside frightened her even though she didn't fully understand it. They heard the men muttering in their own language, and then, just as they had before, the shadows disappeared.

'We're leaving,' Milo declared suddenly.

She looked at him. 'Huh?'

'We're leaving.'

'What? *Leaving* leaving?'

'Yes.'

'Milo —'

'We're not staying here. You're — we're not safe here.'

'What do you mean?'

'Things are getting more dangerous. Those men … I know what they're thinking of doing.'

Kirra stared at him. He seemed so serious, and it was scaring her.

'We can't escape,' she said firmly. 'They'll kill us.'

'No. No, I don't think they will. They need the sequences too badly. And if they do, so what? At least we won't be sticking around to … to see what happens.'

Kirra stared at his set face, his tight jaw, his eyes gleaming in the moonlight. He seemed older than usual as he glared at her through the darkness.

'It's been half a year. Do you want to stay here like this forever?' he asked her. 'What sort of life is that?'

'It's bad, but —'

'It's worse than bad!'

'It's better than being dead!'

Milo frowned.

'If you say so,' he said, looking annoyed.

'I don't think it's a good idea. Not yet, anyway.'

'Not yet? How much longer do you want to rot in here?'

'Milo —'

'You're coming.'

'You can't make me,' Kirra retorted. 'I'm staying.'

'No, you're not.'

'You can't tell me what to do.'

'Look!' he nearly yelled. 'If you're not going to cooperate, I'll drag you out of here. Don't think I won't.'

Kirra, sick of arguing, ignored him.

'Please,' he said. He took her hand. 'Please, Kirra. We've got to try.'

She closed her eyes for a long moment, the memory of Lena's blood running into her hair hitting Kirra with full force.

'I'm scared,' she admitted.

'But … you'll do it?'

'Okay.'

'Okay?'

'Yes, but … we've got to plan it. We've got to go over it and over it. Things could go very wrong, you know.'

'They won't.'

'You don't know that. We've got to account for everything.'

'We will,' Milo assured her. 'We'll do whatever you want. Nothing will go wrong, you'll see.'

CHAPTER FIFTEEN

THE ESCAPE

The following night, Kirra sat in her usual corner, her fingers pattering out an unsteady rhythm on her knees. She kept changing position, drawing her knees to her chest, stretching her legs out as far as they could go, kneeling on them just to stop them from trembling. The space between her heart and stomach felt knotted and queasy, fluttering as though she'd swallowed something alive and whole.

Hushed footsteps along the corridor reached her ears. The lock on the cell door clicked quietly. She took a small, sharp breath. They had been waiting for a recruit to bring their evening meal for hours, but two silhouettes stood in the doorway instead of one. Why two? And where was the food?

The recruits glanced at her, then at the other corner. When they saw it was empty, they went for the handguns in their belts.

This was the sign Kirra had been waiting for and she coughed quietly into the silence.

Milo's hand shot out from behind the door, grabbed the closest recruit's weapon and yanked it away. The recruit was so surprised he barely had time to respond before Milo cracked the gun down on his skull and he crumpled to the floor with a soft thump.

The second recruit had almost enough time to point his gun directly between Milo's eyes, but Milo was quicker, reaching out to trap the recruit's firing arm between both of his. He twisted, ducking out of the way in case the gun fired. The recruit gave a strangled grunt and drew away, giving Milo enough room to tackle him. They fell hard against the cement together, Milo groping for the gun that was still dangerously close to his face.

Kirra shot to her feet, watching the struggle breathlessly. Milo was putting up an impressive fight. In fact, he looked far more agile and combative than the recruit did. He finally wrenched the gun from the recruit's grip and got to his feet, applying a furious kick to the man's chest. It seemed that overpowering him had only taken the element of surprise.

Gun in hand, he glanced at Kirra, motionless against the wall, then back at the recruit, who was clutching his ribs and attempting to push himself to his feet, half-crawling, half-limping towards them. The first recruit was still out cold by the door.

Milo raised the gun, looking down at the winded man, but stopped midway and instead handed it to Kirra. She stared at him, horrified.

'No! I'm not going to —'

'Quick!' he hissed. 'Come on! Now!'

Kirra looked at the recruit as he clambered towards her. Panicking, she raised the gun. It shook in her hands, bouncing about between her fingers. She couldn't do it. She couldn't kill him.

Then she felt Milo by her side, his hand on the small of her back, and watched as he slipped his own finger over hers. He pressed down and made her squeeze the trigger, and, with a bang that seemed to explode into her own heart, she shot the man.

He gasped, his hands going straight to the wound in his throat. There was a suspended moment in which the room was very still, except for the blood spewing from the bullet hole, and then the recruit toppled over onto the floor, fighting to take long, slurping breaths.

Milo took Kirra's hand and dragged her towards the door, still breathing hard from the pain of the scuffle. They didn't have time to think about what they'd done. Someone surely would have heard the gunshot.

They glided along the corridor and into a wide, rundown hall, where old pieces of machinery were left off to the sides and the smell of oil and dirt hung in the air. Milo crouched behind a bank of discarded equipment, pulling Kirra down beside him and together they waited with bated breath, listening for sounds of pursuit. They were perfectly silent, but Kirra was sure the tumultuous pounding of her heart would give them away. They both still held weapons: Kirra's, heavy and cold in her hand; Milo's grip on his looking almost comfortable.

'Why did you do that?' she breathed, blood screaming in her ears.

Milo knew exactly what she was referring to but he continued to stare straight ahead. Finally, he shook his head, his curls rustling over his eyes. 'You needed to do it.'

'But why?'

'Think about it, Kirra! Why did those two come into the cell? They weren't bringing us dinner, and they weren't there for me! Think about it!'

Kirra stared at him, feeling sick. He nodded grimly and turned away.

Milo seemed to decide it was safe, or perhaps that they might not get another chance, and pulled Kirra to her feet. Keeping low behind the cover of the machinery, they sprinted the length of the hall, stopping just short of entering another corridor. They had planned their escape as carefully as possible, but their knowledge of the factory was limited to the corridors between the bathroom, their cell and the graffiti room. To some extent, they were fumbling around in the dark. At any moment they could turn a corner and find themselves in a dead end or, worse, come face to face with a wall of recruits.

Peering into the gloomy corridor, Kirra heard distant voices yelling. The recruits had realised they'd escaped. Milo pulled her into the passageway, heading away from the voices, but his grip on her wrist tightened when they heard someone, close by, heading in their direction.

Kirra stopped an anxious gasp before it left her mouth. Together they darted through an open door into an empty room and listened for their pursuer. The muffled voices were some distance from the lone presence in the corridor, which was moving almost soundlessly. In fact, Kirra realised, they could no longer hear anything at all. Their pursuer must have changed course, leaving the corridor silent. She expelled a grateful breath.

They vacated the room and turned left, eyes scanning for possible exits. A shriek of terror exploded from Kirra's dry lips when she felt a warm hand shoot out to wrap around hers. Poised beside the doorway was Wyles. He spun Kirra into his arms and had a gun to her temple like lightning, watching as Milo froze.

Kirra struggled, an impulse reaction before she realised there was no need. It was Wyles, after all. Gentle, generous Wyles with his chocolates and jokes. Surely he wasn't going to hurt them.

'Place the gun on the floor,' he whispered, his weapon sinking deeper into Kirra's skin, his eyes flicking down the corridor.

Milo didn't move, his expression outraged. He looked between Kirra, the gun at her head and Wyles several times. Kirra swallowed painfully. She wanted to talk to him, tell him that it was alright. This escape attempt had failed, but there would be others.

'I don't have all night,' Wyles said, increasing the pressure at Kirra's temple.

Milo studied him suspiciously. Finally he complied, slowly setting the weapon down. Kirra winced as Wyles tightened his grip on her. It really was all over. Wyles was going to drag them back to the cell, lock them up and leave them there for Latham to deal with, who would undoubtedly find some new and repugnant way of punishing them.

'Back in there,' Wyles said to Milo, indicating the room he and Kirra had just vacated. Milo retreated over the threshold slowly.

'Good,' Wyles muttered, loosening his grip on Kirra to shut the door in Milo's face.

Kirra searched out Milo's gaze just before the door blocked him from view. He looked livid, but she managed a small smile for him. They would just have to try again.

Wyles locked the door with a set of keys from his pocket, then proceeded down the corridor with his arm firmly around Kirra, pinning her to his side, going the same way she and Milo would have fled had they not been intercepted.

'Don't make a sound,' he murmured, coming to a halt at an open door. Kirra felt the fresh night air whipping around her face. They stepped out into a deserted street and, to her shock, kept walking.

'Where are you taking me?' she asked, twisting back for a last glance at the building where Milo was locked away.

'No questions,' Wyles murmured, pulling her along the street.

The smell and taste of fresh air was strange after so many months inside the factory, and the sky, filled with stars, made Kirra feel extremely exposed. Even the pavement beneath her feet felt odd.

Wyles unlocked the back door of a sleek green sedan and forced her inside. The smell of brand new upholstery filled Kirra's nostrils. He closed the door with a thud and proceeded to the driver's seat. Once inside, he reached for a bag and withdrew two tablets and a bottle of water.

'Take these,' he said curtly, handing them to her.

She shoved his arm away. 'No!'

He pulled his gun from inside his jacket and pressed it to her forehead with a resigned sigh. 'Yes,' he said.

One of Latham's recruits would never shoot her, Kirra knew that, but she was beginning to suspect Wyles wasn't all he appeared to be. After a quick review of her options, she took the pills from his hand. She tossed them into her mouth and raised the bottle to her lips, swallowing them down in a single gulp, staring daggers at Wyles the entire time.

'Good,' he said, more to himself than to her, his gun now out of sight. He turned the key in the ignition. 'They won't harm you. They'll just put you to sleep. Don't fight them.'

Kirra was full of questions, not least of which was what had brought about the sudden change in his temperament, but as he accelerated down the street, the factory receding behind them, she started feeling wobbly and sluggish. Her eyes were heavy; her neck felt unable to support the weight of her head. At a rate she would have found vaguely disturbing, the pills did their job and she dropped off into a deep, dreamless sleep.

CHAPTER SIXTEEN

DESMOND RALL

Kirra awoke to the sensation of something soft and comfortable beneath her. Her head started to pound as though on cue, and she opened her eyes a crack only to be blinded by the morning sun. She turned her head away. How long had she been asleep? Her hair was strewn across her face and neck as though she'd been unceremoniously dumped on the white couch beneath her.

A couch? That couldn't be right. She opened her eyes and sat upright, a colossal, heaving effort, and squinted around. The room she was in was long and broad, and nearly everything in it was stainless steel or perfect white. A smooth marble coffee table sat at her feet on a soft ivory rug, and she was facing a spotless kitchen behind a perfectly oval kitchen island.

She rubbed her forehead, feeling ill, and jumped when a side door opened and a man strode into the room. Her eyes widened. It was Wyles. In a flash she remembered the escape attempt. She remembered Milo being locked in an empty room before she'd been rushed away by the man she'd completely misjudged until now.

He came to stand in the middle of the room, watching her from what seemed like a safe distance with a strangely contrite look on his face. He was tall, his skin was very pale and his hair was almost black. His square jaw was covered in its customary dark stubble and his eyes were sunken and weary.

'Good morning,' he said.

Kirra gazed at him for a long time before speaking.

'Who are you?'

Her voice was rough and croaky from sleep. Strangely, she didn't feel all that fearful of him. She was annoyed, yes. Perplexed, certainly. But scared? Not at all.

'Desmond Rall,' he said.

'So ... not Wyles then?'

He smiled. 'No. Not Wyles.'

He had a strange accent, one Kirra couldn't quite place. He sat in a chair opposite her, the light catching his face, and for the first time Kirra realised that his chin wasn't the only damaged part of him. His nose was off centre, and another, much lighter, scar nicked up from his eyebrow into his hairline. He clasped his hands and leaned forward as she stared at him.

'What happened to Milo?' She asked her most important question quickly. 'Did they find him?'

'Who?'

'Milo,' she said. 'You locked him in a room at the factory, remember?'

'Oh ... the kid? I wondered what his name was.'

Kirra's jaw tightened. 'He's not a kid,' she gritted out, looking around. 'Where are we anyway? Why aren't I tied up or behind a locked door or something?'

Desmond Rall gave her a roguish smile. 'I'm not a recruit. I don't work for Latham.'

Kirra froze. 'What?'

'I'm not a recruit.'

'Yes, you are. You've been there for months. I've seen you!'

'Oh, Latham thought I was working for him. Truth be told, I just needed to get close enough to steal you away.'

He got to his feet and strode to the kitchen. Kirra studied him as he filled a stainless-steel kettle with water, all the while whistling between his teeth. She blinked furiously to ensure she wasn't having an incredibly overimaginative daydream.

'You ... you were just pretending to work for him?' she ventured.

'That's right,' Desmond called from the pantry, where he was digging around for something. 'Under the name Wyles.'

'Do you work for the government? Are you going to help me?' Kirra gasped.

Hope inflated her to the point of giddiness, but subsided when he emerged from the pantry with a box of teabags in his hand and gave her another wry smile.

'I do not work for the government,' he said, the hint of a chuckle in his voice, 'whichever government it is you are referring to. As a general rule, the government and I don't *really* get along. I'm a Contractor.'

'Great,' Kirra muttered, disappointment hitting hard. 'What do you want with me?'

He stopped what he was doing.

'What do I want with you?' he repeated. He stared at her over the pristine kitchen island. 'You *are* Kirra Hayward, aren't you?'

'You know I am,' she said, not in the mood for games.

Desmond was still gawking at her. 'You know what the Spencer System is, don't you? Why you're so valuable?'

'The Spencer code has something to do with security systems,' she said, 'but that's all I know.'

The kettle started whistling from its place near the sink. Desmond rummaged through the cabinets, bashing together pots and pans, and Kirra winced.

'You get a sequence of numbers from this code, right?' Desmond hollered to her over the clanging. 'And they become a PIN? Well, that's a very rare skill.'

'Yeah, I've gathered that.'

'Yes, but you don't understand *how* rare,' he said, eventually digging up a mug with a large crimson heart painted on the side and setting it down triumphantly. 'There are only three people in the world who can do it, and one of them, Richard Spencer, is dead. There have been intelligence reports of a woman named Josephine Shaw who's suspected to be a Translator, though it hasn't been confirmed.'

'Why not?'

He shrugged. 'She's disappeared. Then there's the third person, who is currently missing.' He finished with a small grin, looking pleased that the person in question was missing because of him.

'What about Milo?' Kirra said pointedly.

Desmond stopped what he was doing and spun around, his interest evidently piqued. 'The other kid can do it too?'

Kirra gave a curt nod. 'You were there in the factory — how could you not know that?'

Desmond shrugged again. 'Latham's got a sort of hierarchy going on. I wasn't a high-level recruit. When you got to the factory I was given responsibility for bringing you meals. I wasn't cleared to sit in on your translations. I had no idea Milo was anything special at all.'

'Yeah, well,' Kirra said, 'he is.'

'That makes a lot of sense,' Desmond continued thoughtfully, plopping a teabag into his mug. 'See, I thought they'd just grabbed any old kid.'

'What are you talking about?'

'I didn't think Milo was a Translator. I just thought he was a nobody they kidnapped for you.'

Kirra looked up. 'What? Kidnapped for ... what?'

Desmond took a few moments to consider his response.

'Latham put out a worldwide search — that quiz you answered — to find a Translator,' he said. 'He figured if Spencer could do the code, chances were someone else somewhere in the world could too. He went for the youngest candidate he could get his hands on; he thought it would make things easier. And then he met you and he wasn't so sure. So he brought in a kid for you to form a relationship with, so he could use it against you if it came to that. You know, brandish a gun at him, or torture him, and force you to hand over the sequence. The whole torture thing is much more effective when there's leverage involved. He thought if the two of you were locked up for long enough together, you'd do anything for each other.'

Kirra stared at a very precise spot on the coffee table. 'Yeah. They made me watch him … and they made him watch me …' She trailed off before she embarrassed herself. She wasn't sure she'd ever really get over Balcescu's drug.

'I didn't realise Latham continued the search to find a second Translator,' Desmond said, 'but it's quite ingenious now I think of it. He had the opportunity to use you both, and should anything happen to one of you he had the other to fall back on — his own sort of security.'

Kirra was very still.

'So, Milo was really only there because of me?' she asked, her voice barely more than a whisper.

'That was the original idea, yeah,' Desmond said. 'Why else would they need him? Tea?' he asked over his shoulder as he poured boiling water in the mug.

'No, thank you,' Kirra murmured, staring blankly at the floor.

So Milo had been part of Latham's plan for her. The only reason Latham had gone looking for Milo was because he'd thought it would help his cause where Kirra was concerned. Kirra wanted to be sick. The idea was putrid, crawling around in her mind like a parasite. She shuddered. The fact that Latham had orchestrated their bond was … revolting. Milo was her friend, her only source of comfort, and that was exactly how Latham had planned it. Now the thought of being reunited with Milo felt quite sordid.

'Are you alright?' Desmond asked as he resumed his seat across from her, as though they'd been discussing nothing more than neighbourly gossip.

'Fine,' Kirra said. 'Fine.'

'Well, anyway,' he continued, blowing the steam from his tea, 'you're in high demand. Contractors the world over would give their right arms to get hold of you.'

Kirra must have looked baffled because Desmond said, 'You don't know very much about the Industry, do you?'

She shook her head. Desmond nodded and absently scratched the side of his face.

'Richard Spencer?'

'No.'

He made an irritated sound in the back of his throat. 'No one's explained any of it to you?'

She shook her head, wondering what she could possibly need to know other than the fact that Latham, and everyone like him, was evil.

'Okay,' Desmond said. 'Okay. Well … the Industry isn't really like the world you've grown up in.'

'Really?' Kirra said.

Desmond seemed not to notice her sarcasm. 'Yes. That's the first thing to know. It's a sort of community, I guess, built on criminal activity. Assassination, Extracting, Retrieving … that sort of thing. It operates in every country in the world. We don't like to call ourselves criminals — sounds too petty — we go with the title "Contractors" instead.'

Kirra tried to digest this. A criminal community that operated all around the world?

'Now to Richard Spencer,' he went on. 'Spencer was an engineer. A brilliant one. He engineered a brand new security system for regular people, one that was, until recently, completely unbreakable. Usually there are various ways of breaking through a security system, but all our methods are ineffective with the Spencer System. Everything we've tried has failed. Then it was discovered that Spencer had embedded unique disabling PINs for each of his systems into codes. Codes only he could break.'

'Why would he do that?'

'Well, that's the great mystery, isn't it?'

Kirra frowned at him. 'You don't know?'

'No one does,' he said. 'Initially they thought it was Spencer's way of adding another layer of security, but as the codes only provide a means of breaking through the system, rather than protecting it, that theory was shot to hell. Some of us thought that perhaps it was simply Spencer being a control freak. Maybe he wanted the assurance that he could break through his own systems if he so desired. We still haven't worked out why, but the fact of the matter is that the Spencer System is a coveted product. Naturally, every person who has any reason to hide anything — or themselves — wants the protection this system offers.'

'But you said the codes can break through —'

'Yes, but only those of us in the Contracting Industry know that. Spencer's customers — regular people — have no idea about any of this. All they know is that it's marketed as the best security money can buy. It's very difficult for Contractors to stay in business when their targets are safely hidden behind an unbreakable defence. It's become a very frustrating time for us, and we've tried everything to get through the system, but to no avail. We soon found out, however, about the codes. Codes that, when broken, could unlock these systems. It was an incredible breakthrough for all of us, well worth the celebration it caused. Contractors all over the world went hunting for the codes, and we eventually found them, but discovered shortly after that they weren't the sort of thing just anyone could decipher. In fact, they were deemed impossible to crack. This enraged many of us, so when the news came out that the engineer could translate his own code, Contractors all around the world raced to get to him first. Richard Spencer killed himself the day he heard they were coming. Probably the best move he ever made. After all the inconvenience he'd caused, that man was better off dead than what they had planned for him.'

Desmond took a sip of his tea and set it on the coffee table in front of him. 'And so, with Spencer dead, the search for another Translator began, with Latham at the helm. He discovered that there were copies of every code for every system. Now, you can obtain these copies if you pay one of the old Spencer apprentices the right sum of money, but that only gets you the code; none of the apprentices know how to break it.'

'Why not?'

'Spencer never thought to include his employees when it came to his ingenious code idea. He had a bit of a superiority complex, I think. Speaking of complexes,

Latham was, at the time the Spencer System came out, one of the most sought-after professionals in the Industry. He started losing business only days after the Spencer System came on the market. He could no longer break into houses to assassinate his targets, or sneak into their office buildings to kill them at work, or break into their computers to check their schedules. He specialises in making assassinations look like suicides or accidents. It's hard to make a death look like a suicide if you can't get inside the victim's home to place a fired handgun by their side. So he sought out the best mathematicians he could get his hands on. He blackmailed cryptographers, threatened all sorts of analysts, but no one could explain the code to him. Then he had a stroke of genius. He tricked someone into bringing him a prototype of the code, something Richard Spencer had kept very well hidden. Spencer had used it during the development of the code, and it had a corresponding answer sequence attached. Latham's discovery of that prototype will probably go down as the single greatest event in Contracting history because with it, and with it alone, another Translator could be found.

'Latham tasked one of his tech recruits to disguise the prototype code as a puzzle and post it up on a quiz website — the idea was to widen the search as much as possible. Then he waited for someone to submit a sequence that matched the one they had. Shockingly, it was only a week before a match was submitted. And now here you are, deciphering codes and giving correct sequences, and you're like a miracle to the Industry — the key to it all. The solution to our biggest problem.

Everyone is after you, and I'm sorry to say they probably will be for a long time to come.'

Kirra stared at her hands, feeling horrified. *Everyone is after you and they will be for a long time to come.*

'What about Milo?' she asked, struggling to keep her voice balanced.

'Well, no one knows about Milo,' Desmond replied slowly. 'He was an afterthought. A secret well kept by Latham. He'd have liked for you to have been kept a secret too, except that it's impossible not to notice that Latham is operating at full capacity again, taking jobs left, right and centre, most of them Spencer-system-protected. It got out a few days after you were kidnapped — by way of a loud-mouthed recruit, probably — that Latham possesses the only known accessible Spencer code Translator in the world.'

'Are you sure no one knows Milo's another Translator?'

'Quite sure. I didn't even know, and I was there at the factory. Latham's clearly learnt from his mistakes with you and is taking much more care to keep Milo a complete secret.'

Kirra expelled a small sigh of relief. If they ever made it out of this alive, Milo had the chance to retreat back into normality. He could leave it all behind him and move on with his life. She felt like springing to her feet and doing some sort of celebratory dance. Then she wondered why. It wasn't as though she could go with him.

She glanced up at Desmond as he drained his mug. 'And what about you?' she asked coldly. 'Do you get paid to kill people?'

'I used to,' he said. 'Not anymore.'

'Why not?'

'I found it wasn't as rewarding a career as I'd hoped. Now I'm an Extraction specialist.'

'Which is what, exactly?' Kirra asked.

He thumbed the handle of his mug, mulling over how best to describe himself. 'Say someone's been sent to prison, someone wealthy. Their family pays me to get them out and then they go into hiding. I usually extract the prisoner in transit — it's easier that way — but I've had to force my way into a couple of prisons — not an easy day's work. I'm not cheap to hire, and why should I be? If I'm going to set criminals free I like to take a good portion of their money from them first.'

He nodded in her direction.

'Your Extraction was probably the hardest job I've ever taken.'

Kirra glanced around the immaculate apartment. 'Where are we?'

'Madrid. Sorry about the drug; it was easier that way.'

'Easier for whom?' Kirra said, more to herself than to him. 'You could have taken Milo with us. You didn't have to leave him.'

'If I'd known he was a Translator I would have. I didn't think he was worth anything.'

Kirra bristled, but recalled having once felt a similar way.

'Well, he is,' she said.

Desmond gave a small shrug, got up and dropped his mug in the sink. 'We've got to get started tomorrow, but for now you can sleep.'

'Get started?'

'I'm doing someone a favour here, but before that there are a few jobs I need your help with. Really, all I need is for you to crack a couple of codes so I can send them to my colleagues. They're waiting to do a job in Kyoto and then another in Phuket. Also, I need your help here in Madrid. The police have started using the Spencer System on all their prisoner transit trucks. Cedro Aguilar is on his way to a maximum security facility next week and you're going to help me get him away.'

'What did he do?'

'Who cares? His wife is paying me to get him out.'

Kirra, however, found that she did care. She also found Desmond's lack of morals intensely annoying.

'Why do you assume I'm going to help you?' she asked. 'What makes you think I'm going anywhere with you? I don't even know you.'

Desmond observed her from behind the kitchen island, his arms folded comfortably across his chest.

'You don't really have a choice, do you?' he said. 'What else are you going to do? Surely Latham's told you that he's watching your family? Don't delude yourself into thinking he won't harm them if you attempt to make contact. He's prepared to do anything to keep you to himself, so by my count you don't really have any other options … unless you plan on going back to him.'

Kirra glared at her boots. Of course she wasn't going back to Latham. Some part of her knew she ought to be grateful to Desmond, really. He had released her from a life of captivity in the factory, and he didn't seem to be intending to treat her like a prisoner himself. At a time when going back to Freemont wasn't an option, Desmond really was all she had.

He washed his mug, allowing her a moment of private deliberation, which was outstandingly interrupted by the door bursting open with a crash. A young woman strode into the room and, barely looking at them, slapped her black laptop bag on the kitchen island. Kirra glanced apprehensively at Desmond. He didn't act as though this was anything out of the ordinary, so she supposed she wasn't in any immediate danger.

'I think this is going to be harder than we thought,' the woman said, without so much as an explanation or a greeting. 'Aguilar's transit has been rescheduled.'

After failing to receive a response from Desmond, she glanced up and then followed his gaze to the couch. She froze when her sharp, dark eyes fell on Kirra.

'Who is that?' she said abruptly.

'Kirra, this is Mai Luong,' Desmond said. 'She's worked on and off with me for many years. Mai, I'd like to introduce my new friend Kirra Hayward.'

Mai was small and intense to look at. She had shiny black hair styled to sit evenly above her shoulders, and thin, arching eyebrows. She was wearing fitted black slacks and a brown jacket, a fine silver chain around her neck, and two plain silver earrings just visible beneath her hair. She flashed her eyes around the room as though expecting to find someone else there, before locking back onto Kirra and beginning what felt like an alarmingly thorough evaluation. Kirra tried not to squirm.

'Kirra Hayward?' Mai repeated, looking suspicious.

'Kirra Hayward,' Desmond confirmed.

'No,' Mai said with a curt shake of her head. 'That's just a ... No.'

'Interesting, isn't it, how few people know that Kirra Hayward is just a schoolgirl,' Desmond pondered out loud.

Kirra felt a stab of annoyance at his choice of words. *Just* a schoolgirl?

Mai's eyes shot to the door and back, her expression one of frightened vigilance. 'Desmond, are you sure you weren't followed? Are you sure we're safe here with her?'

'I'm sure,' he said.

'Desmond, this is very dangerous! Did you ensure maximum secur—'

'Tea, Mai?' Desmond asked loudly.

Mai glanced at the door, then the windows, and finally at Desmond. 'Yes. Please,' she replied stiffly. She then returned her gaze to Kirra, who was already feeling uncomfortable enough without Mai's hawkish eyes trained on her.

'How do you do it?' she asked abruptly.

Kirra jumped a little. 'What? The code?'

'Of course the code! What else?'

Kirra shrugged. 'I don't know. I just ... can,' she said truthfully.

Mai crossed her arms. 'I can't accept that,' she shot back. 'There *must* be an algorithm!'

Kirra eyed her worriedly. She seemed incredibly put out.

'An algorithm is just a set of steps for working something out,' Desmond interjected when Kirra failed to answer.

'I know what an algorithm is!' Kirra exclaimed. 'I was the best maths student at my school!'

Neither Desmond nor Mai seemed remotely impressed by this.

'But there must be some pattern you follow,' Mai pressed on stubbornly.

'No,' Kirra told her, getting annoyed in return. 'Depending on the succession of characters, certain numbers and letters make sense. I see one number, I write it down. I keep looking and immediately see a letter that just has to follow. There is no pattern. It just … happens.'

Kirra was certain she'd never seen anyone look quite as incensed as Mai now did.

Desmond gave Kirra a small grin. 'Mai is one of the most proficient Analysts I've ever met,' he said. 'It drives her mad that she can't translate the code.'

Mai shot him an enraged glance, her delicate jaw clenched. Then she zipped open her bag and pulled out a sleek black laptop.

'You weren't supposed to get her 'til Friday,' she muttered to Desmond, as though Kirra had suddenly disappeared and they were free to discuss her at length.

'Yes, believe it or not I do remember our plan,' he replied, still unable to contain his smile. 'We had a little problem at the factory. An impromptu escape attempt required a modification.'

'Oh,' Mai replied, and dropped the matter. Her fingers flew across the keys of her laptop with almost inhuman speed. 'Look at this.'

Desmond turned away from preparing Mai's tea and looked at the screen. Kirra watched them curiously as they studied the laptop together, side by side. At the kitchen island, between the elevated microwave, the blender and the coffee percolator, they almost looked like normal people.

'Kirra, come and have a look,' said Desmond, his eyes glued to the computer.

She did as she was told, clambering unsteadily to her feet. She wasn't sure how she felt about being included. It was strange, yes, but a small part of her thrilled to it.

Mai pointed at the map of Madrid onscreen. 'They were holding him here, just outside the city,' she explained. 'But they've already moved him. He's at a station here,' she pointed to the city centre, 'because they're suspicious someone might try to intervene. They're moving him to the maximum security prison on Thursday, not Saturday.'

'Intervene? Who's after him?' Desmond asked. 'His wife is paying us to get him out. She can't want him dead.'

'She doesn't,' Mai agreed, minimising the map. 'And they're not suspicious of an attack. They're suspicious of an Extraction.'

'Really?' said Desmond. 'Amazing.' He didn't look worried; on the contrary, he appeared quite delighted by the challenge it presented. 'Well,' he said, 'we'll just get him away on Thursday. Lucky I pulled Kirra out when I did, or it would have been too late.'

'But I'll need to re-analyse the whole thing! Plus, I don't know the details of the new transit!' Mai protested.

'Set up a meeting with your prison contact,' Desmond said. 'He should be able to get hold of that information. It'll make the Extraction a bit more difficult, but not impossible. Not for us anyway.'

CHAPTER SEVENTEEN

THE RUIZ BAR

Desmond had ushered Kirra into the bedroom as soon as night fell, partly so she could rest and partly so he and Mai could continue discussing their plans in privacy. Kirra had come to a decision while lying wide awake in the room, but it was immediately clear to her that she couldn't proceed alone. Garnering Desmond's cooperation was crucial if she wanted her plans to succeed. She sighed as she shuffled her feet across the bed sheets, wondering how best to phrase her request to Desmond to increase her chances of getting a 'yes' out of him.

She slid out of bed and crossed to the window. The rooftops of Madrid stretched out in every direction. She looked down to the street and watched a woman with shopping bags in her hands hurrying across the road. Kirra's gaze followed her until she rounded a corner and disappeared out of sight, quickening her pace, no doubt en route home.

It seemed an age had passed since Kirra had had a home and parents and siblings. For all intents and purposes she knew her family was long gone, as though wiped out by a flash flood or a freeway accident or a house fire, leaving her entirely on her own. Everything was different now, and by no real fault of her own (other than perhaps her foolishness in submitting the sequence in the first place) her life could never be the same. For some reason, this realisation wasn't particularly upsetting. In fact, it had a mildly liberating quality about it. Kirra accepted it quickly and effortlessly, understanding that her abduction marked the end of an era, like graduating from school, or leaving a job, or getting to the highest level of one of Mitchell's video games and realising there was nowhere else to go.

She soon came to another conclusion: the only person she could rely on now, the only person who could offer her any sort of stability, was trapped in a factory in Germany. It didn't matter that Latham had engineered their friendship. Kirra knew, deep down, that didn't change anything. Latham might have put them in the cell together, but even he couldn't force the things she felt for Milo.

How could she even begin to contemplate escaping the Industry without him there to help her? What would it mean to be free if he was still imprisoned? How could she live with herself?

Kirra knew she had a very serious task ahead of her. Somehow she had to find a way to wriggle free of the Industry forever; and, if she could, to expose Latham to the authorities. But she knew beyond all doubt that she could not do it without Milo. He was part of the equation, a crucial element, as deeply entrenched in all this as she was. He deserved a chance to put things right too. She could go no further without him, and even if she could she didn't want to. Milo was everything now, her one true friend.

Besides, Kirra knew it was her fault he was mixed up in all this. If only she'd cooperated with Latham at the start he wouldn't have gone looking for a second Translator to use against her. Milo would still be in Southampton with his parents and brothers. He'd be at uni, going out, making friends and having fun. Perhaps he'd even have a girlfriend? Kirra despised the thought, but that was the reality of what she'd taken from him. He was missing out on being young. Every day he was in the cell was a day of his life wasted; days he could never get back, all because of Kirra. He'd been pulled into this because of her, so it was her responsibility to see that he climbed back out again.

Kirra crossed softly to the door and opened it just enough for her to slide out into the kitchen where Desmond and Mai were conversing in low voices over the laptop.

'I'll help you,' she told them when they looked up. 'But we have to make a deal first.'

Desmond and Mai agreed to talk to Kirra, but asked for her patience first. They'd scheduled a meeting with Mai's contact who had information pertaining to Aguilar's transit, and they flat out refused to leave Kirra alone in the apartment while they were out.

Kirra thought it was just as much of a risk taking her along but didn't voice her objections. She was determined to ask as little of them as possible before she had to ask as much of them as she could. She followed them out of the apartment building into Mai's little black hire car, and together they drove to a quiet corner bar. Desmond and Mai flanked Kirra, shooting furtive glances down the street and doing a visual sweep of the place before they shooed her inside.

The lit-up sign over the door declared the bar's name to be 'Ruiz', and it was empty save for an older woman wrapped tightly in a cream and gold pashmina. She was reading what looked like a romance novel over her glass of wine. The place smelled strongly of sweet, sugary drinks and was poorly lit and dirty. The carpet was so sticky Kirra had to pull each foot off the ground to take the next step.

Mai cast around for her contact, who apparently hadn't shown up yet, before ushering Kirra into a gaudy velvet booth right at the very back of the bar. Desmond shoved a soft drink in front of her even though she told him she wanted nothing.

'I'm hardly getting you a glass of scotch but, for appearances' sake, you'd better drink something,' he said, sitting down across from her.

The bar, despite being empty, was still a public place and that made Kirra nervous. She tried the soft drink, sucking a mouthful up through a straw, and felt the bubbles fizz and sting in her nose, the sensation quite startling. Her mother was strictly against soft drinks in the house, and no one, not even Olivia, had ever been able to sway her on that rule.

'I want you to send me back,' Kirra said, taking her opportunity whilst they waited for Mai's contact to arrive.

Desmond's glass, which had been on the way to his mouth, halted in midair. 'Are you serious?' he said.

'Yes.'

Mai raised one of her pointed eyebrows, but said nothing.

'Well … that's not an option,' Desmond spluttered, his glass still hovering some distance from his mouth. 'We need you. You aren't going anywhere.'

'I won't help you then,' Kirra said.

Desmond rubbed his eyes and a small, helpless sound escaped him. Mai closed her laptop, which she seemed to take everywhere with her, and perched her chin on her palm, observing Kirra with interest.

'Why do you want to go back?' Desmond said finally. 'You weren't exactly treated well there.'

Kirra palmed the broken watch, which she kept zipped up in the tiny inside pocket of Lena's jacket. 'Milo,' she said quietly.

Mai looked puzzled, but understanding dawned on Desmond's face.

'Oh, I get it. You two were friends,' he said, slouching back in his chair.

'Wasn't that the point?' Kirra muttered. 'So, you can either take me back or,' she paused to ensure they were both listening, 'extract him for me.' Then, just for good measure, she added, 'Please.'

'Look,' said Desmond, 'his value just increased a hundredfold to them because they no longer have you to fall back on. Therefore, they'll have upped the security a hundred times over. So ... we can't get him out for you.'

'But isn't that what you specialise in? Breaking people out of prison?'

'Yes ... but ... this is different.'

'Only because there's no financial gain in it for you,' she said, realising she'd hit the mark when an ashamed expression crossed his face. 'Believe me, I'd pay you if I could. Any amount you asked.'

'I'm confused,' Mai interjected, taking her opportunity amid the silence. 'Who exactly is Milo?'

'Remember the kid Latham brought in to use as leverage against Kirra?' Desmond said.

Mai pursed her lips. 'No.'

Desmond blinked. 'I told you about this,' he said.

'Months ago, yes?' she asked, seeming to dredge up a long-forgotten fact. 'Back at the start of the year?'

'Exactly. Turns out Latham didn't just pull in some random kid. He went back to the code he'd planted on the internet and found another Translator.'

'This kid can also translate the code?' Mai asked.

'Yep,' said Desmond.

Mai looked positively murderous.

'I want that information to be kept secret,' Kirra said suddenly.

'It's not really up to you, I'm afraid,' Mai said, still looking livid. 'If Latham wants it to be known, then it will be known.'

'Why would he do that?'

'If Milo gets away, Latham could release the news of a second Translator to every other Contractor in the world. They'd put all their time and money into finding him, and the moment Milo's snatched up, Latham just has to track down whichever Contractor got to him first and take him back. It would be the easier way of finding him. If Milo stays where he is, then chances are his skills will be kept secret.'

'He can't stay there!' Kirra exclaimed. 'Even if it is the safest place for him! You don't know what it's like being shut up in a cell alone!'

Desmond gazed at her, looking torn. Mai pressed a finger to her lips, her brow wrinkling in thought.

'Kirra, we're trying to understand,' Desmond said earnestly, 'but you can't comprehend the danger you're in. Right now, Contractors everywhere are searching for the least bit of information on your whereabouts. They're climbing over each other to get to you. If Latham decides to use them to find you, there is nowhere you can hide. And Milo will be in the same danger if you free him.'

Kirra pressed her hands to her face. 'Getting separated was the worst thing that could have happened,' she told them, her voice strained.

'Wouldn't the worst thing be dying?' Desmond suggested.

Kirra looked at him, tempted to tell him he was wrong. Instead she remained silent.

Desmond stared at her. Mai was staring too, but it wasn't the contemptuous glare Kirra was becoming accustomed to. Her expression showed a mixture of understanding and compassion. Kirra didn't understand the change, but she didn't dwell on it. She was too busy glowering at Desmond.

'Listen. You either get Milo out and get him to me, or I'll just forget everything I know about the code. It's your choice. You need me, remember?'

Nothing was said for several tense moments.

It was Mai who spoke first, with a very small, 'Des?'

She scrutinised him closely, her sharp eyebrows elevated, until he gave a sigh and threw up his hands in defeat.

Mai returned her gaze to Kirra. 'After we get Aguilar, we'll start planning for your friend. Plans often have to change at the last minute in these situations so ... don't get your hopes up,' she said.

A short, pot-bellied man entered the bar and Mai looked over at him.

'He's here,' she said and got to her feet.

She walked over to the man, clasped his hand momentarily, and the pair slid into a different booth. The conversation that followed was too hushed for Kirra to hear.

'We promise we'll do our best,' Desmond said softly. 'That's all.'

Kirra looked over to the bar, where the young bartender was polishing wine glasses with a scrunched-up wad of newspaper. He had a tiny amber stain on his collar and his sandy blond hair was brushed across his forehead. He kept turning to peer at the small clock on the shelf behind him every few minutes.

'I heard about what happened with Lena,' Desmond said after a moment.

Kirra choked on a sip of her drink. 'You knew Lena?'

'Yes. She was remarkably observant; within hours of

meeting me she'd worked out that I wasn't a true recruit, but she kept my secret very safe.'

'Yeah ... I believe that,' Kirra said, her voice catching softly.

'I know she looked after you, and was killed attempting to help you escape. Kirra, it's important for you to know that it wasn't your fault.'

Kirra swirled her straw around the inside of her glass. 'Yes, it was,' she said hollowly. 'Of course it was. If it wasn't for me she would be alive right now.'

'That's not really true. Lena's days were numbered right from the beginning. She knew too much. They would have killed her eventually. She knew it just as well as they did.'

'At least she might have had a chance,' Kirra murmured.

Desmond leaned forward to still Kirra's trembling hand, his fingers warm against her skin. 'Looking after you was one of the only things she had left,' he said, a measure of true sorrow in his eyes. 'Despite the circumstances, I think you made her happy.'

Kirra stared at an invisible mark on the table, her lip quivering fiercely.

'She made no difference,' she said quietly. 'She was just a servant. Her life wasn't important. Her life didn't change anything. No one except me will remember her, and now there's nothing left of her. No bearing on anything. She made no difference.'

Desmond released Kirra's hand. 'Believe that if you want,' he said. 'Deep down you know what's really true.'

Kirra continued to play with her straw.

'How old was she?' she asked suddenly.

'Twenty-nine.'

'Where was she from?'

'Croatia.'

'What was her last name?'

'Markic.'

'We should go,' Mai said as she strode back to the table. 'I have the details of the trans—' She stopped mid-sentence, staring, aghast, at the window facing onto the street. 'DESMOND!' she screamed.

Kirra barely caught a glimpse of the three men striding towards the bar, simultaneously removing handguns from beneath their jackets, before Mai seized her wrist, yanked her off her chair and flung her onto the floor. Kirra landed with a thud, temporarily stunned, and her soft drink smashed beside her.

Both Desmond and Mai pulled out guns: Mai's from her laptop case, Desmond's from his belt. Mai threw herself in front of Kirra as the three men barged through the door and raised their weapons. Three ear-splitting shots rang out.

One narrowly missed Desmond, sinking into the wall behind him. On the way, it struck the frame of an oil painting of two entwined lovers, sending wood splinters and canvas into the air like misshapen confetti. The second bullet struck a table and sent it toppling, and the third shattered a window.

The bartender plunged behind the counter with a loud bellow of terror. The woman in the cream and gold pashmina dived off her chair and scrambled under her table, her eyes wide and her mouth hanging open to reveal numerous black fillings.

The three men took cover behind the bar counter, resulting in another dismayed yell from the hiding bartender, who seemed to take it upon himself to aid in the battle and started throwing full bottles of wine in their direction.

Mai took her chance while the attackers were out of sight, grabbing Kirra's arm and hoisting her into a crouching position.

'We have to go!' she urged, readying them both for a dash to the door. Kirra gulped down a breath and stole a glance at the counter.

'Move, now!' Mai hissed.

She jumped to her feet and took off, dragging Kirra with her, dodging between upturned chairs as they went.

Another shot rang out; this time it reached its target. Mai gave a nauseating yelp and Kirra was horrified to see blood gushing from a gaping hole in her sleeve.

Mai stumbled to the ground next to one of the booths, out of the line of fire. She pulled Kirra down with her, then used her uninjured right arm to drag herself closer to the door.

Desmond was firing furiously and one of the men collapsed behind the counter, spattering it with blood. Mai transferred her gun to her right hand, her left dangling by her side, blood streaming freely between her fingers.

Suddenly, Desmond seized Kirra's wrist and hauled her to her feet. 'Run!' he barked, urging her towards the door.

They crossed the distance in what seemed like hours instead of seconds. Together they tore out into the night, the bar's front windows bursting into smithereens as bullets chased them. As they surged forward, Kirra looked over her shoulder to see Mai slumped and bleeding between the tables and stools. She was shooting furiously at the attackers' hiding place. Bottles of wine and spirits exploded along the bar and shelf behind it, as though Mai was trying her luck at some sort of carnival game, but Kirra couldn't see whether she'd hit her targets.

Out in the street, Kirra expected to hear the blare of incoming police sirens, yet apart from the sounds of shooting, which steadily faded as they ran, the night was eerily peaceful.

They reached the complex in minutes, Desmond ascending the stairs with great powerful strides and shoving through the door into the apartment. Kirra stumbled in behind him and groped for the kitchen bench for support.

'Shit,' Desmond snarled, scanning the room as though more assailants might pop out at any moment and start firing at them. 'Shit!'

Kirra stared at him. In light of what had just happened, 'shit' seemed like a monstrous understatement.

'You left her. You left Mai behind,' she whispered.

The room was dark, the only light coming from the streetlights outside, which meant Kirra could only just make out the uneasy expression on Desmond's face. He cursed under his breath once more and strode into another room. She watched him go, transfixed. It was as though he couldn't hear her. He returned with two backpacks, and zipped one up on the kitchen island. His hands were quite steady. Kirra could barely believe what she was seeing.

'Are you listening to me?' she bellowed, her voice high and unfamiliar. 'You just left her there! She got hit! Why ... *why* did you do that?'

'No questions,' Desmond mumbled, rummaging through the other bag.

Kirra stood frozen next to the kitchen bench, tears snaking down her cheeks. She didn't know Mai well, and certainly didn't feel close to her, but she couldn't fathom Desmond's apparent ease at leaving her behind in such danger. Didn't he realise she was as good as dead?

'Desmond!' Kirra persisted. She grabbed his hand. 'HOW could you do that? Mai could be dead! Desmond! You just *left* her!'

'Kirra!' he yelled, whipping around and grasping her arms. He gave her a slight shake. 'Stop!'

Stunned at his outburst, she fell silent, her hysteria ebbing slowly. Desmond shook his head as he released her.

'She'll be alright,' he said softly, returning to rummage through the backpack, checking the items inside.

'But ...' Kirra murmured weakly.

'I had to leave her,' he said. 'There was an opportunity to get you away and I had to take it. Those men were going to kill us both and take you away.'

'Did Latham send them?' Kirra asked after a moment.

'I don't know,' Desmond said. 'I think so, but I can't be sure. If they weren't under Latham's employ, it means he's done exactly what we feared. He's released your identity, your previous location, everything, hoping that some other Contractor will track you down for him.'

Kirra felt like she needed to sit down.

'They're coming after me?' she asked in a tiny whisper. 'All of them?'

'We have to get moving. They know our area,' Desmond answered softly, unable to tell her what she wanted to hear.

'But … Mai …'

Desmond handed her a backpack and slung the other one over his shoulder.

'She'll be alright. You'll see,' he said. Kirra wasn't convinced, and, judging by the look on his face, neither was he.

CHAPTER EIGHTEEN

THE M10

Desmond scanned the street several times before allowing Kirra out of the shadows of the complex and into the balmy night air.

'Walk slowly,' he instructed.

Kirra frowned. She'd have expected him to say the opposite. After giving the street another check she slowed her pace. Desmond, who looked around once he realised he was striding ahead, gave her a beleaguered look.

'Not *that* slowly,' he said. He took her elbow. 'That looks ridiculous. You *will* draw attention to yourself that way. Just be calm. Be natural. Look as though you've never done a thing wrong in your life and walk with me.'

Kirra fell into step at his elbow, feeling stupid. He rounded a corner, unlocked the dark green sedan parked there, and bundled Kirra into the passenger seat. He perused the street once more, seemed to decide the coast was clear, and climbed into the driver's seat.

Desmond drove back towards the bar and halted the car a block away from the police tape now strung up around the area. Kirra could hear people shouting orders, and the odd siren still rang out. Broken glass and bits of furniture lined the footpath outside the bar, where police were treading carefully, taking notes. A crowd of excited onlookers had formed, and she peered past them to see an ambulance with a covered body on a stretcher inside it. She shuddered. Mai was amongst all that, and Kirra had no idea whether she was living or dead. She could have been the body on the stretcher for all Kirra knew.

She looked at Desmond from the corner of her eye. His brow was lined, his eyes weary and worried. He seemed calmed by the presence of police though. After a moment they drove away, Desmond maintaining a tight grip on the steering wheel and Kirra took this as a sign not to ask where they were going. They entered what she guessed was the business district of Madrid, with skyscrapers and office buildings standing like sleeping giants amongst the stars. She glimpsed the occasional street sign at junctions but gave up trying to glean any information from them. Desmond didn't seem to pay attention to the signs at all. He seemed to know precisely where he was going.

He finally turned into a car park beneath a towering glass building. All the levels of the car park were vacant, except for the very last. Getting out, Kirra looked around at the hundreds of cars lined up in neat rows. Mystified, she followed Desmond into the elevator and watched, thoroughly confused, as he hit a small black button marked U4.

'U?' she asked. 'Underground?'

'What else would U stand for?'

Desmond didn't look at her as the doors closed, folding his arms as they descended even deeper into the ground.

The elevator eventually gave a sharp *ping* and the doors slid open with surprising speed. Kirra leaned forward, looking out into what seemed to be an ordinary reception area with rough brick walls and thick crimson carpet. Lamps with polished brass stands gave the room a welcoming glow, and two healthy potted kentia palms flanked the elevator.

Kirra followed Desmond towards a woman sitting behind a regal-looking desk. The woman was somewhere in her early thirties, attractive and gave the distinct impression of finetuned competency. Her shiny reddish-brown hair almost blended into the brick wall behind her. She glanced up from the spotless surface of her desk and laid the shiny fountain pen she'd been using perfectly parallel with her writing pad. Her computer cast a soft, rosy blush across her fair features as she watched them politely. On the wall behind her was a sign that read:

Lajos Gerencia SA
Lajos Management Ltd

'Good evening,' she said, her words rounded and rich. 'How may I assist you?'

Desmond narrowed his eyes suspiciously. 'How did you know we weren't Spanish?' he asked.

The receptionist blinked. Kirra could have sworn she saw a flicker of alarm cross her face, yet it was so fleeting she wondered if she'd imagined it.

'I'm sorry, sir?' the woman said, looking genuinely confused.

'Never mind,' Desmond said, with a slight shake of his head. 'I need to speak with Marron Davis.'

The receptionist's expression didn't change whatsoever this time.

'My apologies, sir, but there is no one named Marron Davis in this particular office,' she told him, her voice like an automated recording. 'I am truly sorry for the inconvenience.'

Desmond gave her a strange look before leaning over the desk.

'I know you have to say that,' he said. 'And I know there's no appointment registered, but there's been an emergency. Kindly give Marron a call and tell him Des needs a quick word.'

The receptionist's eyes widened a fraction. Kirra noticed it only because she'd been searching for another break in the woman's composure — anything to indicate that she was real and not some highly convincing robot. The woman's gaze flicked over Desmond and, despite her frozen face, Kirra could tell she was weighing up her options.

'Very well, sir,' she consented finally, lifting her phone gracefully, her perfectly manicured fingers poised delicately on the receiver. She dialled a number and waited, her lips pursed. 'Yes, please put Mr Davis on the line,' she requested, her eyes never leaving Desmond.

Kirra rocked on her feet slightly, looking around as they waited. To the left of the receptionist was a set of intricately carved double doors, a security pad on the wall next to them. To the woman's right hung a thickly framed abstract painting featuring the exact same crimson as the carpet. Kirra chewed her lip. Everything about this place seemed purposeful, as though someone had gone to great lengths to create a welcoming but somehow always slightly distant atmosphere.

'Mr Davis?' The receptionist's voice startled Kirra. She'd been silent for some time. 'Yes, sir. I have a Mr ... er ... Des for you, sir.'

Mr Davis must have said something quite monumental, because the receptionist suddenly dropped her facade.

'Oh, really?' she said, a winsome smile playing at her lips. 'I'll tell him. See you later, Marron.'

Dropping the phone back on the hook, she looked up at Desmond. 'Desmond Rall?' she asked, her eyes ablaze with something very close to adulation. '*The* Desmond Rall? I thought this day would never come.'

Desmond seemed stunned for a moment.

'Are you Nicolette Portier?' he said.

'Oh, please,' she returned, sounding delighted. 'It's Lettie. Sorry about all that. After all the times we've spoken on the phone I should have recognised your voice. Just wait 'til I tell the girls downstairs that Desmond Rall himself came to the MIO!'

Kirra raised an eyebrow, and gave Desmond a quick sideways glance. He looked quite uncomfortable.

'We've had a bit of a problem, Lettie,' he said, guiding her gently back to the serious task at hand. 'We really do need to see Marron.'

'But of course,' she trilled happily, rising from her chair and sauntering over to the double doors. She typed the security PIN into the pad. Kirra couldn't help wondering if it was a Spencer System.

'I'll take you down myself,' Lettie said, pulling open one of the heavy doors and ushering them through. She closed it carefully behind them and took them down a short corridor, past another set of doors and around a corner.

To Kirra's astonishment they emerged onto a balcony overlooking a buzzing open-plan office the size of a stadium. It was totally devoid of windows, which made perfect sense as they were several floors below ground. The walls were the same red brick as the reception area, the light was as warm and inviting, the carpet was the same plush crimson. Hanging from the walls were enormous screens displaying satellite images of Madrid, street maps and what looked like surveillance feeds of the inside of buildings. Smaller screens showed what looked like photos of crime and accident scenes. Kirra could have sworn she spotted the shattered windows of the Ruiz bar on one of the screens before it flicked away to show a platform at a train station.

There were people — so many people — scurrying about the office, having hurried conversations, delivering files and forms to each other. She was reminded of an ants' nest she'd once found by Oscar's kennel in their backyard: hundreds of the little insects scurrying around, bumping into each other, changing directions, carrying tiny parcels as they went. Gazing down at the office activity, Kirra swallowed a hard, anxious lump in her throat. She didn't feel well all of a sudden. Half a year cooped up with only one other person for company had had more of an effect on her than she'd realised. The crowd below felt intensely threatening.

Lettie set off down a flight of stairs into the bullpen, Kirra all the while resisting the urge to ask Desmond if she couldn't just wait quietly in the reception area.

As they weaved their way through the masses, Kirra caught snippets of conversations. An old woman was scurrying alongside a man with greying hair, both of them clutching stacks of stapled files.

'... they're expecting me to drop what I've been doing for decades and work with an entirely new system!' the old woman complained. 'Well, I told them where to go. Long live hard-copy filing!'

'Ramona, we've been using computerised files for the last ten years,' the man said gently, 'and we're still having problems with the amount of paper coming in and out of this office. If you would just switch over, then we could empty the files out of the office next to yours and give it to someone who really needs it. We're all working towards a paper-free office. You know, it's about being environmentally minded —'

'Tell it to someone who cares,' Ramona grumbled. 'I'll transfer to the PIO if it comes to that. They're still doing things the good old-fashioned way!'

'That's because the PIO is intent on destroying the planet!' the man retorted.

Lettie steered them to the left and Kirra was pulled away from the conversation. She tuned in to a pair of young men who were exchanging stacks of folders.

'This one's everything we have on the RedCons in Madrid,' one said, his Spanish accent delicate and pleasant to listen to. 'And these are on the Winthrop Agency and their movements in the last six months.'

'Why so many?' asked the other man, taking the numerous folders and piling them in his arms.

'The Winthrop lot have been on the move since February,' the first man said. 'From what I can gather they're looking for something.'

Kirra realised Lettie and Desmond were striding ahead and she hurried to keep up. Lettie finally came to a stop at a private office.

'Here he is,' she said with a smile. 'I'll see you when you're finished.'

She rapped on the door, spun around and walked away, negotiating a path through the organised chaos with apparent ease. Kirra watched her stop to whisper something to two women loitering by a square cubicle. All three of them looked over at Desmond and giggled. Lettie sashayed on with a very purposeful swing to her hips, but Desmond took little notice. He raised his hand to rap on the door once more. Almost instantly, it was yanked open.

'Desmond! What the hell happened?'

Marron Davis was older than Desmond, although he looked just as unkempt and tired. His skin was such a deep shade of brown Kirra could barely distinguish the several days worth of stubble that coated his jawline. His hair was cropped close to his scalp, his face streaked with worry lines, and his grey suit was crumpled.

His eyes, huge and dark, flickered over Kirra briefly as he ushered them into his highly disorganised office. Desmond took a seat and Kirra followed suit, watching as

Marron sank into a plush, high-backed chair on the other side of the desk, his hand shooting out to stabilise a pile of files that wobbled precariously on the bookshelf beside him.

When Desmond failed to launch into an immediate explanation Marron gave him an impatient look. 'Well?' he prodded. 'What is it?'

Kirra felt her jaw drop. This man, this Marron Davis, was Australian! She heard it in his voice. She immediately wished Desmond wasn't there so she could ask him her own set of questions. Perhaps Marron knew about her situation? Perhaps he could help her? Perhaps he had a special phone number to call, and within hours Kirra would be surrounded by Australian officials who knew how to deal with people like Latham.

'Are you Australian?' she blurted out.

Marron looked at her and frowned, his face wrinkling like a prune.

'Why?' he asked, his hands frozen upon the armrests of his chair.

'You are, aren't you?' Kirra said.

Marron glanced from Kirra to Desmond and back again. 'In a manner of speaking ...' he said slowly.

'Do you know anything about Kirra Hayward?' she asked.

Marron's frown deepened. 'Kirra Hayward? Why?'

Desmond gave a small whimper of distress. Marron noticed it.

'Why?' he repeated, this time addressing Desmond.

'You're not going to like this, Marron,' Desmond mumbled.

'What?' Marron said, his voice rising, his dark eyes darting suspiciously between them. 'What are you talking about?'

Desmond sighed. 'This *is* Kirra Hayward.'

'Jesus Christ!' Marron breathed, his face terrified. 'Get her out of here. Now!'

CHAPTER NINETEEN

EYES AND EARS EVERYWHERE

Marron shot to his feet and crossed to the door. He threw it open.

'You need to leave immediately, Desmond!' he said, his expression very serious.

Desmond made no effort to move.

'Marron, settle down,' he said weakly. 'It's alright, really.'

Marron's eyes looked as though they were about to pop out of his head. 'No,' he said. '"Alright" is the opposite of what this is. You brought Kirra Hayward, *Kirra Hayward*, into my office. That — is — NOT — alright!'

'No one followed us. I made sure.'

'Desmond! You have no idea how *serious* this is. They could be coming right now. All of them!'

Kirra sat still, listening closely to the exchange. Who could be coming?

'Just close the door, Marron,' Desmond insisted quietly. 'I promise we won't be staying long.'

Marron gave Kirra an anxious glance, then heaved a great, defeated sigh. He slowly shut the door, and resumed his seat, eyeing Kirra as though she might contaminate him with a fatal disease.

'We'd better tell the Cautlifs you have her,' he said, moving to pick up the phone.

'NO!'

Desmond's hand shot out to stop Marron's wrist in what looked like an extremely painful grip. The two men stared at each other for a long moment.

'Are you serious, Desmond?' Marron whispered, his eyes wide once more. 'You want me to keep *this* from *them*?'

Desmond let go of Marron and gave a curt nod, his expression suddenly bitter.

'Look, I don't give a crap about the issues you have with them,' Marron said. 'We have to tell them about Kirra Hayward — we have to!'

'Tell them what exactly?' Desmond asked.

'Well ...' Marron shrugged. 'That she's been found. That we know where she is.'

'No, I don't think so,' Desmond said. 'They'll take her away.'

'Probably,' Marron conceded. He didn't seem too bothered by the idea. In fact, it seemed like the very solution to all his problems. He reached again for the phone. 'I'll tell them that we'll hold her here 'til they arrive.'

Desmond's hand shot out again and this time Marron grunted in pain.

'They're not having her!' Desmond snarled. 'You're not telling them anything.'

Marron winced, looking panic-stricken.

'Deceive the Cautlifs?' he said. 'Go the same way as Sam Haffey and Pearl Whittaker? I don't think so!'

Desmond said nothing to that.

'I'm not willing to risk my job over this,' Marron added.

'You'll have to be,' Desmond threatened. 'Or keeping this job will be the least of your problems.'

Marron glared at him. He seemed to understand Desmond's meaning though because he gave a long, low sigh and slumped back in his chair. Kirra, who was tremendously confused, kept glancing between the two men.

'Des ...' Marron began, hunching slightly as though the situation was a literal weight on his bowed shoulders, 'why are you with Kirra Hayward at all? How is it you're not dead yet?'

'Believe me, I'm as shocked as you are,' Desmond said, all traces of hostility gone from his voice. 'We had a problem about an hour ago and I need some information.'

Marron eyed him closely, looking interested despite himself.

'We were ambushed by three Contractors. I don't think they work for Latham, though I can't be sure. I managed to get Kirra away ... but we lost Mai Luong.'

'She's dead?' Marron asked.

Desmond gave an unsteady shrug. 'I don't know,' he admitted. 'Honestly, I don't. That's why I'm here.'

'Wait,' said Marron, his eyebrows knitting together. 'Tell me this wasn't the ridiculous incident we just picked up at that bar? What's its name? Ruiz?'

Desmond looked sheepish.

'You went to a bar with Kirra Hayward?' Marron said. 'Do you have a death wish? What were you thinking?'

'Not an awful lot, evidently,' Desmond replied lightly. 'We needed to meet a contact and we couldn't leave her unsupervised. We thought it would be fine because we didn't think anyone knew where she was. We were wrong, clearly. Anyway, can you give me anything at all on Mai?'

Marron scratched his cheek absently for a moment.

'Alright,' he said, picking up his phone and dialling an extension. 'Who's on the Ruiz thing?' he barked into the receiver. He listened for a moment, observing the buzzing office through the glass panel in his door, then slapped the phone back on the hook without so much as a parting comment.

'I'll send you to Viera Favero,' he told Desmond. 'She's collecting on this one.'

Desmond rose and headed for the door. He opened it and indicated for Kirra to follow. Standing up, she glanced back at Marron.

'So ... you don't have any information about me at all?' she said, seizing what seemed like her final chance to ask.

Marron looked as though he'd rather Kirra didn't address him directly, but after a moment he gave her a compassionate sort of grimace.

'Information is what we do here,' he told her, neatening the contents of a folder on his desk and dropping it onto a stack by his feet. 'We know more about you than you probably do: right now you're the subject of a file the approximate size of a phone book. But let me promise you this: absolutely none of it will make you feel any better.'

Kirra gritted her teeth, not even bothering to mask her disappointment. 'I just thought … because you're Australian, you might …'

'Australian?' He laughed. 'Hardly. I haven't lived there for nearly twenty years,' he said, quashing whatever hope she'd had of him feeling some kind of patriotic bond. 'And just because someone shares your accent doesn't, by any stretch of the imagination, mean they're your friend.'

He turned to address Desmond. 'You have a lot of work to do on her, Des.'

Desmond gave him a rueful smile. 'Not a word to the Cautlifs,' he warned. 'Remember?'

Marron swallowed nervously, but nodded all the same. Desmond tugged Kirra back out into the frenzied bullpen.

'Well, what about Milo Franklyn then?' she called back to Marron. 'Do you have anything on him?'

Marron considered her for several moments. 'Milo Franklyn,' he said. 'The name rings a bell …'

Kirra was going to tell him why, but Desmond dragged her away before she got a chance.

'I thought you wanted Milo to be kept a secret,' he hissed, shutting the door to Marron's office.

'I do!' she said furiously.

'So keep your mouth shut! This office is not loyal to you. Telling them something valuable like that is as dangerous as telling an enemy. Besides, we're in a hurry here,' he said, shoving through a cluster of bespectacled men, all of whom looked put out by his fierce lack of decorum. 'This really isn't the time for nostalgia or reading up on your friend.'

Kirra glared at him. 'But —'

'No questions.'

With the conversation apparently closed, he led her in a zigzag through the office, coming to a stop at an atrociously untidy cubicle.

'Viera?' Desmond called.

Towers of multicoloured files and folders seemed to be growing up between the dividing walls, as though the cubicle was an out-of-control greenhouse. Any bit of partition that wasn't buried behind a mountain of documents was plastered with lists and bits of paper with phone numbers scrawled on them. Atop a steel filing cabinet sat a tiny screen that flashed glimpses of different news programs from all over the world. In the few seconds Kirra studied it she saw at least eight different news reporters and heard just as many different languages. Six telephones, each a different colour, hung from hooks in a row, their little holding lights flashing silently.

As Kirra gazed at the mess, a mass of blonde curls erupted from behind one of the piles and scared her half to death. With hair like that, she'd almost expected to see Olivia.

'Is that you, Des?' a shrill voice asked.

A small, stout woman in a salmon-coloured suit strode out of the cubicle, her golden ringlets bouncing around her shoulders as if they were independently alive.

'You haven't visited for some time,' she added stiffly, glaring at Desmond through tiny round glasses. 'Please remind Flo when you see her that she still has my file on Brigitte Wipplinger. I want it returned for my archives.'

'Ah yes ... well ... she's most likely lost it somewhere in her room, Viera,' Desmond said. 'But I'll tell her anyway,' he promised hastily, catching the incensed look on her face.

Viera Favero gave a defeated sigh. 'I suppose you're right, but that's the last time she borrows from this office. Now, you want some stuff on the bar thing, yes?'

She rubbed her forehead, and eyed Kirra with interest.

'And who's this?' she said.

Desmond cleared his throat.

'Kirra,' he said, purposely not mentioning her last name, something Kirra was tremendously grateful for. 'This is Kirra.'

Viera stuck out her hand. '*Buenas noches*,' she said. '*¿Cómo está?*'

'English, Viera,' Desmond told her. 'She speaks English.'

'Oh, thank god! I've had it with Spanish today! We've picked up a flurry of activity ... I swear, something is going on in Madrid and I've got too many things happening to be worrying about tripping over a foreign language.'

'It's not technically foreign,' Desmond corrected her, looking as though he was enjoying himself. 'We're in Spain.'

Viera inspected him, her hazel eyes sharp. 'Do you want information or not?' she said venomously.

Desmond gave her an apologetic smile. 'Mai Luong was involved in the bar incident. I need whatever you have on her.'

Viera opened one of the topmost files on her desk and searched through it, her lips moving silently. Kirra looked around the cubicle, saw an open file nearby and began reading the pages as covertly as possible. Someone called H A McCoy was apparently a figure of interest, his name circled in thick black marker, a large question mark hovering beside it. There was another folder labelled 'Rae and Wesley Arlo', complete with security footage stills and a family tree. Heather Hertzog's name appeared several times in one file, each mention of her linked to the next with a thin red line; she seemed to be a missing Contractor of some sort.

'Mai Luong …' Viera murmured, dropping the file and taking up another. 'Mai Luong … Mai — oh! Here we are.'

Kirra heard Desmond take a small, sharp breath as Viera scanned the page, her tiny eyes zipping back and forth. She kept them in suspense for far too long before …

'Alright! Mai Luong was taken in an ambulance to the San Ignatius Hospital just after ten thirty. She was alive at the scene, but apparently sustained significant blood loss, enough for her to be pronounced critical. I haven't received further information on her status as yet. Perhaps in the next half an hour — does that suit you?'

Desmond ignored the question. 'So … she was alive?' he clarified.

Viera gave him a surprised look. 'Well, yes,' she said, nodding so that her curls practically ricocheted off her head. 'Do you require her for something?'

'Just about everything right now,' Desmond told her, eyeing the path back to reception and barely containing a grin.

'Desmond,' Viera said in a warning tone, 'San Ignatius is *not* an Industry-friendly hospital. She'll be under guard. They think she's a suspect.'

'I'll bet they do,' he agreed, taking another backward step.

'You can't just go in and snatch her from her sick bed!' she exclaimed, looking at him as though he was likely to do just that.

'No, no, I won't,' he said unconvincingly. 'I just needed to know if she was alive, otherwise Fadil will kill me.'

'Oh yes,' Viera said thoughtfully. 'He could become a problem.' She glanced back down at the file for a moment, tapping her tongue against her teeth.

'Any idea who attacked you?'

'Not really,' Desmond replied.

'Well,' she said, 'it might interest you to know that a break and enter occurred in the same area fifteen minutes before the gunfire at Ruiz.'

Desmond stopped inching backward. 'Really?'

'Really,' said Viera, perusing her file again. 'If you ask me, it's got "Decoy" written all over it. The perpetrator was gone before the police arrived; left a few personalised threats written on the kitchen table and took all the utensils, a pair of roller skates and most of the computer cables. Random enough to have kept the cops busy.'

Desmond didn't seem worried by this news, merely interested.

'Any idea of the Decoy's name?'

'None at all, but if you want to find him I'd start with Gaspara Pueyo, if I were you.'

'Gaspara Pueyo?'

'She keeps track of all the Madrilenian Decoys. Here ...' Viera scribbled an address on a small card and flicked it at him. 'It might be nothing, but it's well worth a look if you're interested.'

Viera's phone rang. She scooped it up with a terse '¿Sí?' and listened intently for a moment before her expression melted into one of unrestrained horror. She dropped the phone back onto its hook, hardly noticing when she missed and it bounced onto the floor, lost between the columns of files.

'That was Marron,' she told Desmond in a whisper, her face deathly white. 'He says your time is up. You've had K-Kirra Hayward here for ten minutes and he said that's ten minutes too many.'

Desmond gave a groan as Viera edged away from Kirra, nearly toppling over a box of papers beside her desk.

'We'd better go,' he muttered. 'Thanks again, Viera.'

He and Kirra made their way back through the surging workers, climbed the stairs and retreated to the reception area. Lettie glanced up at them. She had been ticking names off a list.

'Got everything you need?'

'Just about,' Desmond told her. 'I'll be talking to you shortly, I imagine.'

'I'm counting on it,' she said.

Desmond crossed to the elevator and pressed the button. As the doors flew open and Kirra stepped inside, Lettie called Desmond's name. She spun her computer monitor around so they could see a live video feed of the inside of the elevator.

'That's how I knew,' she said gleefully.

'Knew what?' Desmond asked.

She tilted her head gracefully, her full lips transforming into a dazzling smile. 'That you weren't Spanish,' she said, spinning the monitor back around. 'We have eyes and ears everywhere.'

Desmond gave an appreciative half-smile. 'That you do,' he said as he stepped into the elevator beside Kirra.

'Desmond ...' Kirra began once they were back in the car and driving away from the underground office. Desmond glanced at her and seemed to know what she was going to ask before she did herself.

'Don't worry about it too much,' he told her. 'Those people spend far too much time sifting through the world's demons. They're scared of everything.'

Kirra suspected Desmond was just saying that to make her feel better. It had been an incredibly unsettling experience to have people recoil from her with varying degrees of distress on their faces.

'It's only because you're valuable,' he continued. 'They're worried you'll bring a string of enemies to their door, and not without cause. By the way, you can no longer use the name Kirra Hayward. It's far too dangerous to just throw around. If you have to, use the name Katherine Hammond.'

Kirra stared at him.

'Remember it,' he said. 'You'll need it for later.'

'Katherine Hammond,' Kirra echoed, unsure as to what 'later' meant. Did it mean later tonight or years from now?

'What was that place, anyway?' she asked.

Desmond checked the name of a street before turning into it. 'An intelligence office,' he told her absently. It began raining outside, the soft rumble of thunder reaching Kirra's ears.

'Is it a government thing?'

Desmond looked at her, his face horrified.

'What *is* it with you and the government?' he asked. 'The government doesn't have to be involved in everything! In fact, it might shock you to know how little the government *is* actually involved in.'

Kirra frowned. 'But then —'

'You know, I really don't think you have an appropriate appreciation of the scope of the Industry. It's organised. It's old. It has regulations, rules, traditions and resources. We need no one but ourselves.'

'So that place —'

'Was the MIO — one of *our* intelligence offices,' he said, his eyes flitting between the silent GPS sitting on the dashboard and the rainy road ahead. 'They sift through police radio transmissions, media broadcasts, even the odd newspaper, to collect as much information as they can on any event or topic of interest that might be of use to the Industry. They also liaise with intelligence agents stationed around the city. They'll tell you everything you need to know about anything — for a price, of course. Extremely useful.'

'Is it legal?'

'How is it any different from a really informative news program?' he asked.

Kirra shrugged. 'Because they deal with Contractors?' she guessed.

'Exactly,' he said, giving her a pleased look. 'They don't question their clients or the information they're seeking. They just hand it over quietly and they never take sides. It's not up to them to determine who's right and who's wrong. Their only business is the sale of information. They're very covert agencies. You can't really stumble across them; you have to be told where they are.'

'Who told you?' she asked.

Desmond focused on the road ahead for a moment.

'A member of the Cautlif family,' he said, his voice oddly discontented. 'But that's generally how all of us find out.'

Cautlif? Marron and Desmond had had a short, tense conversation regarding these Cautlifs and whether or not they should be called to take Kirra away.

'Who are they?'

'People,' he said unhelpfully. 'Bad ones. Remember that always, Kirra. Very bad people.'

Sensing that Desmond had little else to say on the matter, Kirra fell silent. She glanced up at the high-rise buildings, then at the faint lights of a jet flickering through the heavy clouds, a great flying ghost over the city. A thought suddenly occurred to her.

'How come Latham can fly around in his jet undetected?' she asked. 'How come he hasn't shown up on ... on some sort of radar or ... or something?'

'He does show up,' Desmond said. 'Only he operates beneath a cover occupation.'

'A what?'

'He has the credentials to prove that he's a remarkably successful executive consultant. He flies around the world visiting his "clients".'

'An executive consultant? What does that even mean?'

'Well, absolutely nothing, but that's not the point. The point is that it sounds legitimate. It's the same with my Extraction business. For external purposes, we're an IT company specialising in firewall software and installation.' Desmond smiled. 'And I happen to have it on good authority that the Estate, for official purposes, is a private college for gifted classical music students.'

Kirra looked at him sharply. 'Should I know what the Estate is?'

'No,' he said. 'In fact, I'd be worried if you did. Secrecy is their speciality.'

CHAPTER TWENTY

LA INDUSTRIA

The address Viera had supplied to Desmond brought them to a leafy part of Madrid, where the roads were wide and the houses grand. Desmond stopped the car outside perhaps the oldest house they'd passed, and drew Kirra towards a high rose-coloured concrete wall. He stabbed the doorbell next to an iron gate and waited. An age seemed to pass before a gravelly voice rang out.

'¿*Sí*?'

Desmond pressed the intercom button and stated his business (whatever it was) in Spanish. At first he seemed to be met with resistance, but then they were unexpectedly buzzed into the front garden. A marble path lined with potted cherry-red cyclamens brought them to the front door, which was already standing ajar, light spilling out into the darkness.

'Good evening,' uttered a throaty, weathered voice. 'Please, come in.'

A small, round woman stood at the foot of a narrow staircase, her hair swept up in a bun, her face festooned with wrinkles, her speckled hands clutching a knobbly wooden walking frame. She looked a bit like an overgrown, ageing owl, though the effect was not altogether unpleasant. She hobbled over to Desmond, the walking frame creaking as she moved, and gazed into his face.

After glancing at the three thickset men positioned menacingly around the hallway, Desmond adopted a stance of polite inquisition. 'Gaspara Pueyo?' he asked.

'*Sí*,' the woman replied. 'They tell me you are Desmond Rall, no?'

He nodded.

Gaspara barely even looked at Kirra. It seemed she had eyes for no one but Desmond. 'You prefer to converse in English?' she asked.

Desmond shot a glance at Kirra. 'Please.'

Gaspara nodded graciously and ushered them into a sitting room furnished with couches and bookshelves that looked as old as she was. The smell of dust and ash tingled in Kirra's nostrils. Gaspara, it seemed, was a fan of macabre interior design: Gothic candlesticks lined the mantelpiece, black velvet curtains framed the front window, and a thick layer of dust covered most surfaces. Once they were seated the old woman offered them drinks, all the while looking intently into Desmond's scarred face.

'Ah … no,' Desmond said at the proposal of beverages. 'No, thank you. We're alright. We're here on an urgent matter regarding a Decoy.'

Gaspara blinked and said nothing. 'Ah ... around quarter past ten,' Desmond continued, 'there was a break and enter near the Ruiz bar and —'

'*Sí,* I know,' she said serenely.

'Yes ... we need to speak with that Decoy. It's important. I'm willing to pay for the privilege.'

Gaspara's gaze finally flicked over Kirra and hovered there for a moment.

'This can be arranged,' she said slowly. 'Though no payment shall be accepted.'

'No ...?'

'No. I will not accept payment from you, Desmond Rall. It shall be my pleasure. Please, wait here. We shall return before long.'

With that she heaved herself off the couch, muttered with her three men, and set off with two of them, the other left to make his intimidating presence quite conspicuous in the hallway. The sound of car doors closing and a powerful engine starting filled the sitting room, and then Gaspara was gone.

Kirra didn't know which question to ask first, but after a warning look from Desmond she kept her mouth shut. They sat together in tense silence for almost ten minutes before the front door slammed open with an almighty crash and a tirade of croaky screams reached their ears.

'¡SUÉLTENME! ¡MAL NACIDOS! ¡SUÉLTENME! ARRRGGHHH!'

Suddenly, what appeared to be a long bag of potatoes was thrown into the sitting room, landing with a thud at Kirra's feet. Desmond had Kirra up off the couch and into the corner before she realised that the bag was actually a teenage boy dressed in the dirtiest clothes she'd ever seen. He scrambled to his feet, his skinny, lengthy limbs more of a hindrance than a help, and threw himself at the door with unashamed desperation. Two of Gaspara Pueyo's men caught him and hurled him back into the room. Gaspara stayed comfortably out of reach behind them, resting on her walking frame and watching the scene between their elbows.

'*¡No he hecho nada!*' the boy yelled. '*¡Déjenme!*'

'*¡En inglés!*' Gaspara snarled.

The boy glared at her, practically frothing at the mouth. His face, like the rest of him, was long and pale, and his short hair was pitch black.

'*¿Inglés?* Yes! Why you take me? Why? Let me go! I did nothing! LET ME GO!'

'*¡Sí, sí!* We'll let you go, but first you must answer some questions.'

But the boy took no notice. Instead, he spotted the window, bolted towards it and hurled himself straight through the glass pane and into the front garden.

Kirra clapped a hand over her mouth, stunned, as glass burst everywhere. Desmond stood stock-still, staring into the front garden as though he couldn't believe what had just happened. Gaspara Pueyo merely rolled her eyes, as though teenagers regularly threw themselves through solid window panes in her presence.

Some rustling, some cursing in Spanish, a thud, a moan of pain and the crunching of glass floated in through the window. There was also what sounded like one of the cyclamen pots shattering before another of Gaspara's men brought the teenager back through the sitting room door. He deposited the boy by the couch and placed himself in front of the now obliterated window to act as a human barrier.

The boy stumbled into the centre of the room, his eyes darting around. He seemed surprisingly uninjured from his hazardous escape attempt. His arms were scratched and small shards of glass glittered in his hair, but that was all.

'You are the *Señuelo* named Tavio?' Gaspara asked.

The boy cast around, panting, searching for another way out. He sized up the two men at the door and seemed to decide against trying his luck with them; a wise move, Kirra thought, as they were both six or seven times his weight. Instead, he lunged at the man at the window. His arms clawed at the velvet curtains before he was thrown effortlessly back onto the couch, which upturned with his weight and slammed with a heavy clunk against the floorboards.

'Tavio!' Gaspara bellowed.

'¡*Sí!*' he yelled wildly, fighting with his gangly limbs to stand. 'I am Tavio, *si*! Now let me out! I am good! I am good! *No Señuelo*!'

'We know you are a Decoy. We *know* this!'

But Tavio didn't seem to be listening. Instead he busied himself with the task of running at the men at the door, apparently throwing caution to the wind and trying his luck with them anyway, massive though they were. One grabbed his arms, the other his legs, and both drew him back towards the couch. Tavio flailed about madly in their grip, snarling and spitting insults. Finally, he was set upright and, after receiving a terrorising look from the men, he quietened down. Desmond approached him cautiously.

'Tavio, you are in no trouble, I promise. I have come looking only for the one who hired you tonight.'

'I am no rat!' Tavio spat out. 'I shall not betray!'

He then walloped Desmond around the face with his fist. Desmond staggered slightly, seemingly more from surprise than anything else, and brought his thumb to his chin, dabbing at it gingerly. Tavio shot well away from him and latched onto a tall bookcase, upturning it between them as a protective barricade, sending books tumbling across the room. The two men at the door rushed furiously at Tavio.

'No!' Desmond held up his hand. 'No, it's alright.'

Tavio was eyeing Desmond worriedly, kicking books away from his ankles. 'I shall not betray!' he declared, sweat gathering on his forehead. 'I shall NOT!'

Desmond blinked. 'I didn't think Decoys harboured any particular loyalty to their employers,' he said in Gaspara's direction.

'They don't,' she confirmed from behind her blockade of men. 'He's merely stalling. He suspects he's going to prison tonight.'

At this Tavio buried his hands in his grubby hair. He hopped on the spot for a moment, looking terrified. 'No prison! I won't go, I won't!'

'No one is going to prison this evening,' Desmond said firmly. 'I am a Contractor. I am on your side.'

Tavio's head snapped up. '¿La Industria?' he whispered.

Desmond nodded. 'Yes. The Industry.'

Tavio's shoulders relaxed slightly. 'And the girl?'

He stared at Kirra, who stared back, transfixed.

'No,' Desmond said. 'She does not belong in the Industry.'

'Then she is not to be trusted!' screamed Tavio.

'She is a *ciudadana*,' Desmond insisted. 'A citizen who is no threat.'

Tavio glared at Kirra, his top lip curling. '¿*Ciudadana*? So, why are you here then, girl? Why? Wanting to make the switch? Want to join *this*?'

He jabbed his thumb at his filthy coat. Kirra could only stare at him, confused.

'Do you like what you have been shown?' he continued venomously. 'Do you still want to switch *now*?'

He seemed enraged by Kirra, as though her presence amongst so many Industry professionals was somehow highly inappropriate and offensive; and as he crept ever closer, Kirra couldn't help but back away, despite Desmond's reassuring presence between them.

'*La Industria* does not seem so pretty now, does it, girl? *Does it*? But you can still run home, where it's safe. Always safe. We are stuck here, stuck here always.'

His unwashed face was sneering at her, his crooked teeth bared. Kirra swallowed nervously, horrified to be so singled out.

'You think you can look at me this way?' he hissed, his black eyes gleaming crazily. 'You think you can look down at me?'

He seemed to be speaking mostly to himself now, muttering quietly in the centre of the room, his grimy fingers tangled in his even grimier hair.

'She is not looking at you,' Desmond said diplomatically. 'Down, up or otherwise. She is a friend of the Industry.'

Tavio did not seem convinced, though he thankfully ceased his demented muttering.

'I will pay you for any information you have regarding your most recent employer, the one who commissioned you to break into that house tonight,' Desmond said.

Tavio visibly perked up at the sound of payment.

'*Sí*,' he said brightly. 'I will tell you all.'

Kirra thought she heard a small noise of disapproval from between the two men at the door.

'What was your employer's name?' Desmond asked.

Tavio giggled. 'Name? No, no. There is never a name.'

Desmond let out a huff. 'Was it the Assassin known as Latham?'

Tavio chewed his tongue for a moment. 'All I know,' he said, 'is that this man was a *bebé*. Very young.'

'How young?'

'How am I to know?' Tavio shrugged. 'I do not know him, so how can I be sure? He is just young. He is anxious, also ... and beaten badly. He says, "Make disturbance here," and he points to a map. He is angry, very angry. Then he calls someone and says to them, "She is at a bar named Ruiz. Bring her to me alive," and then hangs up. He gives me my money and goes away. That is all.'

Desmond stared at Tavio for a long moment before handing him a thick slab of Euros. Tavio hugged them to his chest.

'Thank you, Tavio,' Desmond said.

'*Sí*, my pleasure,' Tavio said earnestly. He peered hopefully at Gaspara.

'You may go,' she rasped.

With a last lingering sneer at Kirra, Tavio scooted past the man, stepped carefully out through the smashed window and stalked off into the night, tucking his payment deep into his pockets.

The two men at the door broke away, and Gaspara hobbled into the room, tossing books out of her way with her walking frame.

'*Señor* Rall,' she said, 'are you satisfied?'

'Yes, thanks,' said Desmond, looking a touch uncomfortable beneath her intense gaze. 'Very satisfied.'

'I am glad. You must know I am a supporter of your cause,' she said. 'And I wish you success in your endeavours. Please understand that you are always welcome here.'

Kirra knew she was again missing something crucial, but Desmond merely smiled.

'I appreciate it,' he returned.

'Well,' he said to Kirra, after they'd bade Gaspara farewell and climbed back into the car. 'That was a colossal waste of time. I thought we'd get a name at the very least.'

Kirra shrugged. At least they weren't any further from finding out who'd attacked them at the bar.

'Decoys,' she began curiously. 'You can hire them to make a scene prior to an ambush?'

'Prior to anything really. An Assassination, a Retrieval, an Extraction.'

'To distract the police?'

'Distract, or at least keep them busy before and during an assignment in the same area. It's only the police in the same area that you have to worry about, really. The ones who are likely to respond fastest to the sound of gunfire or to an emergency call.'

'It's that easy to distract them?'

'No.' Desmond grinned. 'Not always. Sometimes we're under surveillance, though we can shake off officials fairly easily in a few days. For much bigger jobs, we have other methods of distractions. Decoys, though, are a seriously undervalued minority within the Industry. They've given themselves a bad name over the years, but, you know ... they don't *really* deserve it.'

CHAPTER TWENTY-ONE

NO OPPORTUNITY WASTED

San Ignatius hospital was a vast, gleaming structure with its name stamped proudly across it in giant blue letters. It was four in the morning by the time Desmond halted the car in its visitor parking area and gazed up at it, as though trying to decipher from the outside which room Mai was in.

'Thought you told Viera we weren't going to break her out,' Kirra said after what felt like ten minutes of solid staring.

Desmond didn't even look at her as he released his seatbelt from its clasp.

'You lied though,' Kirra muttered unhappily, reluctantly releasing hers as well.

'Without Mai, without her information and her expertise,' Desmond said as they marched towards the entry, 'I can't ensure my Extraction of Aguilar. If we don't extract Aguilar, then we don't extract Milo. So you need Mai as much as I do.'

'I know,' said Kirra.

'Good. Now, it's the middle of the night, so this should be relatively easy. If anything goes wrong, though, get yourself to Vienna.'

Kirra stopped between a ticket machine and a purple four-wheel drive. 'Vienna?'

'Yeah. Take a train or a bus or something.'

He pressed fifty Euros into her hand and strolled into the foyer. He held a hushed conversation in Spanish with a tired-looking man behind the reception desk, then led Kirra down a hallway and into an elevator. Instead of going up, they went down a floor, to the basement.

'Quiet now,' Desmond said as they entered a darkened, low-ceilinged area. 'And stay here for a moment.'

He turned a corner, into an office of some sort, and Kirra lost sight of him. She stood very quietly next to a row of cabinets and a trolley holding packaged gauzes and disposable bedpans, until she heard a short yell of surprise and a heavy thud.

'Okay, Kirra,' came Desmond's voice.

She hurried into the office and gasped. A security guard was lying on his back, motionless, and Desmond was standing over him, gun in hand.

'I just knocked him out,' he said when he saw the shocked look on Kirra's face, plucking something from the guard's chest. 'He'll wake up soon and have no idea what happened.'

Kirra looked closely at the guard but could see no wound on him. Desmond turned to a control panel and fiddled with it until he brought up a security feed on a television on the desk. He flicked through several channels, waiting patiently as the feeds changed angles, until he found a man sitting by an elevator. Kirra wasn't close enough to get a good look, but this image apparently meant something to Desmond. He fiddled some more with the control panel; he seemed to be disabling some of the cameras.

'That should do it,' he said, and ushered her back into the elevator. They shot up several floors to where Kirra guessed the intensive care unit must be. Before the elevator doors had opened all the way, Desmond snaked his gun out into the corridor and shot someone, though there was no bang. Kirra gasped.

'Just put him to sleep again,' Desmond said, indicating a slumped policeman in a chair by the elevator doors. He again plucked something from the man's chest, something Kirra failed to get a look at before it disappeared into Desmond's pocket.

She decided not to badger him about it just now, and instead followed him down the corridor. Kirra hadn't spent much time in hospitals, but she'd always had the impression they were bustling and full of action right round the clock. Apparently she was wrong. The whole place seemed very much asleep, except for the occasional faint beep or buzz of a machine, a low light here, a far-off voice there.

Desmond, who was a little way ahead of her, fired the silent gun once more. Kirra rounded the corner to see another policeman crumpled on the floor by a door. Desmond hauled a chair over to him and Kirra helped heave the man into it.

'They'll be furious at each other for falling asleep on the job,' Desmond said happily, stuffing another something in his pocket and taking the man's keys. 'They never suspect. That's why it pays to do these things in the middle of the night. Fatigue is the number one cause of Extractions.' He laughed at his own joke.

Kirra looked at the officer. He seemed to be sleeping peacefully, along with all the patients in the ward. She could hear the faint tinkling of voices now and see the light of a nurses' station right down the end of the corridor, thankfully far enough away so that no one had spotted them.

Desmond tilted the policeman's head forward so his chin was resting sleepily on his chest, and opened the door. Kirra followed him inside.

There they found Mai, lying propped up in a bed of white sheets, hooked up with tubes to a dozen machines, and her arm bandaged up. Her other arm was handcuffed to the steel bed frame. Upon first glance she looked dead.

'Mai,' Desmond said softly, touching her hand. She stirred and peered at them through tired, unfocused eyes. She was as white as the sheets she was lying on.

'It's been hours,' she said groggily. 'Was there traffic?'

Desmond gave a tight smile as he used the policeman's keys to release her wrist from the handcuff.

'You're as high as a hot-air balloon,' he said, helping her to sit up. 'How much morphine have they got in you?'

'The correct amount,' she murmured, a very faint grin on her face.

Desmond rolled his eyes and began removing a drip attached to a pouch of blood from Mai's arm. Then he unhooked her from all the other machines, pressing buttons on them first to ensure no alarms went off. Kirra fidgeted by the door.

Mai tried to push herself up, but faltered halfway and dropped back onto the pillows.

'Is there an Industry-friendly hospital anywhere nearby?' she asked.

Both she and Desmond seemed to realise that she still required medical assistance. The bandage on her arm was bleeding through.

'No,' Desmond said, thinking hard. Then his face lit up. 'No ... but there's an Intensive not too far from here.'

'Even better,' she mumbled, putting her feet on the ground.

Desmond helped her out of the hospital gown and reached for her clothes, stored in a plastic zip-lock bag in a drawer by the bed. He seemed completely oblivious to the fact that she was only wearing underwear. After several moments of quiet negotiation with her limbs, he finally helped her to slide her injured arm into the sleeve of her jacket.

Mai wobbled dangerously when she got to her feet, but Desmond took her by the shoulders and guided her to the door. Kirra wanted to say something, but it seemed Mai had passed out. He gave her a worried look, and lifted her easily into his arms.

They rode the elevator back down to the basement, right past the sleeping security guard, and to a service exit that took them out into the fresh air. Desmond obviously thought they might draw attention if they were seen carrying an unconscious patient through the foyer.

Desmond placed Mai in the back seat of the car, where she lay deathly still, and drove them quietly away. Kirra turned to look back at the hospital, simultaneously horrified and impressed with what they'd just managed to pull off. It seemed the staff at San Ignatius had no idea what had just happened.

Twenty minutes later, Desmond turned into an almost deserted car park in one of the most derelict areas Kirra had ever been in. The streets were lined with litter and graffiti, and most of the buildings looked abandoned, with windows smashed in and decaying wooden doors. One building, however, looked strangely new. It reminded Kirra of the fancy new complex that had been built the previous year at Freemont Grammar, paid for with the bequest of a wealthy alumnus who had died of avian flu whilst wintering in Vietnam. She glanced at the GPS on the dashboard of the car. According to it, they were at the Cabrera International College. Unlike San Ignatius, nearly all the building's lights were on.

'An international college?' Kirra asked.

'Yeah,' said Desmond. 'You know … where expats send their kids.'

'That's not what it really is, though, is it?'

'Not even a little bit.'

Mai hadn't regained consciousness so Desmond carried her into the complex. There was a man standing straight as a board just inside the door, holding a gun, but Desmond said something to him and he let them through without question.

A young woman padded past them a way down the corridor, her hair wet and a toothbrush in hand.

'Excuse me,' said Desmond. 'Would you be able to point me in the direction of Mr Marquison?'

The woman stopped, a smile she seemed unable to control coming over her face. 'Upstairs,' she said, hardly batting an eyelid at the bandaged, bleeding deadweight that was Mai. 'He'd be in his bureau by now.'

'Thanks.'

Desmond hoisted Mai higher in his arms and ascended the stairs three at a time. The next level up was a bit livelier, with a few people hurrying around, most of them looking as though they'd only recently fallen out of bed. None of the girls wore a skerrick of make-up and all the boys had tousled hair, sticking up just the way Milo's did after he'd tossed and turned at night. The words 'The Marquison Training Intensive, Est. 1973' were stencilled upon a wall in red, and beneath them was the slogan 'No Opportunity Wasted'.

Desmond passed through a set of double doors and vanished into a large office, Kirra trotting to keep up. The office space was filled with many desks in rows, but Desmond ignored them all and made his way to an enclosed room at the end, his pace becoming more urgent.

Kirra knocked on the door for him.

'Coming, coming,' piped an ancient voice.

A little old man with a speckled bald head peered out at them. He blinked tiredly for a moment, his face white and fatigued.

'Oh, hell! Desmond?' he said. 'Is that you?' He put on his glasses and squinted at Mai. 'Oh, dear.'

He hit an intercom by the door, looking oddly delighted. 'Be so kind as to get a stretcher up here,' he said cheerfully. 'And get the infirmary up and running. Make sure Caroline's awake. She has herself a patient.'

In about thirty seconds a young man and a young woman rocketed into the office carrying a thin plastic stretcher. They helped Desmond lay Mai upon it then wasted no time in whisking her away. Mai's bandage was sodden with blood and she still looked quite dead.

'Always have state-of-the-art facilities at Intensives,' Mr Marquison commented proudly. 'Don't know why any of us bother with hospitals, even the Industry-friendly ones. You and I seem to be the only ones who still know that, right, Desmond?'

Desmond smiled, looking utterly relieved to have Mai taken care of.

'I'd love to speak with you, sir,' he said. 'If you're not busy.'

'Busy? I'm nothing but busy with this lot to run around after.' Mr Marquison jerked his wrinkly little head back towards the corridor. 'But you know I'll always spare a moment for you, Desmond. Would your friend care for something to eat?' He turned to Kirra. 'They're serving breakfast in the cafeteria if you're interested.'

Now that she thought of it, Kirra realised she was starving. She glanced hopefully at Desmond.

'You can if you want,' he said. 'This place is secure.'

Mr Marquison laughed. 'Secure? This place is a fortress,' he said. 'Off you go then.'

CHAPTER TWENTY-TWO

THE DEAD END
AND THE DECLINE

Kirra, happy for something to do, made her way out of the bureau. As she went she heard Mr Marquison say, 'Have you heard about Gervis Morris-Daley, Des? Just got promoted to Senior Associate with the Greenfield mob.'

'Aren't they Assassins?' Desmond asked.

'Yes, yes,' said Mr Marquison airily. He had clearly missed the hateful tone in Desmond's voice. 'Gervis studied here with you back in the day, didn't he? Or was he the year before?'

'The year after, actually,' Desmond said. 'Anyway, sir, I wondered if I could discuss something with you ...'

Kirra was out of earshot by this stage and not of a mind to linger and eavesdrop. She went in the direction Mr Marquison had indicated, and followed the sound of tinkling cutlery and the smell of rich coffee to a round room, smaller than she'd anticipated, jam-packed with chairs and tables. A counter ran across the front, full to bursting with trays of delicious-looking breakfast food, and people were roaming about, pouring juice and selecting cereals. The room was hushed and the lamps gave off a warm glow. Kirra supposed it was too early for bright lights and rigorous conversation, though a tall blond boy a little way off proved her wrong.

'I know something you don't,' he said happily to a dark-haired boy sitting at a table closest to the buffet. He slammed his tray down and took a seat opposite the boy. Kirra guessed they were both about seventeen.

'Bullshit,' said the dark-haired boy.

'I do!'

'Go on then.'

'Okay. I just heard ...' He paused for maximum effect. '... that there's a Spencer Translator.'

Kirra tensed by a tray of fresh chocolate croissants.

'No way,' whispered the dark-haired boy. 'Are you serious? Where?'

'They say she's here in Madrid.'

'She? The Spencer Translator's a *girl*?'

'Yep. It's a secret though, so don't tell anyone. No one knows where she is or even who's got her.'

'Course they don't, otherwise the Cautlifs would've jumped on her already.'

'Right. But how cool is that? A Spencer Translator.'

'That's crazy. I wonder how she does it ...'

'She'd have to be mad. To be able to do a thing like that you'd have to be crazy.'

'Yeah,' the other agreed. 'Tried these eggs?'

'Yeah, they're awesome.'

'Best I've had since Seoul.'

Kirra scooped a bit of French toast onto her plate and turned around to find a table. There wasn't a single empty one.

'Spot here, if you like,' called the dark-haired boy she'd been listening to.

'Yeah, plenty of room,' said his blond companion and pulled a chair out for her.

Kirra panicked for a moment. The room was filling fast and there wasn't a quiet spot anywhere. As long as she didn't say anything, as long as she didn't give herself away, Kirra supposed she could eat at their table. She took a deep breath and sat down, though in a seat several chairs away from the one the blond boy had indicated.

'New?' asked the dark-haired boy, immediately scooting closer and bringing his tray with him.

'Um …' Kirra had no idea what to say.

'First Intensive?' said the other, also moving closer. He spoke very quickly. 'You'll be right after you settle in. How good are the donuts? Have you given the berry muesli a go?'

'Not yet …'

'Which room are you in?'

'I'm not —'

'Where are you headed next?'

'Next?'

'Yeah, where's your next Intensive? Santiago or Tehran?'

'I d-don't … I'm not sure,' Kirra stammered, suddenly wishing she'd just stayed back in the bureau with Desmond.

'Only booked in for the one? Our bosses signed us up to as many as possible. Two weeks here, four weeks there,' said the blond. 'We've been on about five together this year. Name's Lev Langston.'

'Bronson Miller,' said the other boy.

'So, you don't stay here?' Kirra asked, snaking her way around telling them her own name.

They looked at each other, then at her.

'Nope, they hold them all over the place, so you get used to travelling and picking up languages and stuff,' said Bronson. 'You're not in training, are you?'

'No,' she said, deciding not to lie. 'I'm here because my ... my friend needs help. I'm not ... I'm just normal.'

They both looked mildly sympathetic.

'That's too bad,' said Bronson.

'But you'd have to be part of the Industry,' disputed Lev. 'They wouldn't let you in here otherwise.'

'My friend is,' Kirra said hurriedly. 'He knows Mr Marquison.'

'Oh. Fair enough then. You know, you should join.'

'I'm a bit young.'

Lev snorted. 'I was picked from a group home last year. Never too young.'

'Picked?' Kirra asked.

'Yeah, by my boss. He was looking for an apprentice to learn his business, join his team. Good thing too, otherwise who knows what might have happened to me. I might've had to become a Decoy.'

Bronson pulled a face. 'A Decoy ... how dismal,' he said.

'Decoys have just given themselves a bad name,' Kirra heard herself saying. 'They don't really deserve it.'

The two boys nodded, half-confused, half-impressed that she seemed to know what she was talking about. Kirra cast around for something else to say.

'So ... so your boss,' she asked Lev, chewing a bit of the French toast. It was delicious. 'What does he do?'

'Field Intelligence,' Lev answered proudly.

'To give to places like the MIO?' Kirra asked, fascinated despite herself.

They both frowned.

'Not part of the Industry, you say?'

'No.'

'You know a fair bit about it, don't you? Sure you're not?'

'Positive. Anyway, you said you were picked from a group home. How were you picked?'

'My boss and his wife just came and told me. Nicer people you wouldn't find. They treat me like their grandkid.'

'They just *told* you?'

'Well, they always ask you first. They sit you down in private, all formal, and give you a choice. But my time was running out at the home, and who's gonna say no anyway? I mean, really. And I reckon I really belong here.'

'I know I do,' said Bronson through a mouthful of crisp bacon. 'When Imogen came and —'

Lev gave a longing moan at the mention of her name.

'Oi! That's my boss you're fantasising about. Show some respect,' Bronson said, even though he too was grinning from ear to ear. 'Anyway, my boss Imogen came and asked me if I'd be interested in a career in Diverting. I said yes — not just because she's hot, but because I really wanted to — and she took me from my house that night.'

Kirra had no idea what Diverting was, but that wasn't what made her mouth fall open.

'Your house?'

'Yeah.'

'But what about your —'

'Oh, she told my folks some fib about me going to some youth leadership school — something weird for smart, eager kids,' he said casually. 'They believed her, even though I was an idiot at school, because she had all these pamphlets and it all looked really legit. 'S'not hard to fool them, though,' he said, his face suddenly grim. 'They hardly ever think too hard about anything but themselves. They'll realise something's up sooner or later, but Imogen will have some fib ready to feed them then too. She says I might have to go back for a bit, pretend I'm on holidays or something, so they don't get too curious, but I won't have to stay for long. Soon they'll get so used to it I won't have to visit at all.'

He pushed a bit of sausage around the side of his plate. Kirra watched him for a long moment, wondering how on earth it was possible for someone to visit their own home.

'But ...' She was almost lost for words. 'Don't you miss them? Don't you wish they knew the truth?'

'Not really. It's been the best since Imogen offered me the job.'

'Apprenticeship,' Lev corrected derisively. 'You don't have a job yet. You're good, but you're not that good.'

'Yeah, well, that's not what your mum said to me last night ...'

They both burst out laughing.

Kirra gave a weak smile. She was sure she was missing something with these two boys. They couldn't possibly *want* this kind of life. It was absurd to say the least.

She looked around the cafeteria. There was a table of girls in one corner, all laughing loudly and shovelling down toast, bleary-eyed and croaky-voiced. At the next table, a skinny boy was holding a spoon extremely awkwardly and trying to grip his bowl of cereal. There appeared to be something wrong with his fingers.

'He's new,' the boys at Kirra's table said together.

'And a first-timer,' said Bronson.

'He looks a bit miserable, doesn't he?' said Lev.

'He does. We'll talk to him after breakfast. What do you say?'

'Yeah, why not?'

The spoon slipped from the skinny boy's fingers and clattered into his bowl, milk splashing up all over him. He tried to rub it from his eyes with his fingers, but winced and used the backs of his hands instead.

'Here ya go, buddy,' called Lev, tossing a wad of napkins onto his table. The boy smiled gratefully, took one and began dabbing the milk off his T-shirt.

'Poor bugger,' said Bronson softly. 'Should've asked him to our table. It's crap being new. His parents only dropped him off last night.'

'His *parents*?'

They nodded, looking confused again.

'Sure,' said Lev. 'I think they were both CIs.'

'Huh?'

'Corporate Invaders.'

Kirra had no idea what that was either, but didn't want to ask.

'So, exactly what do you do here?' she asked.

They grinned.

'Learn the life of a Contractor.'

'So ... a criminal?'

They shook their heads.

'We don't like that,' said Lev.

'No,' agreed Bronson. 'Sounds too ...'

'Petty?' said Kirra. 'Yeah, I know. But how do you get picked? How did your boss —'

'Imogen,' Bronson offered.

'Yes. How did Imogen know where to find you?'

They both cracked wide smiles.

'Gotta show some potential, that's the thing. Only you don't know you're showing it, do you?' said Lev, suddenly looking thoughtful. ''Cos you don't even know what the Industry is yet.'

'Potential?'

'Sure. It all depends on the sorts of things you're already good at. Some stuff you can't be taught.'

They both spoke as though convinced they were making complete sense. Kirra, however, wasn't following at all.

'What do you have to be good at to be an Extractor?' she asked.

'Evasion,' they both said immediately.

'You must be adaptable,' Lev added, 'and have good instincts.'

'To be an Analyst?'

'Gotta be perceptive, I guess,' Bronson told her.

He nodded to a table where two neat-looking boys sat across from a girl with braces. The three of them were conversing quietly. 'They're training to be Analysts. I think you have to be great with numbers and puzzles and have a photographic memory or something. They're insane. You ask them anything and they have the answer ready to go.'

'What about Assassination?' Kirra asked after a moment. 'Who's training for that?'

The question was met with silence. They both looked stunned.

'The Marquison Training Intensive doesn't run classes for training Assassins,' Lev said quietly, as though worried someone might overhear the indecent topic of their conversation. 'But there's only really one trait required for Assassination.'

'What?'

'To be able to kill people — lots of people — in cold blood ...' Bronson said. 'You have to be unfeeling, I guess. How could you be anything less?'

They both looked uncomfortable. Feeling awkward, Kirra asked, 'What about you two? What are you good at?'

It was Lev who answered first, looking cheerful once more. 'I'm neat and thorough,' he said. 'I like to order things and keep track of them. When I was younger I started to collect newspaper clippings, a sort of weird hobby. I liked to follow stories on investigations and whatever and save all the articles in a folder so I could piece it all together once it was resolved. Like a jigsaw puzzle. Kept me busy, I guess. When I started to dig through stuff on the internet, my boss and his wife showed up. Wondered if I wanted to get into Intelligence, you know, collecting and organising info.'

'Right,' said Kirra.

'And Diverting is all about being good at deception, really,' Bronson told her. 'Lying and document fabrication, that sort of thing. I used to be great at lying. Best in my class, and great at forgery ... used to write my own notes from my mother and fake all my report cards, 'cos I was crap at school, you know. Anyway, I got in a bit of trouble for telling pretty big lies and faking important people's signatures ... something about fraud ... then Imogen heard about it, turned up and nabbed me. Says I'll be great once I know a couple of languages. I guess having a bit of bad in you helps too. You're no good to anyone if you're all good; then again, you're no good if you're all bad either.'

Kirra ate the last of her French toast, working very hard to understand that last comment.

'They just know, don't they?' Lev mused, after downing a glass of chocolate milk in one go. 'Somehow they just know.'

'They do,' agreed Bronson with a nod.

'Know?'

'Yeah, they just know where you are.'

'And,' said Lev, his voice suddenly shrouded with significance, 'where you're *meant* to be.'

Well, that settles it, thought Kirra. The pair of them had been brainwashed. They had to have been. They were both insane, talking about a life of crime as though it was something wonderful, something desirable. Thankfully

Desmond chose that moment to reappear, and Kirra felt relieved. She was fast running out of things to say to the two boys.

'Finished?' he asked her. She nodded gladly and got to her feet.

'Bye,' she said.

The boys waved her off merrily. Then they caught sight of Desmond and their mouths fell open simultaneously. As they walked away, Kirra heard Lev whisper, 'Whoa. *Whoa*. Was that ... was that Desmond Rall?'

Desmond escorted Kirra back into the bureau, where Mr Marquison sat at one of the desks in the open area.

'Desmond tells me someone's after you,' he said kindly, pulling out a chair for her. She sat next to him. 'Someone who ordered those men to seize you at the Ruiz bar.'

'Yes,' she said. 'So ... you know who I am then?'

He smiled kindly. 'Secret's safe with me, Miss Hayward. I'm not a Contractor anymore. I merely make my money by educating them. Besides, Desmond wants it to stay hushed, and I'm hardly going to go against him of all people, am I?'

'Er ... no,' Kirra said, wondering why it would be such an unwise idea. It seemed everyone knew something about Desmond that she didn't. 'I guess not.'

'Now,' Mr Marquison continued. 'You suspect the person pursuing you is Latham?'

'Well, he is,' Kirra answered, 'but Tavio said another person was behind the attack, meaning someone else is after me as well.'

'Tavio?' Mr Marquison asked.

'The Decoy,' Desmond told him, sitting on his other side. 'All we know about Kirra's most aggressive pursuer is that he is relatively young and obviously a Contractor.'

'I've had my most senior Intelligence student draw up a list,' Mr Marquison told them, before calling out in a voice that seemed to reverberate through the building, 'Felicity!'

A girl with a pointed chin and an elongated neck materialised at the door and entered the room with military formality. A golden plait dangled down her back.

'This is Felicity Klein,' Mr Marquison announced. 'One of my best. I'm most proud of her because she's just secured an internship at the MIO. She starts in two weeks' time.'

Felicity looked a little embarrassed, though thoroughly pleased with what seemed to be a momentous achievement.

'Mr Marquison. Sir,' Felicity declared, 'I have two likely names to offer you from our database. Both of them young Contractors, both of them familiar with or native to the city of Madrid, both rumoured to be here at the present time.'

'Excellent,' said Mr Marquison, leaning back in his chair. It seemed even he was a little taken aback by her intensity.

'The first is Guillermo Valdez.' Felicity opened a white folder and took out an enlarged photograph of a thin, weedy-looking boy with red welts on his neck. His hair was a mess, his teeth were crooked and he made for an altogether unimpressive sight. 'He is nineteen and only this year opened an Assassination agency in Madrid.'

Kirra, Desmond and Mr Marquison all leaned forward in their chairs to gaze at the photo. The boy moped back at them.

'He doesn't really look ...' began Kirra.

'... like the man we're after, somehow,' finished Desmond.

Felicity turned the photo back and took a better look herself. 'He matches the criteria,' she said with a small shrug, seeming to take Kirra's and Desmond's lacklustre reaction personally.

'What are his rates like?' Desmond asked.

Felicity flipped to the first page of the folder. 'He doesn't charge high,' she said. 'He's cheap, in fact.'

'Well, that settles it,' Desmond told the room, clasping his hands behind his head and leaning back.

'It does?' asked Kirra.

'Yes,' he said. 'If Guillermo Valdez doesn't charge high, then he doesn't have the means to hire recruits. The men who ambushed us were hired recruits.'

'I think it's safe to toss him back in the database,' Mr Marquison told Felicity. 'Who's the second man?'

'Hector Grant,' she said. 'Twenty-three years of age. Owns the second most sought-after Assassination agency in the entire Industry. His prices are astronomical, but his services are first rate. He visits Madrid several times a year.'

Felicity held up another enlarged photograph and Kirra shuddered in her seat. Staring back at her was a mean-faced man with blond hair, strong, broad features, a weathered tan and the most cunning and sinister-looking amber eyes she'd ever seen. Hector Grant was tall and strapping and looked an awful lot like the muscular actors and models in the posters plastered all over the pink wallpaper in Olivia's room. Though he shared physical similarities with Olivia's poster boys, Kirra had to concede that this man looked incapable of grinning good-naturedly the way they all did for the camera. Instead, he stared out from his photograph with a self-assured sneer.

'Business has been slow for him,' Felicity told them. 'He's been suffering severely due to the decline.'

'The decline?' Kirra asked.

Felicity frowned at her. 'Yeah,' she said, losing her formal manner for an instant. 'The decline ...' She raised a contemptuous eyebrow, as though anyone who required an explanation of something so basic wasn't worthy of being in the Marquison Training Intensive, let alone Mr Marquison's own bureau.

'The Industry has been in a recession ever since the Spencer System became popular,' Mr Marquison said. 'We've all suffered a serious slump in business because of it. You can't take a job you know you can't complete. Thus, the decline.'

'But there's hope,' Felicity said excitedly. 'Rumour has it that there's a Translator. Someone who can break the code and get through the Spencer System. It's just a question of finding the person and —'

'And what, Felicity?' Mr Marquison cut in.

Felicity stopped and stared hard at the ground, looking as though her entire reputation as Mr Marquison's finest student depended on a correct answer.

'And getting them into a position where they *have* to

translate the code ... for *everyone*,' she said, 'otherwise we'll be in decline forever.'

Kirra was sitting straight-backed in her chair, feeling very tense. For some reason she'd assumed Felicity already knew she was a Translator; that Mr Marquison had told her so she could compile the list. Obviously he hadn't; and after what Felicity had just said, Kirra was immensely grateful Mr Marquison had seen fit to keep his best student, and everyone like her, out of the loop. People who thought Kirra ought to become public property needed to be kept as far out of the loop as humanly possible.

Mr Marquison seemed to be thinking along the same lines.

'If that were to be the case, the Translator would be dragged all over the globe,' he said. 'They would be scrutinised by those who wish to understand how, precisely, the translation works; and come under constant threat from those wanting to further their own careers by seizing the Translator and keeping them all to themselves. The Translator's entire existence would become a battle for privacy, normality and peace.'

Felicity looked as though she had plenty to say in reply, but chose to refrain out of respect for Mr Marquison. Instead she nodded. 'Anyway, Hector Grant has been losing business for a while. His movements are probably more aggressive than ever.'

She turned back to Kirra. 'Why is he after you anyway?'

'We're not certain it's him, Felicity,' Mr Marquison said. 'Was there anyone else?'

'I only shortlisted those two. The search turned up fragments of another matching file, but it had been deleted. Probably the remains of a RedCon or something.'

'Well, there's nothing we can do about that, I suppose. Alright, Felicity, you can leave the files with me and go off to breakfast.'

She placed the folder before him and gave a curt bow. 'Thank you, Mr Marquison, sir,' she said, and marched off.

'It's not Hector Grant,' Desmond said as soon as the door was firmly shut.

'How do you know?' Kirra asked.

'Because,' Desmond replied, 'Hector Grant detests Decoys. He thinks they're money-scrounging scum, that they impede what otherwise would be an efficient, highly professionalised Industry. He would never hire one.'

'Do you think it's the other one then? What's-his-name?' Kirra asked.

Desmond glared at the files on the desk.

'No,' he said. 'Guillermo Valdez just doesn't have the means to pursue you.'

'Who then?' Kirra asked, feeling her temper rise.

'We have no reason not to believe it's just Latham.'

'Yes, we do!' Kirra said loudly. 'Latham's not young! Tavio said the man who hired him was young.'

Desmond shrugged. 'He could have sent any one of his recruits to do the negotiating with Tavio. Let's face it: Latham has the means and the drive. It's him. He's just waiting for the right moment to take you back.'

'So what do we do?'

Desmond gave another shrug.

Mr Marquison drummed his fingers upon the folder, then tucked Felicity's files away.

'Take care,' he said, rather unhelpfully. 'Nothing more for you to do, Miss Hayward, than to take great care.'

CHAPTER TWENTY-THREE

ANTON AND FADIL

Once their visit with Mr Marquison was over, Desmond drove through the streets of Madrid, taking detours and doubling back to ensure they weren't being followed. After what seemed like hours of weaving in neat little circles he headed for the outskirts of the city and it was there they found a suite in the quiet Jacinta de Santo Hotel.

That very evening Mai was escorted to their room by two girls from the Marquison Training Intensive. Kirra stared as one rattled off Mai's prescribed medications and the other changed her bandages at the table with perfect handiwork.

'They're training to be Industry doctors,' Desmond muttered to Kirra as the girls packed up their equipment and marched out of the suite. 'They jump at opportunities like these.'

Mai's condition had improved since Kirra had last seen her, but she was by no means recovered. Her face was pale, her fingers shaky and there were dark circles surrounding her eyes. She couldn't move her arm at all, and looked constantly like she was on the verge of throwing up, but it didn't matter because she was alive. Wonderfully and incontestably alive.

Desmond engulfed Mai in a light embrace once the Intensive girls had left and ushered her to the leather couch by the television, then went about making her a cup of tea into which he heaped several teaspoons of sugar. After handing her the cup and a plate of the leftover takeaway noodles he'd shared with Kirra, he sat down and scrutinised her anxiously, beating his fingers against his knees.

Mai hunched in her seat, looking frail and much, much older than her years. 'So, I hit the other two,' she began, 'just after you made it out of the bar. Then the police and ambulances were there. I pretended I couldn't speak Spanish or English just to avoid questioning. Then they had me in the hospital, gave me a couple of shots of morphine and tried to sort out what to do with me. They had my surgery scheduled for first thing in the morning. Then you showed up, thank god, though you certainly took your time.' She swallowed, something that seemed a difficult undertaking. 'Anyway,' she went on, 'I got the transit details. Four o'clock on Thursday — they're moving Aguilar in an armoured truck to maximum security.'

'Great,' said Desmond. 'The thing is ... we're going to have to be more careful from now on. Latham's on our trail. I'm sure he sent the recruits for Kirra at Ruiz, so he knows roughly where she is. We're going to have to keep moving as much as possible.'

Mai nodded and brushed sweat from her forehead, wincing slightly as she moved.

'Are you alright?' Kirra asked.

Mai raised her perfectly arched eyebrow, looking at Kirra for the first time. 'I will be,' she declared. 'They did a good job at the Intensive. There was blood loss, but nothing too dire.'

The problem with that, Kirra thought, was that it did look dire. Very dire, in fact. She had never seen anyone look so ill in her life. She gave Desmond a pointed look.

Desmond rubbed his forehead. 'Mai ... you know I had to —'

'Of course I do,' she said. 'Don't apologise. I would have done the same thing.'

Kirra stared at her; she felt as if her guilt was radiating through her skin.

Mai gave her a humourless smile. 'You are more important than you allow yourself to admit, Kirra. Your value is far, far greater than ours.'

Kirra shifted uncomfortably. She didn't want to be more valuable than anyone, or indeed more important; nor did she want near strangers to almost sacrifice their lives for her safety. Truth be told, being near-invisible in Freemont had suited her far, far better.

Due to the events following the meeting at the Ruiz bar, Desmond had temporarily forgotten his two colleagues waiting for codes. But the next morning he approached Kirra where she was curled up on the couch watching children's cartoons in Spanish.

'Kirra,' he began, his tone a little too friendly, 'I need your help now.'

She looked at him and then at the bright white papers in his hand. She let the television remote slip from her fingers.

'Desmond … I don't want to do it,' she said honestly.

After visiting both the MIO and Marquison's Training Intensive, countless frightening thoughts had churned through her head. Before, she'd understood that she was special, but now it seemed she couldn't escape the fact that she was urgently important, and in grave danger because of it. The fear in Marron Davies' eyes as he'd looked at her was something she couldn't push to the back of her head, and the things Felicity Klein had said lingered as well. The Industry was plagued with a downturn in business and Kirra, and Kirra alone, could pull them out of it. She was coveted by just about everyone, it seemed, and the speed with which Latham's recruits had found her at the Ruiz bar frightened her. Would she have to be on the move for the rest of her days to avoid them, and every other Contractor on her trail? What sort of life would that be? She didn't want to help Desmond with his code. She knew if she never laid eyes on one again it would be too soon.

Desmond sat next to her, his expression a mixture of determination and patience.

'I know it's been difficult, but please …'

Kirra suddenly felt furious with him.

'I don't want to do it!' she yelled, standing up just to get away from him. 'I just want to go home!'

Mai, who was working at her laptop at the table, attempting to type with one hand, looked up, interested by the outburst.

'You know I have a family,' Kirra continued angrily, pacing around. 'I have a brother and a sister, and right now my mother and father think ... Well, I don't know what they think, do I? If I help you now, when do I get out of this? When can I go home?'

Mai propped her chin in her hand and watched as Kirra collapsed into a chair beside her at the table.

'What *is* this fascination with your family?' Desmond said coldly. 'It'd be better for you, for me, for *everyone*, if you forgot about them.'

She stared at him. 'What? How could —'

'They can't help you here! They really can't help you anywhere, and the sooner you get a grip on that the easier everything will be.'

They glared at each other across the table.

'Kirra, you know Latham's watching your house,' Mai intervened, attempting to sound kind but instead coming across a bit pained. 'He's waiting for you to reach out to them. In fact, he's hoping for it. You'll be doing your family a favour by forgetting them ... for now, at least.'

Kirra closed her eyes and dropped her head into her hands.

Desmond took a seat opposite her and sighed. 'We will always endeavour to protect you, Kirra, but we need your help in return. Believe me, right now, you can do with friends like us.'

Glancing up, Kirra was met with two beseeching faces. She looked away, feeling lost. Then, she remembered what was really at stake: Milo's rescue. That was the most important thing. Who cared if the code made her feel sick? Who cared that it made her skin crawl? Day after day, Milo was alone in the dark, with nothing but his thoughts for company. She shook her head in quiet surrender and reached for the two codes.

'I need a pen,' she muttered.

In a flash, Mai laid a ballpoint by the paper. They were both watching her with unblinking eyes, unashamedly exhilarated at the prospect of seeing the unbreakable code broken.

Kirra concentrated on the first code and watched as the sequence formed immediately, no longer fascinated as to why and how it happened. She scribbled the string of numbers and letters along the bottom of the first page in her unsteady cursive, then moved on to the second page.

When she'd finished, Mai scooped the two pages up.

'I couldn't believe it before,' she whispered, her eyes scanning the paper with wonder. 'I didn't think it was possible.'

'I wish it wasn't,' Kirra said irritably.

'Des,' Mai continued, ignoring her, 'did you see that?'

Desmond nodded, astonished. 'I knew it was true … but to actually see it,' he said, taking the pages from Mai. 'It's amazing. I'll ring Anton and Fadil.'

Grabbing his phone and rising from his seat, Desmond started pacing excitedly.

'It's Des,' he said into the phone. 'I've got the codes. Are you ready?'

Kirra listened as he relayed the sequence slowly and clearly, and then did it all over again with the other code.

He snapped the phone shut and turned back to Mai and Kirra.

'They should have both jobs done by tomorrow,' he said. 'Kirra, you've no idea what you've done for us!'

Failing to feel any measure of pride or satisfaction whatsoever, Kirra faked a smile and turned away. Returning to her position on the couch, she wrapped her arms around her knees and closed her eyes. The sooner Desmond's Extraction in Madrid was complete, the sooner she would be reunited with Milo. *But then what?* a little voice quizzed her nosily. *What will you do then?* They would run away, of course. Spend a few days in each place before moving on, constantly on the lookout for pursuers. Perhaps, one day, if they were careful and covered their tracks, they'd be able to slow down, find somewhere to call home, attempt to get on with their lives, albeit quietly and in total secret? She'd never go back to Freemont, never be able to explain it all to her family, but at least she'd protect them this way. And she'd have Milo. She wasn't sure she could ask for more than that.

The next day Desmond and Mai, ensuring their weapons were within easy reach, escorted Kirra out of the hotel. Desmond had explained that they couldn't spend more than two days in one location, which suited Kirra fine as she was beginning to find the yellowish decor of their suite stifling.

'Fadil and Anton booked a new apartment. They'll be arriving there tonight,' Mai announced after reading a message on her phone.

Kirra glanced at her from the back seat of the car. She was still horribly pale and made all her movements with considerable care. Kirra had also noticed her taking copious amounts of painkillers and cautiously redressing her wound every few hours. She ignored a twinge of shame, reassuring herself that Mai had chosen to protect her at the bar. Kirra hadn't asked.

The new apartment building was much older and far more welcoming than the last hotel. The afternoon was warm and sunny, but their suite was cool and the furniture comfortable. Kirra took her place in front of the television as Mai set up her laptop at the table.

Three hours into a series of reality shows that Kirra couldn't understand, there was an abrupt knock at the door. Desmond glanced through the peephole and let out a breath of relief before letting two men into the room.

One was young and swaggered in with a twisted grin, assessing the apartment and looking impressed with what he found. His eyes were the colour of cork and glowed brightly, enhanced by a piercing in his eyebrow. His skin was a dark bronze colour and his clothes mismatched and baggy. He wore his chestnut hair in long dreadlocks, bunched together at the nape of his neck with a perishing elastic band.

'Nice place,' he said appreciatively.

His eyes landed on Kirra with unabashed interest for a moment, but then he noticed Mai and her bandaged arm and Kirra was suddenly all but invisible.

'Oh my,' he muttered. 'This'll be interesting.'

The second man was tall and muscular and had thick, black hair, a hard, straight nose, and dark striking eyes.

'Desmond,' he said quietly, his voice low and rich. 'Why have you been moving around so much? Where is —'

He stopped abruptly when his eyes fell on Mai, who had carefully risen from her chair and was doing her utmost to keep her arm out of sight — an impossible task given the sling. The man examined her from a distance, his expression changing into something quite foreboding.

'And it begins,' the younger man murmured happily to no one in particular, striding to the kitchen and yanking open the mini bar.

Kirra recognised his accent as Scottish. There had been a Scottish exchange student, Jason Nolan, in her class last year. He had gone out with Cassie Cheng's short and snooty friend Matilda Young a couple of times, their relationship a brief source of interest around the school for the three months he was there.

'Fadil,' Desmond began, addressing the man by the door, whose eyes were still glued to Mai.

Kirra supposed the bronze-skinned man with dreadlocks was Anton. He lounged against the kitchen counter, picking carefully at a chocolate bar and observing the scene with cheerful interest.

'What happened?' Fadil demanded, his voice dangerously quiet.

'It's fine,' Mai said, taking a tentative step forward. 'It's healing perfectly.'

'*What happened*?' Fadil repeated.

'We had a situation the other night. We were ambushed but we all got away. Mai was injured, obviously, but she's been treated and she's on the mend,' Desmond said.

Fadil tore his eyes from Mai and fixed Desmond with a glare. 'She was shot,' he snarled, as though he hadn't heard a word Desmond had said. 'Why?'

'We weren't in control of the location,' Mai hurriedly explained. 'We were tracked. They tried to take Kirra, and I was just caught in the middle. But it's over now. Everything is alright. I feel fine. Great, really.'

That was a blatant lie. Anyone could see that Mai, ashen-faced, slightly breathless and very feeble, was a long way from 'great'.

'Kirra Hayward?' Fadil asked, looking both interested and startlingly alert at the mention of the name. Mai nodded before turning to Kirra herself.

'Kirra, this is Fadil, and this is Anton. They work with us.'

Fadil, looking anxious, said, 'But have you increased security —'

He was interrupted by Anton choking on a bit of chocolate and coughing noisily in the kitchen. 'Holy shit!' he yelped. '*That's* Kirra Hayward?'

'She's a little younger than we imagined,' Mai conceded, dropping back into her chair. The effort of standing to placate Fadil seemed to have exhausted her.

'No kidding,' Anton said. 'Should I run out and get colouring books or something?'

Kirra didn't know whether to be offended or not as Anton strode over to the lounge and openly gawked at her. It was then Kirra realised how young he was himself. He looked in his early twenties.

'You know,' he said conversationally, 'it's a miracle you're still alive. Truly, it is. What's your secret?'

'Being a Translator,' Kirra said obviously.

'Oh right,' came the reply. 'Of course. You're no good to anyone dead.'

'Anton,' Desmond said warningly.

Anton ignored him and flopped onto the couch. He extended his suntanned hand to Kirra, grinning warmly despite his taunting. 'Anton Disraeli,' he said.

He smirked when he noticed her inching away from him.

'Oh, no, you've got it all wrong,' he told her in a broad stage whisper. 'Fadil's the one you want to be scared of, particularly as his girl took a bullet for you.'

With that, he opened another chocolate bar and took a dainty bite, seeming to forget about Kirra altogether.

Attempting to be covert, she glanced over her shoulder. Fadil, Desmond and Mai had gathered in one of the bedrooms and were just visible through the open door, having a hushed and heated argument. She could just make out the use of her name. She watched them for a few moments before Desmond threw his hands up in the air and walked away. He went into the other bedroom and shut the door with a slam.

Returning her attention to the argument, Kirra saw that Mai was pacing around, gesturing furiously and chastising Fadil in what sounded like it might be Arabic. Fadil yelled back at her, each of them shouting over the top of the other, before Mai, in her anger, tried to raise her bad arm to jab him in the chest. She gasped at the attempt and, very suddenly, the argument was at an end. After a moment in which she glared hatefully into his eyes, Mai allowed Fadil to draw her into his arms.

Kirra averted her gaze and experienced a quick pang of longing for Milo, but told herself not to dwell on it. It was only a matter of days before she would see him again.

Later that night, Desmond intercepted Kirra on her way out of the bathroom.

'Feel like an excursion?' he asked hopefully.

She snuck a quick look around the place. Mai and Fadil had locked themselves in one of the bedrooms, and Anton was sprawled across the couch, chortling loudly at another reality TV show that really didn't look funny at all, his filthy shoes resting on a pillow as he placed chips, one by one, on the tip of his tongue.

'Yes,' she said firmly, 'I do.'

Desmond looked pleasantly surprised by her answer. 'Thought you could do with some time away from our dear young friend.'

They made it to the car without incident, an achievement in itself, and Desmond drove them away. As he fiddled with the radio, Kirra seized the courage to ask her most burning question while they had some privacy.

'Desmond?'

'Mmm?' he said distractedly, hovering between two Spanish stations with a confused look on his face.

'Why do you think I'm a Translator?'

'I have my theories,' he said. 'But I don't think any of them has particular weight.'

He gave her a decidedly sympathetic look, as though Kirra had been diagnosed with a terminal illness and doctors were yet to find a cure.

'Why do you think there are only four of us?' she went on.

'Three now,' Desmond reminded her. 'Richard Spencer's been dead for a while. There's just you, your friend Milo and that Josephine Shaw woman.'

'Right,' Kirra said, wondering for a second where 'that Josephine Shaw woman' was. 'But there are billions of people on earth, and there isn't some secret algorithm that the three of us shared. We can just do it. I've never heard of anything like that.'

'I seem to remember you telling me you were the best maths student in your school,' Desmond said. 'Perhaps your mind is so adept, so practised, at looking at problems that it can't help but subconsciously find a solution to every problem it sees.'

'But you said Latham made all sorts of mathematicians and analysts look at the Spencer code and they came up with nothing. They'd be as practised at equations as I am, if not better.'

'It's what I would call an elite skill, and a very selective one. Latham may have just asked all the wrong people.'

'You mean more people might be Translators and he just didn't find one?'

'Well, he didn't have any way of knowing who they were or where to look for them, especially when they wouldn't have known that they were Translators themselves.'

'So you're saying there might be more like me and Milo?'

'Who knows? I personally think so, yes,' he said after a moment. 'Out of the, as you say, billions of people on earth I definitely wouldn't rule out the possibility of others gifted with this special way of looking at the code. They're lucky, I suppose, that they didn't attempt that online example as you did.'

Kirra imagined, just for a moment, that it had been one of the other students in her school, and not her, who had been cursed with the most highly sought-after skill in the Contracting Industry. What if it had been Phillipa Corbel's meek friend Joanne Gaskell, who was excellent at maths, though of course, not quite as good as Kirra? Would Kirra then be at home right now? Or perhaps at school, handing in an assignment and taking a moment to wonder where her missing classmate had gone to?

'Still doesn't explain why I can do it in the first place,' she said.

'In the way some people can … I don't know … sing and others most definitely cannot — there mightn't be a very remarkable explanation for it,' he said. 'I may be wrong, of course.'

'Sing?' Kirra repeated in a disbelieving tone.

He smiled. 'Yours is a gift on a much more exclusive scale, clearly.'

It was only as they were ascending a dusty flight of stairs within an old apartment block smeared with spray paint and grime that Kirra thought to question where this excursion was taking them.

'To visit a Reloader,' Desmond told her, wrinkling his nose as he pulled his hand away from the banister to see his palm coated in grease.

'What's that?'

'It's exactly what it sounds like,' he said, finding Apartment 4 on the second level and rapping his knuckles

235

on the door. 'Don't leave my side!' he added over his shoulder.

'Who's there?' came a raspy reply from beyond the door.

Desmond cleared his throat. 'Do you stock Gravers?'

The door flew open, and Kirra was hit with the stale stench of smoke and sweat. She took an unconscious step backward to avoid it. A man stood at the door, a squat, stinking man, wearing nothing but a pair of stained trackpants and a browning singlet. He held a lit cigarette between two thick, stubby fingers and his straggly moustache contained remnants of whatever Kirra supposed he had had for dinner.

'Fanuco?'

The man, who had been leering at Kirra, turned his shiny, sweaty face towards Desmond. 'Who wants to know?'

Desmond made an impatient noise in the back of his throat. 'My name really does not concern you in the slightest,' he said haughtily. 'I require ammunition. Am I in the right place?'

The man, Fanuco, gave a gurgling little laugh.

'People are never in the right place when they come here,' he said, grinning slyly, 'but yeah, I got ammo.'

Desmond followed him inside, ensuring that Kirra wasn't far behind, and shut the door in her wake.

Once inside, Kirra could taste the foul stench she'd only sniffed at before and her eyes stung and watered. It was putrid. Desmond appraised the apartment with disgust and looked as though he was trying to breathe through his mouth. The paint was peeling off the walls and the moth-eaten furniture was piled with mail and newspapers. A straggly cat of indeterminate breed meowed softly from the corner. Fanuco squashed his cigarette into an overflowing burgundy ashtray and lit another.

'So, Gravers ammunition?' Desmond asked again.

Fanuco raised his eyebrows. 'Gravers, eh? I might stock 'em.'

He turned to hurry off down the corridor, but froze after his first waddled step. He swivelled around.

'You aren't an Assassin, are you?' he asked suspiciously.

'Why?'

'Well, I got an order a couple of days ago, see. I'm not allowed to sell ammo to any Assassins in this area.'

Desmond frowned, interested by this. 'Why?'

'They don't want some runaway kid killed or something. Said she wasn't to be hurt.'

Kirra dug her hands into her pockets and concentrated hard on a congealed drop of something that looked like gravy on the floor.

'And who made that order?' Desmond enquired. 'Latham?'

'Latham? Who's he?' Fanuco asked. 'Nah, this one didn't give a name. He sounded far too young to be ordering anyone about, but he said my cheque was in the mail as long as I didn't sell anything to any Assassins round here.'

Desmond nodded, and shared a look with Kirra.

'Well, I'm not an Assassin,' Desmond said.

'How do I know that for sure?'

'You don't,' Desmond informed him, stepping forward and slipping a roll of notes into Fanuco's puffy hand.

He eyed it for a split second before … 'Luckily, I'm a trusting man.' Then he took another long look at Kirra. 'Who's that?'

'My assistant,' Desmond said, without missing a beat.

Fanuco nodded, a twisted smile coming over his face.

'Wish she was my assistant,' he muttered and preceded them down the corridor towards a room closed off by a roller door.

Kirra and Desmond left the building with several heavy bags hanging from their shoulders. Fanuco had supplied them with boxes of bullets and several guns of varying sizes and degrees of power. As Desmond piled the bags into the boot of the car he caught the curious look on Kirra's face.

'Reloaders aren't to be trusted,' he said. 'Everything they sell is stolen, and they'll do anything to make a quick buck.'

'The order about me,' Kirra said after a moment, 'came from the same person who paid Tavio, didn't it?'

Desmond closed the boot with a thud. 'Sounds like it.'

Kirra felt her stomach twist. 'Some recruit of Latham's?'

Desmond gave her a quick encouraging look. 'He won't get you, so don't worry. No matter how many recruits he has, young or old, he won't get you.'

'How do you know he won't?'

'Because I'll kill him before he gets the chance.'

'Well …' said Kirra. 'That's reassuring.'

'I knew you'd think so.'

CHAPTER TWENTY-FOUR

THE EXTRACTION OF AGUILAR

Thursday was creeping up quietly and Kirra felt herself growing tense. Thursday was the day she was required to provide an on-site sequence. The last time she'd done one of those, she'd ended up lying trapped beneath the rubble of a half-destroyed office building, so naturally she had her misgivings.

So far, Kirra had been content to stay in the apartment, reading magazines and watching TV. Apart from the visit to Fanuco, she hadn't urged Desmond or Mai to take her out anywhere. The crowds in the city streets made her uncomfortable, the sun outright bothered her, and at times she caught herself almost missing the safety of the cell. Four walls and a tiny window with bars? She chided herself. How could anyone ever miss that?

On Thursday morning, Anton strolled into the apartment with a bag of groceries. Kirra, who was sitting at the kitchen counter reading a Spanish cooking magazine, watched him layer ham, salad, mayonnaise and pickles between two thick slices of bread in a slow, methodical fashion that she found quite irritating. He took a small, gentle bite and appraised Kirra thoughtfully as he chewed. She tried to ignore him, wondering how he could possibly eat. She was so nervous about Aguilar's Extraction that she thought she might spew all over the place.

'Have you decided yet?' Anton said.

Kirra looked up from the magazine. 'Decided what?'

'If you want to be a Retriever or an Analyst.'

She blinked.

Anton tilted his head to the side. They watched each other for a moment.

'You don't know what I'm talking about, do you?' he said.

'No,' she replied. 'Should I?'

'Hmph,' said Anton. 'Guess they haven't told you about the Estate yet.'

He took another bite. Kirra sat up slightly in her seat, remembering that Desmond had mentioned the place the night of the Ruiz ambush.

'What's the Estate?'

Anton grinned. 'Oh, you know,' he said, his voice suddenly low and mysterious. 'A top-secret sort of place.'

Kirra raised a sceptical eyebrow. 'Is it?' she said in a bored tone.

'Well,' he continued, 'that's what Flo says anyway.'

Kirra said nothing and flicked through the pages of the magazine. She knew she wasn't going to get a straight answer out of Anton about anything.

'So, what's so special about this Milo kid then?' he ventured after a pause. 'Why do we need to rescue him so urgently?'

'He's not a kid,' she said, averting her gaze from his moving mouth. His strange, meticulous way of eating annoyed her.

'Right, right,' Anton said hurriedly. 'What's so special about this Milo *guy*?'

She thought for a moment, and was tempted to say that Milo was her best friend, but that didn't seem right. It implied that she had an array of friends, and Milo was merely her favourite of the bunch.

'We have a lot in common,' she told Anton evasively.

'Well, you're the only two accessible Spencer code Translators in the world,' he said. 'I'd say you have a fair bit in common.'

Kirra glared at him. 'I have no friends and I can't go home,' she informed him in what she hoped was a casual tone. 'Milo is all I have. So I have to save him.'

Anton watched her through wide eyes, chewing slowly. He swallowed — an understated, measured occurrence — and took a breath. 'Is that all then?'

Kirra's jaw clenched.

'We've been through a lot together. We were imprisoned for months,' she told him angrily. 'We were inside the Bachmeier building and —'

'The one that half-collapsed?' Anton interrupted, astonished.

'It didn't collapse,' Kirra said quietly, her eyes scrolling over a non-stick frying pan advertisement. 'It was bombed.'

'I thought so,' he said. 'They passed it off to the media as poor construction, but it was clearly an Industry job and — wait ... you were *inside* it?'

Kirra nodded.

'Actually *inside* it?'

She nodded again.

Anton blinked. 'But that's awesome!'

Kirra remembered the exact moment she'd realised she was trapped beneath a propped-up concrete slab buried deep beneath the debris. She also remembered wondering if she would live to see the light of day again.

'Didn't feel so awesome,' she told him moodily, closing the magazine and stalking off.

They were to embark on the Extraction of Aguilar at three in the afternoon, ready to intercept his transit at four. Desmond spent the entire day drilling the plan into Kirra's head. She listened carefully, memorising all his directions word for word. She didn't want to give Desmond a reason to think she was incompetent or perhaps not worth the time he'd taken to Extract her.

Before lunch, Desmond slipped an envelope into Kirra's hand. She opened it to find a perfect replica of an Australian passport, complete with a photo of herself, one she remembered posing for. It had been taken in Year Nine, outside the Hewitt Hollandale Memorial Library in a makeshift photo booth brought in for the annual school photo day.

'How did you get this?' she gasped.

'It was on your high school's intranet,' he told her. 'I've had it ready for months.'

Kirra turned the document over in her hand, running her thumb over the embossed coat of arms. 'Is it real?' she asked, staring at it, fascinated.

Desmond gaped at her. 'Of course not!' he said, as though it was the most absurd question he had been asked in his lifetime. 'Katherine Hammond's a little different to Kirra Hayward.'

Kirra read the passport closely. It gave her a fake name, a fake address, a fake date of birth. According to this passport she was eighteen years old and her birthday was on the twenty-seventh of October.

'Who is Katherine Hammond anyway?' she asked.

Desmond shrugged. 'A phantom profile,' he told her, checking the contents of his backpack one last time.

'A phantom ... what?'

'A profile of a person who doesn't actually exist. We slip them into the system to use for things just like this. Katherine belongs to you now.'

'Won't they realise?' she asked after a moment.

'With enough money you can fake anything. Even a real passport,' he said easily. 'Nobody will question that document because I've given them no reason to.'

Kirra accepted this and secured the passport in her pocket. She returned her gaze to Desmond and after a moment he caught her staring.

'What now?'

'Why do you do it?' she asked.

He seemed to know precisely what she was talking about.

'Come on,' he urged weakly. 'No point in questions like that.'

'Tell me,' she said.

He expelled a frustrated breath. 'It's a job. We've all got to have them.'

'Most people have law-abiding jobs.'

'That's what you want?' he said. 'You want to be *law abiding*?'

Somehow he managed to make this sound oddly derogatory, as though people with such moral aspirations were to be regarded with a measure of sympathy.

'You know,' he said, 'rules are all about control. The people who make them rarely follow them.'

Kirra wasn't certain she agreed with this viewpoint. She had never felt oppressed by rules before and had always found such ideologies a bit juvenile, especially when they were harboured so stalwartly by the regulars of Friday afternoon detention at Freemont Grammar.

When she said nothing, Desmond smiled.

'You know, I used to ask myself all these questions too,' he admitted. 'But the deeper you get into it, the less you need to justify it. It's a job, in the dullest sense of the word. The shock will wear off,' he promised, 'and you'll understand then.'

'I will?'

'Most certainly.'

Kirra nodded and wondered how best to broach her next worry.

'Desmond,' she began, 'I — I shot someone. One of the recruits in the factory.'

She expected him to say something consoling, something that would make the guilty pangs in her stomach go away, but instead he gave an unconcerned nod.

'You'll get over it,' he said firmly, and went to put the kettle on.

Kirra frowned at the floor, certain that wasn't the kind of reassurance she had been fishing for.

'Were you defending yourself?' he asked.

She looked up and nodded.

'Then, yes, you'll get over it.'

He turned away to find the teabags and a mug.

Fadil suddenly strode through the front door, his brow furrowed, and cast around for Mai. He saw her in the bedroom and stalked inside, shutting the door behind him.

Fadil tended to ignore Kirra; in fact, he had yet to say anything to her at all. He did, however, watch her when he thought she wasn't aware, evaluating her carefully from a distance for long periods of time. His interactions with Desmond and Anton were limited to short and stilted conversations, and he spent an awful lot of time perusing a bank of files stored on his phone, with a darkly concerned look on his face. The only time Kirra noticed a change in him was when he was with Mai. He seemed stricken by her brush with death, and made it his business to ensure she had everything she needed at all times, as well as forcing her to take her painkillers four times a day like clockwork.

Once Kirra had caught them arguing: Fadil had been insisting that he needed to change Mai's bandage; and Mai, who loathed sympathy, had been attempting to swat him away so she could do it herself with one hand. Eventually Fadil had won the battle and Kirra had observed from the couch as he set about his task. Mai had watched him closely too, her expression something Kirra couldn't quite fathom. Joy, perhaps? An emotion so strong and so infused with love that it didn't suit the tense, businesslike atmosphere of the apartment at all.

Kirra wasn't sure what she thought of Anton. He seemed a bit too young and carefree to be a part of the business she despised, yet he apparently took his profession seriously enough, because just before they left for the Extraction he intercepted Desmond in the kitchen.

'She's coming, Des?' he asked, his voice a little lower than normal.

Kirra could hear them perfectly from the couch, where she was pulling on her boots, though she kept her eyes glued to the carpet.

'Yes,' Desmond said shortly. 'We need her.'

'But ... do you think it's ... sensible?'

'Sensible?'

'Des ... she's been locked up for ages. Ages and ages! She might be a bit ... you know ...'

'No, I don't know,' Desmond challenged.

'*You know*,' Anton urged, making a swirling motion with his index finger beside his head. Desmond raised his eyebrows, not remotely amused.

'Is the word you're looking for "traumatised"?' he offered patiently.

'Well, I was going for "bonkers" but that'll do,' Anton said, pleased that Desmond was getting his drift. 'How do you know she's stable and won't ... you know ... screw things up?'

Desmond stole a glance at Kirra. He caught her watching him, and as their gazes met he seemed to regard her with something almost akin to pride. Kirra was surprised by this and felt a small measure of appreciation for Desmond that she'd not felt before.

'Curiously,' he informed Anton as he slung his bag onto his back, 'she's fine.'

With that, Desmond strode to the door and held it open, waiting patiently for Kirra to follow.

They took two cars: Desmond's dark green sedan, which Anton drove alone, and a silver van, which everyone else piled into comfortably. Kirra couldn't sit still, so great was her excitement. As soon as this Extraction was over they would be on their way to Dusseldorf.

The two vehicles had been driving in line through the streets of Madrid for less than fifteen minutes before Mai looked down at Fadil's phone.

'We're closing in,' she said quietly. Kirra looked at her, startled. Already? Mai reviewed the phone again, before telling them that Aguilar had just started his final transit to a maximum security facility outside of the city, and that they would come in view of him in only minutes' time.

'There's the truck,' she said shortly after, pointing to a nondescript white transit truck ahead of them on the straight, empty highway. As they got closer, Kirra noticed a security pad on the van's rear door. Her heart started thumping.

'Okay, Anton,' Desmond said into his phone.

Anton accelerated down the highway and overtook the transit truck at full speed. He swerved in front of it and came to a sudden stop, causing the truck to screech to a halt to avoid a collision. Immediately Anton was out of the car, a gun trained between the two drivers.

Fadil stopped the van, and ran to provide Anton support, a gun in each hand. Desmond climbed composedly out of his seat, nodding to Kirra to go with him.

'We have to do this quickly,' he said, zipping up his jacket.

Kirra attempted to quash her nerves. She was determined to prove Anton wrong.

'You need this, Des,' Mai said, tossing him Fadil's phone. She climbed back into the van, in no condition to aid in the Extraction. Kirra spared her a quick glance. She seemed as unfazed as Desmond was, sitting comfortably in her seat and glaring at them as though she resented not being able to help.

Striding towards the back of the truck, Desmond dialled a number and waited.

He said the truck's serial number aloud to the person on the line, reading from a small label by the van's licence plate. Then he passed the phone to Kirra. 'The code will come up in a moment. Read the sequence out to me.'

Kirra glanced at the screen. Sure enough the code was looking back at her, the columns of numbers and letters that were now so familiar streaming down the page. At once the sequence began to form. She read it out to Desmond, taking care to get every digit and letter correct.

'That's it,' she told him when a new character failed to reveal itself.

Desmond typed in the sequence and punched a little green button at the bottom of the security pad. With a tiny beep the door unlocked and Desmond hauled it open.

'Incredible,' he whispered, before drawing his gun and nosing it inside the truck at the two men who sat there looking terrified.

One was a security guard, spitting instructions hurriedly into a mobile phone. Desmond wasted no time in taking it from him, tossing it to the ground and flattening it beneath his foot. He then turned to Aguilar, who, despite his haggard face and bloodshot eyes, was younger than Kirra had imagined. Desmond reached for the guard's keys and uncuffed him. Aguilar, who seemed to have been expecting the intervention, jumped from the truck and watched Desmond lock the guard back inside. Desmond then escorted him to the green sedan, pushed him into the driver's seat and dropped the keys into his lap.

'You're free,' Desmond said. 'So drive.'

Aguilar, who was sweating profusely by this stage, didn't need to be told twice, slamming the door shut and fumbling to start the engine.

Amid all the commotion Kirra had failed to notice the other car on the highway that had quietly crept up on them, and when a gunshot rang through the air her heart nearly stopped.

Desmond, Anton and Fadil abandoned the transit truck and ran back to Kirra, taking cover beside the silver van. Aguilar, who had stalled the sedan in panic, now zoomed away. The two new arrivals, hanging from their car windows, started to shoot after him. Kirra knew they were definitely Latham's recruits, as she recognised both of them from the factory. She watched with bated breath as Aguilar's car swerved dangerously, then dragged off to the side of the road where it rolled to a stop. Kirra could see a revolting explosion of red near the driver's seat and knew that Aguilar was dead.

For a single moment she felt relieved. Maybe the recruits were only after Aguilar for whatever reason, and not her? Maybe they would drive off and let them be? But when the two men reloaded their weapons and turned with unmistakable purpose towards the silver van, Kirra knew how ridiculous that notion was. They'd only killed Aguilar to get him out of the way.

Desmond, Fadil and Anton immediately opened fire on the recruits. Kirra stayed hunkered down out of sight. She had yet to see evidence of Latham, but knowing he'd sent the recruits was enough to terrify her. He knew where she was and it was only a matter of time until he recaptured her.

'We can't let them take her!' Mai yelled, reloading her gun. Despite Fadil's look of warning she jumped out of the van and joined the firefight with gusto.

Anton grabbed Kirra by the shoulders and brought her to her feet. 'Hi,' he said, thrusting a silver gun into her palm. 'Once you've finished panicking you might want to give us a hand and try shooting someone. What do you think?' He didn't wait for an answer. 'Excellent. The safety's off.'

Kirra gazed down at the weighty weapon in her hand, and then back at the four people fighting for her. Without another thought she peered around the van, spotted a recruit, gripped the gun with two hands, took aim, fired and missed, the recoil reverberating down through her arms. She couldn't quite believe her first emotion was disappointment.

'You might want to keep trying,' Anton urged, reloading his gun and shooting madly.

Kirra followed his lead. Finally, to her great surprise, she hit a recruit — though she acknowledged it was through spectacular luck rather than skill. He crumpled to the ground beside his car, motionless, and she stared at the body.

'That's the way!' Anton roared gleefully. 'Keep it up!'

She kept shooting until she was out of bullets, but it didn't matter because Mai had hit the other recruit. He was still alive, but clearly not for long, twitching compulsively on the ground and pressing his hand to his heart. Kirra fought the bizarre urge to cheer. She looked back at Desmond and Fadil, who were stowing their guns and climbing back into the van.

'We need to go. Right now,' Desmond ordered. 'More could be on their way.'

Kirra's face fell. She had almost expected to be congratulated.

She strapped herself into her seat, and Anton slumped down next to her, his eyes bright as he caught his breath. They sped away from the scene, rocketing along the highway for several kilometres before Anton let out a long, happy sigh.

'Did you see that?' he asked the others.

No one paid him any attention.

'Hello?' he called. 'Did you see Kirra? She got a recruit, right in the face! Blood everywhere!'

'We saw, Anton,' Mai said. 'You did well, Kirra.'

'Well? WELL?' Anton spluttered. 'That's not even the word! She ... she —'

'Yes, yes, Anton, she's a natural,' Desmond said absentmindedly from the driver's seat. 'She'll make a great Contractor one day.'

'No,' Kirra said, not caring one bit if she killed the light-hearted mood, 'I'll *never* be a part of this! Not ever.'

Anton slung his arm over her shoulder, chuckling. 'Never?' he said, shoving her lightly. 'Don't lie to yourself. You already are.'

CHAPTER TWENTY-FIVE

DUSSELDORF

After Aguilar's disastrous Extraction, it took Kirra a while to notice they were heading back to Madrid. She glanced at Desmond as they passed an enormous highway sign.

'Uh ... Desmond?' she murmured, pointing over her shoulder. 'Desmond, Germany is that way.'

It seemed that Desmond hadn't heard her. He kept driving, eyes firmly ahead.

'Desmond,' she said, louder this time. 'Milo's in Dusseldorf. You need to turn around.'

No one answered her. Kirra caught Desmond and Mai exchanging a small, guilt-ridden glance. Suddenly, she couldn't breathe.

'Why aren't we going to Dusseldorf?' she asked, her voice growing in volume.

'Kirra,' Mai began, 'it's not a good idea.'

Her heart plunged into her stomach. 'What?' she breathed.

'Don't get upset,' Mai said quickly. 'You have to look at it from our perspective. We'd be walking into a death trap! A factory full of Latham's recruits? There's no sense in it.'

Kirra felt feverish all of a sudden. Sweat was gathering at her temples and her mouth was drying at an astonishing rate.

'Desmond?' she said urgently, deciding to ignore Mai altogether. 'What's going on?'

He caught her gaze in the rear-view mirror.

'Kirra ...' he began softly, though he didn't get to finish. Kirra was stunned when Fadil turned in his seat to face her for the first time, looking down his long nose, his gaze stoic.

'There is no reason for us to risk our lives in Dusseldorf,' he said, his voice a low, impassive rumble. 'We do not need this Milo Franklyn person. We will not be visiting Germany today.'

He turned back to face the road, assured that his was the final word on the matter.

Kirra stared at the back of his head, horror-struck. They weren't going to help her? They were going to leave Milo for dead? She wondered if they'd ever really considered the idea at all. Had it only been to trick her into cooperating? If things were reversed, if Milo was with these Contractors, these *traitors*, and Kirra was still at the factory, she knew what he would do. She knew exactly. He wouldn't stop until he had ensured her escape. He wouldn't stop until they were reunited again.

They had to take her back. They had to listen to her! There was nothing else for it. Kirra had never had a tantrum before, but if there was ever a time for one, it was now.

Enraged, she twisted in her seatbelt. 'NO! YOU CAN'T DO THIS!' she yelled, kicking the empty seat in front of her with enough force to cause a perturbing crunch within the upholstery. Anton winced and shifted away from her.

'Settle down, Kirra,' he said uncomfortably. 'There's nothing we can do.'

'Please!' she said, realising she was not above begging. 'Please! I'll do anything! *Anything!*'

With every moment they were travelling further and further away from Milo, and she was completely outnumbered. She had never felt so betrayed in all her life. Staring at the back of Desmond's head, she took a rasping breath. 'Desmond! You promised!'

Mai turned to her. 'We promised we'd do our best,' she corrected.

'This is *not* your best!' Kirra fired back bitterly. 'Desmond … you promised! I gave you what you wanted! Now help me! You promised!'

The car swerved into the emergency lane and came to an abrupt standstill. Desmond gripped the steering wheel tightly, gazing at Kirra in the rear-view mirror, his expression something close to shame. He sighed deeply.

Fadil glared at him.

'Desmond,' he said warningly. 'We agreed on this.'

Desmond rubbed his eyes. 'I'm changing my mind,' he said. He spun the van around and headed for the French border.

Kirra was frozen in her seat, stunned into silence. She couldn't believe it. He had listened to her! She felt faint with relief.

Mai was very quiet. Fadil sat glaring ahead, his face dark. It was Anton who spoke first as he gazed out the window.

'That was cool, Des,' he said quietly. 'Very cool.'

The trip to Germany was long and, for the most part, silent. Desmond and Anton took turns driving, and stopped every few hours at roadside cafes. Kirra had a feeling Fadil did not elect to drive for the same reason Desmond failed to ask him. Perhaps if he did, he would turn around once again and drive them all away from Milo.

Mai nudged Kirra awake when they turned in to a hotel for the night. It was there she sat down with Kirra at a wobbly little table, free of her laptop for once.

'This is going to be very dangerous,' she warned, her hands cradling a cup of tea. 'You must be prepared for all possibilities.'

Kirra tried to find the scent of Lena's cheap perfume on the collar of her jacket. It was fading now. Soon it would be gone.

'Yeah, I know the risks,' she said.

'Things could go very wrong. Latham could recapture you, Kirra. It's not too late to call it off.'

'If we aren't successful in rescuing him,' Kirra said, 'I want you to leave me there.'

Mai stared at her. 'You know we won't do that.'

'If you were me, would you want to stay?'

Mai swallowed quickly. It was only after meeting

Fadil that Kirra had finally understood Mai's unexpected willingness to help her rescue Milo.

'Kirra,' Mai began tentatively, 'you're so young. Perhaps your feelings stem from your imprisonment. Perhaps in another life you wouldn't look twice at Milo.'

'Maybe, but this isn't another life, is it?'

'You're right,' Mai agreed. 'But it's also the only one you have.'

Desmond, who had more knowledge of the factory than anyone else, Kirra included, drew a rough plan of the building. He showed Kirra the position of the cell, where the bathroom was and then along the passage to the graffiti room.

'Whatever happens,' Desmond said over the table, 'we cannot get separated. Latham has at least ten recruits on-site at any given time. Alone, we have no chance.'

Fadil, who had been sitting in silent disapproval, cleared his throat.

'We really have no chance either way,' he declared. 'This is the most senseless thing any of us has ever done.'

Kirra stared at the map uncomfortably. She was aware of the blatant risk, aware that these new acquaintances of hers were about to put their lives in serious danger, and she dearly wished she had been able to find some alternative. However, rescuing Milo was non-negotiable, and she had to use whatever resources came her way.

'Kirra helped us when we asked for it,' Desmond said firmly, his eyes on Fadil.

Fadil's disdainful gaze coasted over Kirra. 'Well, it wasn't particularly worthwhile,' he pointed out. 'Or perhaps you've forgotten, Desmond? Our assignment was shot in the head.'

'Whatever the outcome of the Extraction, Kirra played her part. It's time for us to play ours.'

'And who knows?' Anton added, rocking on two legs of his chair. 'Pro bono work might be fun.'

Kirra stopped herself from rolling her eyes. As long as he bolstered their numbers, Anton could adopt whatever attitude he wished.

Much later, in the very dead of the night, Kirra stood in the dark at the window, watching two figures trudging up and down the street below. They repeated the process over and over, in no apparent hurry to get anywhere it seemed, every so often looking up at the buildings towering either side of them.

'They're looking for you.'

Kirra jumped. She hadn't realised Desmond had arrived by her side.

'Are you sure?' she whispered, her breath casting a light fog across the glass.

He nodded. 'They've been doing a sweep of the whole area. They spotted the van before, but we outran them. They're Latham's. He's redoubled his search efforts.'

Kirra looked at him. They had been followed since their re-entry into Dusseldorf? She hadn't known that. Desmond must have been expecting it though, because he'd handled the pursuit so effortlessly that his passengers hadn't even noticed. She shuffled slightly towards him, standing in his shadow.

'How did Latham know where I was? How did he

know we were Extracting Aguilar? Or that we were at the Ruiz bar?'

'I've been thinking about that,' Desmond said. 'Maybe someone at the MIO informed him? My best guess is that they might have bugged my phone whilst I was posing as Wyles. It's all I can think of. The phone's been destroyed, so they won't be able to locate us so accurately again.'

'Destroyed?'

'I broke it apart and flushed it down a toilet.'

He smiled at her expression. 'What?' he said. 'I challenge you to come up with something more effective than a toilet.'

They stood together for a moment, both smiling in the dark, until the two figures regained their attention.

'I really wish I'd known,' Kirra said softly after a moment.

'Known what?'

'That Wyles was really you all that time.'

'What kind of difference would it have made?' he asked.

She shrugged. 'You were really decent to us,' she said. 'To me.'

Desmond watched the two men double back once more, his face suddenly dark.

'I could never stop Balcescu and his drug,' he said softly. 'The one time I discouraged it they became suspicious. I couldn't afford to be scrutinised, or I would have had to give up the assignment. I'm sorry.'

'Don't apologise,' Kirra said hurriedly, annoyed that the conversation had taken this morose turn.

For her, being reminded of the regular cruelty at the factory was almost worse than experiencing it in the first place; the memory made more humiliating by the fact that Desmond seemed to want to blame himself for something he'd had no power over. In fact, Kirra was thrilled he had never attempted to intervene. If he had, they would probably have disposed of him, just as they'd disposed of Lena, and Kirra would still be a prisoner at the factory, forced to help Latham week after week. At least this way she was free and had access to resources that would help free Milo too.

'How long exactly has the Industry been active?' she asked, to change the subject.

Desmond grinned at her. 'Active?' he echoed, chuckling at what Kirra had thought to be an appropriate term.

She clenched her jaw. 'How long has it been going on for then?'

'Crime is hardly a modern invention,' he said. 'However, the first ever record of an organised, united community was a century ago. Before that it was every man for himself.'

'A century ago? Really?'

'Sure. It was mostly thievery and con-artistry back then,' he said. 'Why so interested? I thought you didn't want anything to do with the Industry.'

'I don't,' she assured him irritably. 'It's just ... weird, isn't it? My whole life I've heard nothing about it.'

'Yeah, well, frankly that doesn't surprise me. Your entire life has spanned sixteen years, and you've spent most of it holed up in a classroom learning ... Well, whatever it is you've been learning.'

'With all that goes on,' she continued, partially ignoring him, 'you'd think someone would have noticed something. Someone might've picked up on it, at least.'

'We hardly publicise its existence,' he told her. Those who hire us can see it at work, but they're never going to tell anyone, because they'd be telling on themselves at the same time.'

The two men crossed the road below, and Kirra thought they might have even looked up at the very window she was hiding behind.

'Do you think I'll ever get away from it?' she said.

She heard Desmond take a deep, deliberating breath.

'I hope you will,' he said. 'I really do. The thing is … the longer you're involved in it, the harder it is to get out. So let me give you this advice: the very second you recognise such an opportunity, take it. Passage in and out of our community is enormously complicated, but you're yet to make any sort of voluntary commitment to it. You could, with any luck, make a clean departure one day.'

She wondered if she'd just imagined the tone of envy in Desmond's voice. She looked back down at the men on the street.

'They'll move on shortly,' he promised her, turning away.

The pair reached the end of the road, and stood beneath a streetlight, gazing into the distance as though trying to decide whether or not to give up on this particular street and go scour the next.

'For now, though,' Desmond added, 'stay away from the window.'

The next night, Kirra found herself sitting in the silver van outside the factory in Dusseldorf. Fadil and Mai were loading their guns and accessorising themselves with ammunition, speaking Arabic together in low voices. They had gifted Kirra with her own handgun and additional ammunition, which she now tucked into the inside pocket of Lena's jacket, mentally running through the quick reloading tutorial Anton had given her. She hoped she wouldn't have to use the gun, but she was more than prepared to if the need arose.

Desmond and Anton were going over the plan one last time. Kirra, who knew it by heart, returned her attention to the structure before them. The factory was a huge, flat-roofed building amongst a jungle of rundown warehouses. The narrow street was empty save for a couple of cars and a dim streetlight, and the only sound was the buzzing of traffic from a distant freeway. Milo was in there somewhere, sprawled in the cell they had shared for so many months. Kirra wondered if he was thinking of her, trying to guess where she might be and if she was alright. She felt her heart flutter slightly, the prospect of being this close to him thrilling her to the core. Of course, this giddy feeling was shrouded by another very different one. Fear.

No one else seemed scared. Desmond and Anton appeared unruffled as they discussed final details; Mai and Fadil even shared a private smile, as though they were about to head out to do a bit of shopping, not to carry out a risky, unpaid Extraction. Kirra was terror-stricken. What if it all went wrong? What if Latham caught them? What if Milo was killed before they could save him? What if she was killed?

'Alright,' Desmond said, addressing the group. 'That's the closest entrance to the cell.'

He pointed to a door, oddly pristine, near the corner of the street, then fished around in his pocket for a set of keys.

'I can open it, and the cell itself, so I'll go first. Any recruits we meet on our way need to be dealt with quickly. We get to the cell, get Milo, and then get out. It shouldn't take more than a minute. Are we all clear?'

'No, I'm not,' Anton declared, delicately placing a stick of pink chewing gum into his mouth, then tightening the elastic band holding his long dreadlocks in place. 'You lost me back when you were going over it that other time.'

Desmond looked at him. 'Which other time? I've gone over it dozens of times.'

'Exactly,' said Anton.

Desmond ignored him.

CHAPTER TWENTY-SIX

THE EXCHANGE

Slipping out into the night air, Kirra zipped up her jacket and kept her hand near her gun. She was determined this Extraction would go perfectly and didn't want to leave anything to chance; not to mention the fact that she wanted to demonstrate her ability to be professional, especially as Desmond had been reluctant to allow her to accompany them.

'It's never a good idea to be personally invested in an assignment,' he'd warned. 'Perhaps it would be better for you not to be involved.'

'Not involved?' she'd spluttered. 'Desmond ... I'm definitely coming.'

He'd shrugged. 'Okay, but stick to the plan.'

Sucking in a deep breath, she crossed the street and proceeded to watch closely as Desmond unlocked the door. Soon, all five of them were tucked inside the gloomy, narrow corridor, weapons in hand. There was no immediate sign of Latham or any of the recruits, so Kirra relaxed slightly. If they continued along this passageway it would bring them to the cell, to Milo.

They stole along the corridor, listening for oncoming footsteps or voices. The pack stopped abruptly, and Kirra looked up, faced all too soon with the door she knew so well. Desmond punched a security code into the number pad, and then turned the key in the lock. Kirra swallowed. In the next moment, Milo would be back by her side. Desmond pushed the door open softly.

Kirra allowed her eyes to adjust to the darkness within the cell. Milo was probably asleep, in the corner they'd shared for so many nights. The corridor light trickled into the space and Kirra felt her face fall. She couldn't see Milo anywhere.

Desmond cursed under his breath. 'He's not here,' he whispered.

Everyone but Kirra turned back into the corridor, abiding by the plan. When Kirra stayed precisely where she was, Mai returned and took her arm.

'Kirra, remember what we agreed!' she urged. 'If he's not here, we leave it for another day.'

Kirra barely heard her. Where was he?

Mai started to drag her back down the corridor, and she allowed herself to be steered away until a sickening sound met her ears. A moan of pain echoed through the factory, growing steadily into a scream. Kirra stopped dead. It was Milo. They were torturing him. She gasped for breath. He'd never screamed like that before. What were they doing to him? Without thinking, she tore away from Mai's grip.

'No, Kirra!' Desmond groaned.

She ignored him, already sprinting down the corridor, gripping her gun fiercely. She gave no thought to the open doors she passed, or the fact that any number of recruits might hear and see her. All she could think of was Milo and putting a stop to the pain being inflicted upon him.

She flew past an open door and felt her heart stop when she heard shouting. Two recruits raced from the room, weapons in hand, bellowing in a foreign language, obviously raising the alarm.

Kirra gasped and fumbled for her gun, but it hardly mattered because one of the recruits toppled to the ground as though of his own accord, blood spurting in bursts from the wound in his chest. The other recruit lurched forward with a dreadful squeal, gripping at his heart, his eyes bulging. He buckled to the ground and ceased to move.

Behind them, Desmond lowered his gun. Mai, Anton and Fadil were with him, all watching Kirra in horror.

'Leave it, Kirra,' Anton implored, his face deadly serious. 'Just leave it.'

More shouting erupted from the open door, followed by the appearance of several more recruits. Fortunately for Kirra, they were facing Desmond and the others, and assumed them to be the only trespassers in the building. They wasted no time in opening fire on the small group, who gave back as good as they got, taking cover in nearby rooms. By some miracle, none of the recruits noticed Kirra, and, keeping as quiet as possible, she hurried away from the firefight towards the graffiti room.

Another of Milo's spinechilling screams met her ears. Hot tears flooded her eyes. How could she save him?

Latham and Balcescu and however many recruits would be waiting for her in that room. Really, she didn't stand a chance. She needed help, a plan, something, *anything*.

Panicking, she turned a corner and slumped against the wall, rubbing her eyes feverishly. Another of Milo's broken screams met her ears and she shuddered. She knew exactly where he would be, exactly how to get to him, but without the others there was nothing she could do. Bursting into the graffiti room unaccompanied like a wild hero wasn't going to help anyone. Still, she couldn't just leave him.

Another cry of pain echoed through the corridor. Casting around, Kirra's eyes fell on a door opposite her. It was bright yellow. After a moment she frowned. She had never noticed the door before, although there was a lot of the factory she hadn't had access to, so that wasn't such a surprise. Just as she was turning away, resigned to the torment of having to leave Milo, she froze. A soft glow was shining from the crack between the yellow door and the floor. She took a slow breath and, amid the strain of the Extraction gone wrong, something in her hazy mind slid into place. All in an instant, she had a new plan. Kirra pushed the yellow door open. It was a bedroom, the soft light coming from a lamp on a bedside table, left on even though the person in the bed was fast asleep. Kirra hurried over and threw back the pale blue sheets.

Simone Latham stirred, her eyes blinking heavily. She peered up into Kirra's face for a moment, confused, and then scrambled into a sitting position.

'What do you think you're doing?' she cried. But Kirra ignored her, grabbed her arm and dragged her out of bed.

'Let me go! Right now!' she started to scream, but Kirra clamped a hand down over her mouth, and brought her gun into the lamplight. Simone's eyes widened, and her muffled protests stopped at once.

'Don't cry,' Kirra said, 'or yell for help. I'll shoot you if you do.'

Simone stared into Kirra's eyes for a moment, as though trying to determine if she could be taken seriously. Kirra glared back. Another of Milo's yells found her ears, and she gave Simone a quick shake.

'Come on,' she said, and pulled Simone out into the corridor.

Milo looked down at the three broken and bleeding fingers on his left hand. They were almost numb now, but when Balcescu had snapped them with a pair of pliers Milo was sure he'd never experienced pain like it before. Blood still streamed from his broken nose and trickled down his throat. His eye was throbbing, a black and blue stain rippling across his face. Two recruits stood by the door, looking on. Their guns were in their hands.

Milo watched anxiously as Balcescu drew a small scalpel from one of his instrument trolleys. He felt the blade as it was pressed beneath his eye.

'You know, Milo, I'm beginning to think last week's escape *was* something you planned for her,' Latham said. His voice was dangerously quiet. He was standing next to Milo's chair, looking furious. 'I think you're hiding something from me.'

'Wyles,' Milo panted. 'He's helping her. I've had nothing to do with it.'

Latham ignored him and nodded at Balcescu, who made to dig out Milo's eye with his scalpel. Milo tensed, clenching his teeth, readying himself for the pain.

'Papa?'

Milo looked up, astonished, as Latham whirled around to face the open door. The two recruits reached for their guns and Balcescu released the scalpel from Milo's eye.

'Simone!' Latham barked, his eyes wide. 'What are you doing here?'

Simone stood at the threshold in her pastel peach nightgown, her feet bare on the smooth floor, sleep in her eyes, her long hair tousled.

'Papa ...' she whispered again, tears gathering. 'P-please help m-me.'

Latham froze when his eyes found the gun pressed to her temple. Kirra stepped into the light, hauling Simone closer to her, her hand around her neck as she used the girl as a human shield.

Kirra glanced at Milo, her eyes flickering over his blood and bruises. She wanted to smile at him but found she couldn't quite manage it under the circumstances.

'Let him go,' she said to Latham, tightening her grip on Simone, her nails digging into the girl's skin. Simone's body grew rigid and Kirra pushed away an odd sense of satisfaction in causing her pain.

She inched forward. Her determination, strong as it was, couldn't silence her conscience. What she was going to do seemed an unforgivable act. Yet as soon as she'd seen the yellow door she'd known it was her only chance of saving Milo; and with each step towards his agonising moans she had felt bolstered by her decision. They were hurting him — but not for long, not now she had Simone.

Gazing at the dismayed expression on Latham's face, Kirra was certain her plan would work.

'Simone ...' Latham breathed. He glanced at Kirra, his lips twisting furiously. 'Get away from her, Kirra.'

His voice was quiet, malevolent and sure, and he watched her with an irritating sort of presumption. Kirra could tell there was no doubt in his mind that she would listen to him.

She heard distant shooting down the corridor. The firefight was travelling in their direction and she felt overwhelmed with gratitude. The others were still fighting for her. They hadn't abandoned her yet. They were defending her, waiting for her!

The two recruits in the graffiti room raised their weapons, preparing for the incoming confrontation. Kirra ignored them, feeling as though she was made of steel. Latham's daughter was her hostage. She was practically invincible.

'No,' she said to Latham, digging her gun into Simone's hair. 'Not until you release Milo.'

Latham glanced at the silent figure slumped in the chair.

'Let's be serious with each other, Kirra,' he said. 'I know you aren't going to murder a child.'

Milo caught Kirra's eye and she saw that he was watching her with awe as he sat in ruins, completely exhausted.

'I don't want to,' she whispered, her voice so soft it was almost lost in the length of the room.

Latham didn't respond, but Kirra knew he was listening ...

Simone whimpered, wriggling half-heartedly in Kirra's grip. 'Papa ...' she mumbled into the thick silence, tears spilling down her cheeks and splashing onto her nightgown.

'Don't move, Simone!' Latham commanded her, his hand jerking towards her as though it was taking all his will to stay where he was.

'Let him go, Latham, or I will kill her,' Kirra said, clenching her gun hand to stop it from trembling. 'I swear I will.'

Latham's gaze slid from Kirra to Milo and back again. He studied his daughter, his eyes betraying his sudden uncertainty. He needed Kirra and Milo, but it was clear that he was not prepared to lose his daughter over this. Kirra wanted to laugh at him. She wanted to ask him if perhaps he now regretted putting a gun to Lena's head and blasting her away from Kirra forever. She wanted to ask if he regretted using Milo against her for so many months, or if, at this exact moment, he regretted stealing Kirra away from Barrie Avenue in the first place.

Kirra felt a strange desire bloom inside her. An idea that rose up, twisting and sprouting like a plant in sunlight. It would be so easy to kill Latham's daughter right now. He had taken so much from Kirra; why shouldn't she take something from him? It would make them even. It would make up for everything. Perhaps even for Lena?

Simone whimpered again, and the sound made the murderous urge recede slightly. Revenge wouldn't fix things, Kirra thought. It wouldn't resurrect Lena, or get her home.

'Alright, alright, I'll allow Milo to go with you,' Latham said suddenly.

Kirra wondered if he'd sensed the bloodthirsty ideas dancing inside her head.

'Balcescu, release him,' Latham ordered, gesturing towards Milo. 'But be assured, Kirra, I'll see you again very soon.'

Kirra watched in astonishment as Balcescu unbuckled Milo from the chair. Milo couldn't seem to believe it himself, scrutinising Latham with wide, confused eyes. Once free, he climbed laboriously to his feet and stood gazing at Kirra.

'Alright,' Latham said, a small measure of tension evaporating from his voice. 'Let Simone go, Kirra.'

She shook her head quickly. 'No, not until we're out of here. Simone will come with us. When we're far enough away, we'll stop and let her out of the car.'

'I won't agree to those terms!' Latham snarled, stress erupting all over his plump face like a rash. He seemed to be succumbing to the pressure of the situation quite spectacularly, something Kirra found she very much enjoyed.

'You have to,' she said smugly.

She turned to find Milo staring at her, his expression a kaleidoscope of raw emotion. They stood together, completely free for the first time, and Kirra knew that she had never felt as jubilant in all her life as she did right then.

'Let's go,' she said quietly.

Milo walked gingerly to the door, keeping one eye on Latham, apparently convinced he was going to try something underhanded. Latham's expression was nothing short of murderous. Balcescu and the two recruits remained where they were, seemingly stunned.

Kirra began to back out of the room, shielded by the weeping Simone. She could still hear gunfire within the building. They needed to meet up with Desmond and the others as quickly as possible so Kirra could tell them they could retreat. She had Milo. It was over. They could go home — though wherever that was to be now, Kirra did not know.

CHAPTER TWENTY-SEVEN

CROSSFIRE

Kirra and Milo fled down the corridor, steering Simone in front of them, straight towards the firefight. Milo wiped at his nose with the back of his uninjured hand, spitting out a glob of blood as they hurried along.

'Kirra,' he began, his voice thick, 'that was —'

'I know,' she said unsteadily.

They rounded a corner and entered the wide hall they'd taken refuge in during their first foiled escape attempt. Recruits were pouring into the room from various entrances, guns at the ready. The place was quickly becoming a battlefield. Kirra spotted Desmond and Anton crouched behind packing containers, firing at the incoming attackers. Mai and Fadil were close by, sheltering behind an overturned steel table. The room was littered with the bodies of recruits and Kirra felt rather than heard Simone gasp at the sight.

Kirra and Milo, Simone between them, sidled as close to Desmond as they could get without placing themselves in the line of fire, then they too squatted behind pallets of what appeared to be supplies for the factory: boxes of food and ammunition crates.

'Desmond!' Kirra yelled over the gunfire. He whirled around, spotted Milo by her side and nodded. He yelled to Mai and Fadil, who also noted Milo's presence with a good deal of relief on their faces. All they had to do now was find a safe way out.

They were outnumbered by recruits and Desmond motioned for Kirra to help. She drew her gun away from Simone and took aim, shooting several times before chance intervened and a recruit collapsed. Simultaneously sickened and glad, she watched him die and took aim for another man. Simone held her hands clamped to her ears, watching with wide, distraught eyes as lives were lost around her.

The shootout continued, and with each passing moment Kirra panicked a little more. The longer they were stuck here, the more impossible a safe escape seemed. She looked over to see Fadil, armed with a small machine gun, kill a string of recruits in one go. Now they were only faced with a few men, most of whom seemed to be running low on ammunition and took cover to reload. Desmond, Mai, Fadil and Anton took the opportunity to do the same.

And then Latham entered the hall.

Simone glanced up from her hiding place, her eyes falling on her father. 'Papa!' she screamed, and jumped to her feet and darted across the room towards him, her arms outstretched.

Latham's head whipped around. He screamed at her to stay where she was, but she didn't listen.

Kirra watched the girl move, almost as though in slow motion. She wasn't exactly certain what happened next, only that it happened very quickly. Both sides, their weapons reloaded, opened fire once more, failing to register that Simone had entered the firing zone. She fell to the ground, blood cascading over her chest.

Horrified, Kirra glanced at Latham. He looked as though he couldn't move. He couldn't speak. He could only stare at his unmoving daughter.

Desmond's hands, slippery with sweat, grabbed Kirra and hauled her towards the door, taking advantage of the sudden ceasefire. As they ran, the recruits recovered from the shock of what had just happened and resumed the fight with fervour, chasing them with bullets. Kirra burst into the corridor, with Milo by her side. Desmond and Anton were just behind them, and Mai and Fadil were bringing up the rear. One last glance back showed her that Latham had yet to move, still transfixed by the image of his daughter sprawled on the floor.

The recruits rushed past him, their bullets peppering the walls of the corridor as Kirra and her companions ran for the exit.

Desmond shoved open the door at the end of the corridor and fell into the street, pulling Milo with him. Kirra looked back to ensure the others were still close by. She saw Anton, just a few feet behind, and ... Kirra felt her heart stop. Mai was standing still, gazing at Fadil, who was lying at her feet, clutching at his stomach. Blood flooded out from beneath his hand. Mai's face betrayed no emotion as Fadil reached out to her. Like lightning, she tucked her small hand within his just as his body relaxed and his eyes rolled back in his head. His fingers slipped gracefully from hers, his life parting his body.

The recruits were almost upon them. Anton cursed loudly, ran to Mai and hoisted her into his arms. He raced out into the street, Mai curled against him, and slammed the factory door firmly behind them. Desmond had already started the van and was yelling for them to hurry.

Milo stood hunched by the open side door, waiting for Kirra. She climbed into the back row of seats and watched as he negotiated the step and the other seats to sit beside her. As he pulled on his seatbelt, she could see that his fingers were swollen and purple.

Anton pressed Mai into a seat and buckled her seatbelt. He fixed her with a very sad look before flinging himself into the passenger seat and pulling the door shut. Desmond hit the accelerator, the silver van screamed down the street and Kirra turned back to watch the factory fade into the distance.

CHAPTER TWENTY-EIGHT

SOUTHAMPTON

Kirra wasn't sure how long they'd been driving before Mai recovered enough from her shock to begin crying quietly. The change was small, but Kirra, who had been watching for it, noticed.

'Mai,' she whispered, leaning forward in her seat. Her guilt felt as though it was multiplying within her, expanding into a heavy lump in her stomach. It felt as if she'd been force-fed a bucket of gravel. She knew there was nothing she could do or say to ease Mai's grief, but she needed to tell her how sorry she was anyway. Kirra knew she had been reckless, knew Fadil was dead largely because of her.

'Don't,' Mai said without facing her, another tear gliding down her cheek. 'Don't say anything.'

Kirra recoiled uncomfortably and leaned into Milo, who was staring out the window. The only thing that eased her guilt was the fact of his presence, safe and sound, by her side.

'We should have killed Latham,' he muttered. 'We ... we should have used the chance we had. It was so stupid not to kill him.'

Anton twisted round in his seat. 'His kid was shot. Believe me, buddy, you'll get another chance.'

He made his way down to the back of the van with a first-aid kit, and wrapped Milo's broken fingers tightly with a springy white bandage. He handed Milo two strong painkillers, which Milo was reluctant to take at first, but accepted after a few moments.

Kirra gazed out of the window, observing the wild countryside, the morning sun, its glow warm on her face. She sensed Milo fall asleep beside her, his hand rigid and fragile in his lap. Even asleep he looked exhausted.

Kirra wanted to tell them all how thankful she was, but with Mai working so hard to keep her grief at bay, it seemed downright insensitive. What she really needed was to talk things over with Milo: discuss what had happened, assess the danger they were now in, and, of course, acknowledge, even celebrate, the fact that they were alive and together. Yes, everything would be alright once she talked to Milo, but until he woke, she was content to rest against him, feeling, for the first time in a long time, hopeful.

'Are you sure there's nothing on him, Viera?' Desmond said, his voice strained.

Kirra, surprised to realise she'd fallen asleep, stretched slowly in her seat and listened to the hushed phone call.

'Are you very sure?' Desmond said, rubbing his forehead. 'Well, where the hell did he come from then? Aren't you supposed to know these things?'

Viera rambled on for a bit while Desmond stared silently ahead.

'Why am I asking you?' he said. 'Well, Marron said he'd heard the name before so I thought … I don't know what I thought! Look, I'll have to ring you back.'

He ended the call, dialled another number and waited several moments for an answer.

'It's me,' he said. 'I'll have her there tomorrow, but first I need to make a detour.'

He closed the phone gently, trying not to wake his passengers. Anton was slumped beside him, snoring softly. Mai sat with her eyes closed, her cheeks still stained with tears.

Kirra stared at Desmond, catching his eye in the rear-view mirror. 'What is it?' she asked him.

He simply pressed his finger to his lips and drove on.

They'd arrived in Paris, and he was weaving slowly through the empty dawn streets. He brought the car to a very gentle stop in a street lined with shops and Kirra looked at Milo. He was still asleep, his mouth hanging open slightly. She smiled. The painkillers must have been strong.

Desmond was already out of the car. He slid open the side door and beckoned for Kirra to join him on the footpath. Anton, who had woken with a snort just after Desmond stopped the car, watched with avid interest. Kirra slipped out into the fresh air and Desmond shut the door behind her. He folded his arms.

'Still have your passport handy?'

She reached into her pocket. 'Yes.'

'Good. I need to go to England and you need to come with me.'

Kirra raised an eyebrow. 'What for?'

Desmond sighed. 'I need you to trust me on this,' he said. 'Can you do that?'

She stared at him. 'Yes.'

He stared back. 'Well ... that's good.'

It seemed as though he had been expecting her to say something to the contrary.

He motioned for Anton to open the passenger door.

'What?' Anton whispered, looking thrilled to be part of the conspiratorial exchange.

'This is yours,' Desmond said, tossing him the phone he'd used to call Viera.

'Why did you take it?'

'I destroyed mine. Down the toilet.'

'Why?'

'I suspected bugging,' Desmond said simply. Anton nodded.

'I want you to find somewhere to stay here,' Desmond continued, 'and don't do anything until we get back.'

Anton looked as though he was about to launch into another series of questions, but then, seeing Desmond's cold expression, seemed to think better of it. He nodded and shut himself back in the van.

Desmond looked down the street. 'We need a taxi,' he said, hoisting his backpack onto his shoulder.

Kirra froze. 'Milo isn't coming?'

Desmond shook his head. 'It's just us,' he told her tightly.

'But … why?' Kirra spluttered. She'd only just been reunited with Milo. How could she leave him again so soon?

'You said you were going to trust me with this, Kirra,' Desmond reminded her.

She nodded.

'Milo will be perfectly fine with Mai and Anton. We have to leave now; there's not a lot of time to explain.'

Kirra took a last longing look at Milo's sleeping form. She nodded resignedly, and less than a minute later Desmond shepherded her into a taxi and they were speeding away.

'Southampton?' Kirra asked. 'What's in Southampton?'

'No questions.'

'I hate it when you say that!' Kirra said grumpily.

Desmond smiled.

He had just purchased two return tickets to Southampton, England, at Charles De Gaulle airport. Kirra had been slightly startled when he had stepped up to the desk and started conversing in perfect French with a young woman in an ugly blue uniform. How many languages could he speak?

Now they were striding towards the ticket gate, late for a flight that had already been boarded. Kirra nervously ensured her very fake passport was still tucked safely in her pocket. She had thought for sure that airport security would descend from upon high to arrest her as her details were checked at Customs, but the fatigued man at the desk had merely gazed at her tiredly before smacking a stamp onto one of the pages. He'd handed the passport back to her without another glance and nodded for the businesswoman behind her to step forward. As they hurried away, Desmond had given her a deeply affronted look. 'You really didn't think it would work, did you?' he'd said.

On board the plane, Kirra curled up comfortably in her seat. There was plenty of room, with just about every second seat spare. Desmond still wouldn't answer her questions, seeming to have developed a serious bout of deafness.

When they arrived in Southampton, he led Kirra outside to the taxi rank. 'I have an apartment booked so we'll head there first to change,' he said.

'Then what?' Kirra asked hopefully, climbing into the cab and clipping her seatbelt in place.

'I'll have to find you some clothes first,' he muttered to himself. 'Excuse me!'

The driver glanced over his shoulder, his nose bulbous and red.

'Could you take us to the nearest shopping centre, please?'

It was late afternoon by the time they reached the apartment Desmond had rented, and Kirra dumped the shopping bags on the table. Desmond had forced her to buy a new pair of jeans and a soft cream cardigan, both of which were overpriced and far too old for her.

'You can't look like a homeless person,' he said.

'I don't look like a homeless person!'

Desmond wrinkled his nose. 'Yeah ... you do. None of your clothes fit properly and ... Well, do something with your hair,' he said, before pushing her into the bedroom to change.

Kirra, who couldn't have loved her red jacket more if she tried, saw this as an insult to it and very nearly to Lena's memory. Nonetheless, Desmond had something planned and Kirra knew she'd probably draw more attention to herself if she didn't change her clothes. So she ripped off the labels and pulled on the jeans and then the cardigan — the cashmere tickling the skin of her forearms. She tied back her hair with a gold crab clip Desmond had plucked off a counter display and tossed in with the other items as they'd paid the cashier at the shop.

'Just here, please.'

Desmond was already clambering out of the cab before Kirra had even noticed they had come to a stop. She unbuckled her seatbelt as Desmond pressed fifty pounds into the driver's hand.

'If you would just wait here,' he said, 'I'll double that on our return.'

They crossed the street — she saw a sign that told her it was called Ridge Way — and Desmond held open the gate to Number Twenty-three, an old house that had clearly been renovated and re-rendered to look startlingly new. There was no garden, only large charcoal slate pavers leading to the door, separated by small sections of white pebbles in which tiny cacti grew. The overall effect was stark and standoffish, and Kirra wondered if this was a dental clinic. It certainly looked like one.

Desmond rang the doorbell and a tinkling chime echoed faintly through the house before a woman swept open the door and peered at them from a long, white hallway.

'Good afternoon,' Desmond began, his voice lighter than usual. 'My name is Patrick Gately and this is Katherine Hammond. You must be Carla.'

When Kirra said nothing Desmond nudged her shoe.

'H-hello,' she stammered.

The woman, who was middle-aged and strikingly beautiful, looked Desmond up and down several times. She was black, her eyes as dark as the charcoal slates in her garden, and her lipstick was shimmering pale pink. Her raven hair was tied up in a loose knot at the nape of her neck, and she was dressed in a sharp grey suit, accessorised only by a fine silver necklace.

'Yes, I'm Carla,' she said, her voice very controlled, as though every syllable was measured perfectly before it passed her lips. 'May I help you?'

'We'd like to come in, if that's alright with you,' Desmond said, his tone polite yet firm. 'Is your husband home? We'd really like to chat to you both.'

Carla didn't seem completely convinced by Desmond's charade and Kirra honestly couldn't blame her. If a scarred man and a unkempt teenager came to her own front door she'd probably debate the merit of letting them in too. It seemed, however, that Carla decided they were relatively harmless, because minutes later Kirra found herself perched on a pristine couch in the living room, a fine hand-painted china cup of milky tea cradled between her palms, and still very confused as to what exactly they were doing there. The living room itself was quaint and cosy, with a pretty bay window and warm sage-coloured curtains. There was a framed watercolour of yachts moored in a bay hanging perfectly straight by the doorway, and a polished baby grand piano standing beside a filled-in fireplace. Carla's husband, a meek-looking man who introduced himself as Neil, came to sit reverently by his wife's side.

'What can we do for you?' Carla asked.

Desmond placed his teacup gently on the granite coffee table.

'Katherine and I were hoping you could fill us in,' he began, 'on your son.'

'Which one?' Neil said.

His voice was flimsy, almost apologetic, bolstered only by what seemed to be a substantial amount of pride at the mention of one of his sons. Desmond frowned but managed to conceal it before the couple noticed.

'Well, your middle son,' he said, his tone implying that this should have been obvious. 'Milo.'

Kirra's cup clanked down hard on its saucer, the tea slopping over the sides. Before she had time to properly recover, Desmond had steadied the cup, mopped up the small spillage with his napkin and was turning back to address the couple once more.

'Do forgive us. Katherine gets the wobbles when the weather's too hot,' he told them as they stared at her, startled. He shot an extremely meaningful glance Kirra's way.

She ignored him. Carla and Neil were Milo's parents? She was sitting in Milo's house? She scanned the mantelpiece and the bookcase. There were plenty of photos, but none of him. Instead, there was one of a boy —

286

who resembled Milo a little — dressed in a well-fitted suit and leaning against a bar with a warm grin plastered on his face. There was one of a younger boy playing soccer; judging from his position, it looked as though he was about to score a goal. A photo on the bookcase showed the two boys together at a younger age, both dressed in blue, both standing proudly before a goal net.

Kirra closed her gaping mouth and returned her attention to Milo's parents, scrutinising them. Neil was tall, and Carla had obviously bequeathed her eyes to her middle son, but other than that Kirra would never have realised that these two people had produced Milo.

'Oh,' Neil replied, noticeably less animated than before, 'we thought you might be here about another scholarship for Eli. They've been pouring in since he finished school.'

Kirra glared angrily at her half-full teacup. She knew all about Milo's younger brother, Eli. He was spectacularly talented at soccer, something she felt Milo had always resented. She shuffled her feet on the carpet, feeling indignant on his behalf, and hoped that if some stranger ever visited her parents and asked about their missing daughter they would provide a vastly different reaction to that of the Franklyns. The mention of Milo didn't stir any real reaction in them at all. In fact, they seemed content to continue talking about Eli. Thankfully, Desmond seemed just as concerned by this odd behaviour as Kirra was.

'Of course you must be very proud, but I *am* interested in Milo,' he persevered. 'When did you last see him?'

'Oh, Milo's been gone for a while now,' Carla told them.

Kirra shook her head slightly, unable to believe what she was hearing. The Franklyns sounded as though they had no idea that their son was lost at all. When she thought of all Milo had been through, Kirra was outraged on his behalf. His parents were so blasé about his disappearance, as though it was a spare set of keys that was missing and not their son. Why weren't they searching for him? Why weren't they worried sick about where he was and if he was alright?

'He's been gone a while now?' Desmond repeated slowly.

Kirra glanced at him. He was nodding, but she could tell he too was furiously trying to make sense of things.

'Yes. We weren't surprised at all when he left us a note saying he'd taken a job abroad,' Carla carried on.

'A job?'

She looked at Kirra sharply, surprised that she'd finally spoken.

'Yes,' she said, before turning to her husband. 'Something to do with chemistry, wasn't it?'

Neil nodded. 'Science was about the only thing he put any effort into,' he said disdainfully. 'He sends a letter occasionally; very brief ones. I suppose he travels with the job.'

Kirra just stared. Absolutely nothing they'd said so far made sense. But then, quite suddenly, she realised she understood it all. They didn't know. The Franklyns didn't know their son was missing. Latham must have organised the note to avoid another police inquiry, and had maintained the ruse by sending letters every so often updating Carla and Neil with false information.

But it wasn't just Latham's cunning plan that chilled Kirra to the core. It was the apparent ease with which it had worked. Milo's parents had taken it at face value; they'd clearly never questioned the circumstances, hadn't wondered why their son never actually called. Maybe they'd never even read the letters properly and cottoned on to the fact that they weren't written in his own words.

The Franklyns made Kirra feel suddenly ill. She wondered if she could hurdle the coffee table, throttle the two people sitting opposite her, and then somehow make it to the bathroom before throwing up everywhere.

Desmond looked startled by this new piece of information. He took a sip of his tea to buy himself time to gather his thoughts.

'To be honest, I think his brothers were quite relieved when we found the note,' Neil said just before draining his cup. 'Milo's always been so ... so difficult.'

There was an awkward silence.

'Difficult?' Kirra finally managed.

'Oh yes,' Carla said softly, 'since he was very small. He's always been so jealous of Josh and Eli, you see, *so* jealous of all their achievements. He seemed to repel other children as well. I mean, I'm sure at least some of them at school wanted to be friends, but he would have none of them. He insisted upon being alone. I can't count the number of times his teachers called us in to discuss him, sick to death of his behaviour. The more it happened, the more humiliating it became. I'm quite sure it was all a cry for attention — being so dreadfully difficult — I can't think why else he did it.'

'And we knew all about him, of course,' Neil added. 'We hardly needed his teachers to keep telling us. We lived with his antics day in and day out. It only got worse as he grew. His teachers at high school told us he picked fights for no reason at all. He always said the other kids insulted him, but it happened so often we came to realise that he was the instigator, the root of the problem. And then he finally went too far and put another boy in hospital ...'

'He had become absolutely unpredictable and far too much of a strain on the family,' Carla said regretfully. 'And it became so upsetting for us, and quite embarrassing. So, yes, I think our boys were thankful when he finally left.'

'Eli can really focus on his football now,' Neil agreed. 'And Josh on his job.'

Desmond nodded. He seemed to be absorbing the information very calmly.

Kirra, on the other hand, felt like taking every photo frame in the room, every photo of Milo's brothers in their school uniforms, every one of them grinning or playing soccer, and smashing them, one by one, over Neil's and Carla's heads. After all that had happened and all he had been through, Milo had no one looking for him. No one at all. His parents, who obviously hadn't taken the time to really get to know their son, were actually rejoicing in his absence.

Milo had mentioned that he hadn't been very happy at school, but if he had been ostracised and teased to the point of violence then things had been much more serious than he had let on to Kirra. He'd told her everything else — indeed, Kirra suspected she knew more about Milo than the two people sitting opposite her — so why hadn't he told her this? Possibly the memories were too raw, too humiliating? Perhaps he was embarrassed by his past? But Kirra didn't care! Surely he'd known that. She didn't care one bit. After all, she too was wildly embarrassed about her own friendless situation. She understood what it was like! She understood so well.

With a sudden surge of urgency, Kirra realised she needed to be in Paris, to be with Milo, right now, that very instant. She had to tell him she was forever on his side, and that no matter what, he would never have to return to this cold house in Southampton and wonder if anyone at all cared about him.

'Where did you say you were from again?' Neil asked Desmond.

'Milo's university,' Desmond answered promptly. 'Katherine here was a friend of his, and I was his teacher. We just wondered what had happened to him.'

Neil nodded, looking curiously at Kirra. 'A friend?' he mused out loud, his forehead wrinkled. 'From university, you say?'

'Yes,' Kirra said as defiantly as she possibly could, though of course Neil had no idea why. 'His best friend, actually.'

Milo's father looked puzzled, but didn't dispute it.

'He sends photos occasionally,' he said after a beat of silence, getting up and opening a desk drawer beside the bookcase. He rummaged around for a moment before handing Desmond a thin wad of photographs and resuming his seat. 'You can keep them, if you like.'

Kirra barely heard the exchange. She was staring ahead of her, loathing Mr and Mrs Franklyn, loathing their tidy living room, their photos of their sons, their hideous slate and white-pebbled garden, their whole lives. She distantly registered Desmond flicking through the pictures, but she was too disturbed to take any interest.

'We'd best be off,' Desmond said, his voice no longer light and inquisitive.

Carla nodded and showed them to the door.

'Enjoy the rest of your studies,' she said serenely to Kirra, 'and do see it through. No price can be placed on a proper education.'

The door closed, the breeze helping it along, and Kirra trod back over the slate pavers, resisting the urge to flatten one of the ugly cacti beneath her feet — before realising there was no need to resist at all. She squashed one under her heel.

They didn't speak in the taxi on the way back to the apartment. Kirra was too deep in thought and Desmond seemed to be the same. Night was falling. Kirra wanted to ask Desmond what the significance of the meeting with the Franklyns was, but the words wouldn't form and so she stayed silent.

Desmond opened the door of their apartment and grabbed the phone on the stand by the door without bothering to turn on the lights. He tossed the photos onto the nearby couch and jabbed his thumb across the number pad.

'What the hell!' He slammed the phone down. 'It's not working.'

Kirra couldn't understand what he was so stressed about. It wasn't like he really knew Milo. If anyone should be upset for him it was her.

'Listen, I need to make a phone call down at reception. Lock yourself in and stay here,' Desmond said, already marching back down the corridor. 'And keep away from the windows!' he barked.

Kirra did as he asked, closing the door and snapping the lock in place. She flicked on the lamp by the faulty phone and dropped onto the couch, feeling exhausted and miserable and missing Milo terribly.

The photos strewn across the upholstery caught her eye — the photos some recruit had posted to the Franklyns. She scooped them up and looked through them. Every single one was a snap of a tourist attraction. There was the Eiffel Tower at sunset, an Italian piazza, a temple in Laos, even the Sydney Opera House. She sighed. It was all so depressing. And then she came to a photo that made her hands freeze.

Milo was standing in an aircraft hangar by a large private jet, giving a forced smile to the camera, though his eyes betrayed him. They positively glared. Kirra blinked. Her mind couldn't work fast enough to make sense of this. Then she noticed, in the distance, a woman's figure. She was so far away that she wasn't really even a part of the picture. Her back to the jet, she strode towards an open door with some long-forgotten purpose. She wore a blood-red jacket and had long dark hair.

Kirra stared, horrified, at the photo. Lena and Milo had never met. Lena had been killed before Milo had arrived at the hangar.

CHAPTER TWENTY-NINE

THE REAL MILO FRANKLYN

'Kirra.'

She let out a small shriek and leaped off the couch. 'Milo?'

He was standing next to the bathroom door, a strange sort of calm emanating from him. Kirra blinked at him. How long had he been in the apartment? Why hadn't he said anything? Why had he been hiding? For a moment, she forgot the photo on the couch.

'You visited my parents,' he said softly, his eyes flicking disapprovingly between her new cardigan and her neatened hair.

Kirra gazed at him. There was something wrong with his voice. There was something wrong with all of him, really. He was looking at her as though he'd never seen her before in his life, as though he was meeting her for the first time. He had changed his clothes and was dressed in a clean pair of jeans and a black T-shirt. His face was still bruised, but devoid of filth, and the stark bandage Anton

294

had bound his fingers with was gone, a plain black strip of injury tape in its place. In his other hand was a gun.

Kirra didn't gasp or stumble backwards. She simply stared. Milo was here with a gun. Nothing — *nothing* — was making sense.

And then she remembered the photo.

Before she could manage another word, Milo started to speak, but it didn't sound like him. The words were flat and lacked any trace of emotion. He stared at her as he spoke, as though transfixed.

'It's quite astonishing how easy it is to get Wyles out of the picture,' he mused. 'A destroyed phone? A severed landline? And he thinks himself your protector.'

'Desmond,' Kirra said.

'What?'

'Desmond,' she said, louder this time. 'His name isn't Wyles. It's Desmond.'

'Irrelevant, wouldn't you say?'

Kirra's hands were trembling as she reclaimed the photo from the couch. Her thumb glided over Lena's image.

'Who are you?' she whispered.

'My name *is* Milo Franklyn. But I'm not a Spencer Translator. I work for Latham.'

Of course, she'd known it already. Denial had ripped through her at first. Perhaps there was some other explanation. Perhaps Latham had ordered him to stand there and endure having his photo taken so more evidence of his well-being could be sent to Southampton?

'You've met Carla and Neil,' he said, 'so I don't need to explain my life in Southampton to you. Needless to say, it wasn't the place for me. I was at university precisely three days before I met Latham. He offered me a job and a way out of there, and I took it. It only helped that my new profession was something I already excelled at, enjoyed even. I had just turned eighteen. That was more than three years ago.'

'You're really twenty-one?' Kirra asked.

He nodded slowly. 'And Latham's longest-serving recruit so far. All the rest have been pathetic. They always are. Idiots who think they know how to handle themselves, tripping over each other to get their hands on the biggest pay cheques they've ever seen. The dumbest ones die within days, weeks if they're lucky; most quit soon after they've been sent on their first assignment. They tend to get emotional after that. They really have no idea what it takes.'

Kirra stole a glance at his gun. Part of her still didn't believe what she was hearing. It simply wasn't true. Perhaps it was a cruel joke or her mind playing tricks? Perhaps it was a nightmare? The worst one she'd ever had.

'For the important assignments, Latham sends me or he goes himself,' Milo said. 'He trusts no one else. That's why he assigned me to you. I suppose my age didn't hurt either.'

Kirra's throat was dry. Her hands were clammy. Her heart seemed to be going much slower than usual, a lazy staccato of beats struggling and spluttering like an old car engine failing in cold weather.

'I have to give him credit,' Milo continued. 'He really didn't leave anything to chance. He gave you time, more than enough time, to realise how terrible it is to be alone, and then, when he felt you'd had almost enough, intelligence records of me were deleted, my hands were cuffed and I was placed in the cell. Latham and I agreed on certain things I had to do to ensure you believed I was like you. Talk about rescue, chat about our families, that sort of thing. Of course, you had to believe I could do the sequence as well. We had to bond over something, had to share a common curse. That was very important.'

Kirra nodded. She didn't want to, but it seemed she wasn't in control of herself anymore.

'All those times when Balcescu injected you,' she murmured, 'he gave you something else.'

Milo chuckled. It was a cold, slippery sound that seemed to twist and knot around her neck.

'You have such faith in my acting skills, Kirra. No. You had to believe, without doubt, that I was really suffering. The times I watched them torture you before writing a meaningless sequence on the page were to maintain my cover. To make you believe that I too was a Translator. And it was imperative that you did believe. Without you and your cooperation, without the sequences, we have no business. Without a business, I have no job. Without a job, I would still be in Southampton.'

His eyes clouded over for a moment with such hatred that Kirra couldn't stop herself from feeling sorry for him, the way she had at the Franklyns' house. But she had to remind herself that she was feeling sorry for the Milo she'd got to know during their time in the cell, and this ... this wasn't the same Milo.

'Of course, Latham was right in thinking he'd need to assign someone to you. He is an especially good judge of character. He must have seen something in you that concerned him. Say you only responded to the torture while it was still shocking? After that, what if you resisted?

'I'll be honest — even after meeting you, even after the little fight you put up in Barrie Avenue the day we came to take you, I thought Latham was wasting his time. I was sure you'd tolerate half a second of that drug before giving us what we wanted, and you did, but only after you'd held off as long as you could, just as Latham expected you might. Naturally, you'd resist again and again until it killed you, and we couldn't let that happen. Not when you're so priceless. Thankfully, though, people like you are predictable. You'll normally respond to the suffering of someone else. Latham knew that, and so did I. That's when I began my assignment with you.'

Was the room warm? Or was it chilled? Kirra couldn't tell. Was it daytime or night? She knew nothing, really. The idea that he was one of the masked men who had plucked her right out of her old life was eating away at her. She wondered if he'd been the man who'd hoisted her into the air? The one who'd dragged her into the van? Possibly the man who'd jabbed her with that syringe? She shuddered and took an unsteady breath before a terrible thought struck her.

'Mai! Anton!' she gasped, remembering that Desmond had left Milo in their care. 'Did you kill them?'

'Your friends in Paris? I should have,' he replied. 'But escaping them wasn't particularly challenging.'

Kirra moistened her bottom lip with her tongue, relief flooding her.

'When they took you away for those three weeks ...' she began.

'Latham was pleased with the results I'd been getting with you,' Milo said. 'He thought I deserved a break from the cell and gave me a couple of jobs, an excuse to stretch my legs.'

'Those people who died. The men and that woman ...'

'Just jobs,' Milo said. 'Latham never usually sends recruits on solo assignments. Only me.'

'You killed them?' Kirra asked.

He raised an eyebrow. 'Yes.'

'Y-you just shot them?'

'Yes.'

Kirra swallowed nervously.

'After you disappeared with Wyles,' Milo continued, 'Latham was certain I'd had a hand in it. He was furious. He convinced himself that I knew where you were, that I'd orchestrated the escape. He tried to beat the truth out of me the night you left the factory. I told him over and over again about Wyles, but he wouldn't listen. Wyles was just a low-level recruit, after all. A nobody, really. Why would he of all people betray Latham?'

'Desmond,' Kirra murmured.

Milo raised his strapped fingers to touch his blackened eye. It looked several days old. 'Eventually, he gave me the benefit of the doubt, and a chance to prove myself. He sent me to collect you and I would have succeeded if not for your friends in that bar. I shouldn't have been surprised, though. It was almost foolish trusting those men I hired with such a simple task as snatching a teenage girl. It proved to be far too taxing for them.

That woman — Mai, is it? She fought very bravely, particularly for an Analyst.'

'You put that warning out to the Reloaders about me?' Kirra asked. 'You hired Tavio? That was all you?'

He nodded. 'I, unlike most of my colleagues and competitors, never underestimate the value of a Decoy, nor do I assume the worst of a Reloader. Everyone is good for something.'

'You're the young one they all talked about,' she said slowly, overwhelmed by how much sense it all made. 'It's been you every time. Felicity Klein didn't pull up the file of you because Latham had it deleted.'

He gave another slight nod. 'The next team of recruits I sent were killed on that highway. I was enraged by their incompetence, but I couldn't get you myself without ruining my cover. You see, we planned to keep using it. It doesn't matter now, not with the way things have turned out in the last few hours. Anyway, I returned to Dusseldorf empty-handed and my failure made Latham suspicious once again. He thought I let you go, thought I allowed you to slip by. He was furious with me. He thought I was hiding something from him, and tried to torture the truth from me. But when you turned up on your little rescue mission, I was vindicated. Desmond himself was there, which proved my story to be true.'

He gave a grim smile.

'Using Simone was an interesting idea of yours. I've never seen Latham so shocked before. He's a quick thinker, though. He realised he could save his daughter and ensure your safe return in one move. So he let me go — first to dispose of your annoying new friends, and then to bring you back to him. Which I would have done if you hadn't run off to Southampton with Desmond in such a hurry. I'm sure you can imagine what a nasty surprise that was for me to wake up to. Thankfully, it wasn't hard to find out where you'd gone. Viera Favero is exceedingly helpful if you approach her the right way.'

'She told you I'd gone to Southampton?' Kirra said, her voice unfamiliar and quiet.

'Yes. Intelligence agents aren't loyal to their clients. If you're willing to pay for it, they'll tell you anything.'

Kirra knew there was no point in feeling betrayed. She knew money was the only thing that mattered in the Industry.

'I really wish you hadn't used Simone like that though, Kirra,' he said. 'She's not dead, by the way.'

Kirra's head whipped up. 'But … there was blood.'

'She was struck in the shoulder, so I think she'll pull through. Balcescu's operating on her right now.'

Kirra wasn't sure she cared whether Simone lived or died, all she could focus on was Milo. She'd been locked up for six months, nearly five of them with Milo, and she was just realising now that their time together had been a carefully crafted ploy. Which meant Milo Franklyn didn't really exist and nothing they'd shared had been real.

Perhaps she should have listened to Latham all those months ago, just after he'd murdered Lena. *Connections are dangerous in this world you now live in. They will only serve to limit you and hurt you.* She wondered if he had been trying to tell her, in his own way, that she would make the same mistake again, and that he, Latham, could always — *would* always — outsmart her.

Lost in thought, Kirra suddenly realised Milo was still talking.

'Latham's furious about Simone. You can imagine how much that's changed things. You see ... it's personal now.'

'No shit it's personal,' Kirra said furiously. 'It was personal the moment he put a bullet in Lena's brain.'

Milo looked at her for a long time, as though she'd said something very interesting.

'I wondered why you never wanted to discuss Lena,' he said after a while. 'It struck me as very unusual. You rambled on about everything else, the most mundane little things from your Freemont life, things that nearly bored me to sleep, but never her. I wasn't there that night, but I heard she died for you. Surely that had some sort of impact —'

'I wanted to keep her just for me,' Kirra cut in. 'Just one thing I didn't have to share with you.'

Milo looked as though he didn't believe her reasoning one bit.

'You brought me that article,' Kirra said suddenly.

'Yes,' came the curt reply.

She blinked at him, waiting for more.

'It was only printed because I rang in the sighting of you in Sydney. That was my primary intention in the country. The inquiry into your disappearance was getting out of hand, you see. The police had started poking around, forming lists of the places you'd been, the websites you'd viewed at home and at school. They weren't likely to track us down, but we can never be too careful. The false Sydney lead distracted them.

'Your family's alright,' he added after a pause. 'Mitchell even goes to school most days now. You don't really look like any of them, you know. Mitchell, a little, but that's all really.'

'Stay away from them!' Kirra snapped suddenly. The mention of them had sent fear cutting through her like a knife.

Milo smiled, looking amused. 'That's not up to me,' he told her. 'I go where I'm told.'

'Why did you try to escape with me?' Kirra asked suddenly. 'It doesn't make any sense.'

Her numbness was trickling away; she knew she wouldn't be able to hold herself together for much longer, so she needed to ask her questions quickly.

Milo's expression changed; he seemed embarrassed, almost disgusted with himself, and angry too. A vein pulsated amongst the bunched muscles in his neck.

'I tried to get Latham to stop the recruits before they messed with you,' he said, his voice far less controlled than before. 'Latham said it was out of his hands. I couldn't ensure it wouldn't happen, and he wouldn't do anything, so ...

'It was easy to hate you,' he said suddenly. 'Like I've always hated everyone. You dismissed me so quickly, but it didn't bother me. You were just another person who had no time for me. I expected that to be the case, and it's why I was shocked when Latham chose me for the assignment. Someone who'd never formed a bond with anyone before in his life? I told him I was the wrong choice, but he wouldn't listen to me. And at the start, you proved me right. You turned away from me, brushed me off like I was dirt on your shoes. It was so easy to hate you … Then you started to change. It was exactly what we wanted, but that didn't make it any less surprising to me. You seemed to warm to me more and more every day, and we started getting close during the nights. It was astonishing; I kept waiting for you to realise that you really didn't like me at all.

'Then the recruits started hanging around outside the door — you remember? Once Lena was gone, there wasn't a woman around, and they turned their attention to you. They were discussing how best to separate us so they could get you on your own. That wasn't a necessary part of the plan. During my three weeks out, I warned them off and they listened. But once I was back in the cell, there was no guarantee they'd remember my threats. I knew they wouldn't hold off for much longer, and that they'd decided to risk it. They came in, remember? We had to get away …

'I'm glad we didn't succeed, though,' he said after clearing his throat. His face was less intense now, his expression returning to the slightly removed stare of earlier. 'I'm glad Desmond intervened. I blamed the whole thing on him, actually — the dead recruit and the unconscious one we left in the cell. Latham believed me in the end or else I'd be dead too.'

Kirra felt a tear reach her top lip. When had she started crying?

Milo tilted his head to the side. 'I have to take you back,' he told her, his voice businesslike. 'That's just how it is.'

Kirra knew that if she went with him it would mean the end of her life. Latham would take what he needed from her before avenging the damage she'd done to his daughter, and Kirra didn't imagine his vengeance would be merciful or quick. She wondered if Milo knew this. Of course he does, she thought dejectedly.

She turned away from him and moved towards the naked window. Desmond's voice nagged somewhere in the back of her mind, but she didn't care. She needed to put some space between herself and the man she'd thought her friend. The room was silent for a while.

'Do you hate me?' Milo asked.

It seemed an odd question, but one Kirra answered truthfully. 'Yes.'

He said nothing for a moment, before: 'That's fine.'

Was it? Kirra supposed it was. It certainly wouldn't change anything.

She felt him take several steps towards her, saw him looming over her in the reflection in the window. 'Latham expects me to take you back,' he said. Kirra didn't face him. She knew it was unwise to have her back to him. Still, she couldn't move.

It was then that a distant *ping* reached her ears. It came from out in the corridor, floating merrily into the room. She felt Milo tense behind her as he heard it too. The elevator! Now she could make out the sound of Desmond's footsteps coming towards the room, his phone call over and done with, and she felt terror wash over her. Milo knew Desmond wouldn't back off, wouldn't hand Kirra over without a fight. Would Milo kill him then? Would he shoot Desmond and then drag Kirra away? She needed to call out, to say something! She needed to warn Desmond before he walked in on them and got himself killed.

But when she turned away from the window, she found there was no need. The room was empty; she was quite alone. Milo had calculated his chances and decided to leave it for another day.

CHAPTER THIRTY

VIENNA

'I told you to lock this!' Desmond blew in, slammed the door behind him and bolted it. 'You just left it open? What the hell's wrong with you? And get away from the window!'

He grabbed her wrist and twisted her away before pulling the curtains shut. Then he caught sight of her face. 'Kirra! What happened?'

Shakily, she pressed the photo into his hand. 'He was here,' she whispered.

'What?' Desmond looked around wildly. 'Milo was here?'

'I know,' she breathed, ignoring him. 'I know now. I know he's a recruit.'

Desmond's hands shot out to take her arms. He obviously thought she might crumble. Instead, Kirra stood very straight, and pulled away from him.

Later, Desmond placed a cup of tea on the table by

the couch. Kirra ignored it. He watched her closely for a long time.

'You might not be sure of many people now, Kirra. In fact, you might never really trust anyone again,' he said softly. 'But I think it's important you know that you can always be sure of me.'

Kirra didn't sleep at all in the apartment, and Desmond seemed to understand her need to get away from it as quickly as possible. They left first thing the next morning, and returned to Southampton Airport. They were silent for the entire flight back to Paris, and Kirra was glad Desmond didn't try to speak with her. She spent the time wondering what she was going to do now. For the first time, she was completely without a plan. She had no money and nowhere to go. She knew no one outside of Australia, no overseas relatives or family friends, and even if she did, it wouldn't be safe to go to them.

She cast a sidelong look at Desmond. He didn't seem intent on leaving her. Perhaps she would stay with him, work with him, and give him the sequences for his extracting business. It wasn't an ideal future, but at least she wouldn't be cast off to fend for herself. She wouldn't be left completely alone.

They disembarked in Paris, and took a taxi to a hotel where they met up again with Anton and Mai. Mai retreated to her room shortly after their arrival, leaving Anton to hurriedly recount the tale of Milo's disappearance between nibbles of a French pastry.

'I parked the car, turned around and he was just gone,' he said. 'We thought someone had snatched him up, went crazy looking for him, but no sign. Tried to call you,' he said to Desmond, 'but you'd flushed your phone. Remember? Down the toilet.'

They wasted no time in returning to the silver van. Mai took the front seat with Desmond, seeming unable to look anyone in the eye, and Kirra was left to ride in the back with Anton.

She didn't ask them where they were going, and slumped down in her seat, curling up in Lena's red jacket and drifting off to sleep.

Hours later, she awoke to find they were passing through city streets. It was late afternoon, and people were leaving work, hurrying to their cars or bicycles. She scanned the passing buildings, and blinked whenever they passed monuments, opera houses or great sweeping structures that looked like palaces. Desmond was resting in the passenger seat. At some point Anton had taken his place at the wheel. Mai's still form suggested she too was asleep.

'Where are we?' Kirra asked Anton quietly.

'Vienna,' he told her. 'Pretty, isn't it?'

The van left the city, zipping past orchards and green fields before slowing as they approached a solid four-metre hedge that seemed to stand quite alone in the countryside.

Kirra sat upright as Anton pulled off the quiet country road and halted alongside the hedge. Now she could see a pair of imposing gates amid the barrier of leaves, a security pad on one of the gateposts.

Anton leaned out of the driver's window and punched a series of numbers into the pad, then flung a stray dreadlock behind his ear as he waited. The little light at the bottom of the security pad flashed red. He cursed loudly and tried another code. The red light flashed once more. He cursed again before stabbing the intercom button with his thumb.

'Oi!' he bellowed. 'Open the gate! It's just us!'

There were several surveillance cameras perched atop the gates. They swivelled to eye the van for a moment and Kirra thought she heard a resigned sigh float faintly through the intercom. A buzz sounded and the iron gates opened.

Anton drove the van up a snaking gravel path. Kirra frowned as they passed several trenches dug deep into the earth between the trees, shovels lying idly beside them. They looked almost like open graves. Then she pressed her fingertips to the window, her mouth agape. Before, the hedge had hidden the place from view, but now, through the trees and out-of-control undergrowth, she caught glimpses of what looked like an abandoned sandstone mansion. Anton had clearly brought them to an old museum, or maybe a strange, secluded library shut down for renovation. Kirra counted four storeys, as well as smaller wings that branched left and right off the main structure. Spilling out on either side were wide sandstone terraces lined with potted plants: ferns, oleanders and marigolds toppling out over their ceramic edges.

'Anton, where are we?'

He ignored her and brought the van to a skidding halt in a circular driveway. Desmond climbed out and reviewed his poor effort at parking.

'It was hired, right?' he clarified. 'Back in Madrid?'

'Yeah.'

'You might want to be more careful.'

Anton dropped out of the driver's seat and slung his rucksack on his back. 'Why? It's not like they're ever getting it back,' he said with a shrug.

With the topic apparently laid to rest, he set off for the wide sandstone steps leading up to the front door: a huge wooden slab with a brass handle.

Desmond slid the passenger door open for Mai and Kirra. When Mai reached for her bag, he snatched it away from her and hauled it onto his own back before she could protest. She gave a small shrug and followed Anton towards the door. Desmond looked at Kirra, who remained in her seat, feeling out of place and extraordinarily confused.

'Well?' he said tiredly. 'Coming?'

She slid out into the evening air, the setting sun warming her face, and took a long look up at the mansion. 'What is this?'

'The Estate.'

But it wasn't Desmond who answered her. Having just limped out of the front door, a man stood on the steps, staring down at her. He was short and broad, and was leaning on a cane.

Kirra froze where she was.

'You,' she said quietly. It was the man from the hospital after the Bachmeier bomb. The man who'd said he was on her side, who'd said that he was going to help her. Over time Kirra had begun to believe he was a figment of her imagination, but there he stood in the sunset, real as could be.

He staggered down the stairs, past Mai and Anton, and extended his hand.

'Vaclav Falk,' he introduced himself for the second time. 'Come in, Miss Hayward. There's a lot we have to discuss.'